ADVANCE PRAISE F(

"A fanciful, slow-burn grumpy/sunshine tale, ideal for readers who enjoy escapist romance." —*Library Journal*

"Laugh-out-loud funny and romantic beyond the scope of space and time, *Change of Heart* is another total winner from Falon Ballard. I have never met a heroine I've cheered for so hard."

—Annabel Monaghan, author of *Same Time Next Summer* and *Nora Goes Off Script*

"The perfect blend of wit and romance. I love my rom-coms with a slice of magical realism and *Change of Heart* delivers in spades. Imagine *Pleasantville* and *The Hating Game* had a book baby. I adored this book; Falon Ballard at her best."

—Sophie Cousens, author of *Is She Really Going Out with Him?*

"Laugh-out-loud funny, heartwarming, and with a heroine who commands every room she enters . . . I couldn't put *Change of Heart* down. I want to live in Heart Springs, I want Cam Andrews in my corner, and I want this story to be adapted into an actual Hallmark movie."

—Sarah Hogle, author of *Old Flames and New Fortunes*

"*Change of Heart* is the badass feminist rom-com that fans of *Pleasantville* and *The Stepford Wives* will love. It's funny, sharp, and a slow burn that will keep you on the edge of your seat."

—Erin La Rosa, author of *The Backtrack*

"Full of her signature charm, steam, and laugh-out-loud moments, Falon Ballard's newest fully delivers. *Change of Heart* is perfect for anyone who has ever wanted to see the big-city Hallmark villain rewrite the narrative and become the unexpected heroine of her own story. I devoured this in a single, delicious sitting!"—Holly James, author of *Name Your Price*

PRAISE FOR *RIGHT ON CUE*

One of *Elle*'s Best Romance Books of 2024

"Falon Ballard injects the Hallmark rom-com with some much-needed acidity in this Hollywood co-stars-with-benefits sparkler."—*Elle*

"Ballard's lively and fun rom-com will have readers hoping that these two have their second chance."—*Booklist*

"Ballard delivers a feisty and fast-paced Hollywood fantasy in this addictive contemporary."—*Publishers Weekly*

"Ballard creates a winning romantic comedy full of simmering chemistry. A fun and sexy ode to rom-coms, full of joy and chemistry."—*Kirkus Reviews* (starred review)

"Full of winks to the rom-com genre and packed with steamy tension."—*Library Journal*

"Falon Ballard is a master of chemistry-filled banter and lovable characters!"—Sarah Adams, author of *The Cheat Sheet*

"Falon Ballard is the queen of sharp-wit and swoony romances. . . . I will devour everything she writes and beg for more."—Mazey Eddings, author of *The Plus One*

"*Right on Cue* is a perfectly crafted rom-com. . . . Ballard is *right on track* with this delightfully satisfying read."
—Sophie Sullivan, author of *Ten Rules for Faking It*

"Falon Ballard's writing sucks me in like a best friend sharing a juicy story. . . . This adorable, charming, and spicy romcom will hold you captive until the very last page."
—Meredith Schorr, author of *Someone Just Like You*

PRAISE FOR *JUST MY TYPE*

"[A] charming ode to writers' passion and love."—*PopSugar*

"A compulsively readable second-chance romance that's full of pining and laughs."—*Kirkus Reviews*

"This entertaining rom-com from Ballard . . . is one of healing and emotional growth as much as romance."—*Publishers Weekly*

"A great showcase for Ballard's talents. Romance readers—of all types—will be immensely entertained."—*BookPage*

"A unique and humorous tale. Ballard hits all the right notes in a second-chance romance with smart, appealing lead characters."
—*Booklist*

"This spicy, tropey read will have most rom-com fans declaring, 'It's just my type of book!'"—*Library Journal*

"Falon Ballard delivers a page-turning second-chance romance bursting with crackling banter and delightful characters, anchored by a layered, emotional, and sexy love story at the center."

—Ava Wilder, author of *How to Fake It in Hollywood*

"*Just My Type* sparks with enemies-to-lovers wit and dazzles with Los Angeles flair."

—Emily Wibberley and Austin Siegemund-Broka, authors of *The Roughest Draft*

"With its sharp writing, hilarious banter, and delightful characters, *Just My Type* is an absolutely perfect romantic comedy."

—Lacie Waldon, author of *The Layover*

"Everything about Falon Ballard's writing cuts straight to the heart. . . . *Just My Type* is an unputdownable showstopper!"

—Courtney Kae, author of *In the Event of Love*

"With the perfect swirl of lovable characters, sizzling chemistry, and perfectly crafted humor, Ballard's sophomore novel is a story you won't want to put down."

—Denise Williams, author of *How to Fail at Flirting*

PRAISE FOR *LEASE ON LOVE*

"[A] fun and light read."—*USA Today*

"Laugh-out-loud banter, smart characters, and heartfelt charm . . . this rom-com has it all!"—*Woman's World*

"[A] cozy romance."—*PopSugar*

"[A] quirky, heartwarming contemporary romance . . . This is a treat." —*Publishers Weekly*

"A fantastic read . . . a sharply funny roommates-to-lovers, opposites-attract rom-com." —*Booklist*

"[A] charming story of new beginnings and emotional growth . . . Readers who enjoy female entrepreneurs, found family, and gentle romantic leads will enjoy." —*Library Journal*

"The romantic beats and the slow-burning attraction between [Sadie and Jack] are things to savor." —*Kirkus Reviews*

"A delight on every level . . . A beautiful love story about finding something precious that seems out of reach."

—Denise Williams, author of *How to Fail at Flirting*

"A hopeful, heartwarming debut. With a relatable disaster of a protagonist and an adorably nerdy hero, this opposites-attract, roommates-to-lovers romance is a true delight."

—Rachel Lynn Solomon, author of *Business or Pleasure* and *The Ex Talk*

"*Lease on Love* warmly and wittily underscores that none of us are perfect, but we are all worthy, we are all enough: we all deserve to be loved, not just by others, but by ourselves too."

—Sarah Hogle, author of *Twice Shy* and *You Deserve Each Other*

"A crackling, compulsively readable debut about forging new career and romantic paths, finding strength in found family, and discovering what it truly means to be 'home.'"

—Suzanne Park, author of *Loathe at First Sight* and *So We Meet Again*

Also by Falon Ballard

All I Want Is You

Right on Cue

Just My Type

Lease on Love

CHANGE *of* HEART

A NOVEL

FALON BALLARD

G. P. PUTNAM'S SONS
NEW YORK

PUTNAM
— EST. 1838 —
G. P. Putnam's Sons
Publishers Since 1838
An imprint of Penguin Random House LLC
penguinrandomhouse.com

ISBN 9780593712924 (trade paperback)
ISBN 9780593712931 (ebook)

Printed in the United States of America
1st Printing

Book design by Shannon Nicole Plunkett

To all the “unlikable” girls: May you find supportive, kind, compassionate partners who aren’t threatened, but instead inspired, by your ability to kick serious ass.

CHANGE *of* HEART

1

I spot Dr. Ben Loving the moment I step through the door of Two Hearts Café. I'm late, but I don't bother apologizing as I slide into the seat across from him, shooing him back into his own chair when he tries to stand to greet me. He's not bad looking, if you're into the boy-next-door vibe. He's white with thick brown hair and deep brown eyes, plus a wide smile that's a little too friendly and charming. Amazing bone structure, I will give him that.

"Campbell, I presume?" There's no hint of annoyance with me in his tone; it might even be tinged with a hint of humor, but I'm sure it won't take long for the lightness to slip away and the irritation to take hold.

"Cam. Nobody calls me by my full name except for my grandmother." Campbell was my grandmother's mom's last name. It never sat right with her that her mom gave up her name when she got married, and so Grandmother insisted I carry the name in her honor. Agreeing to bestow me with the moniker is one of the few things my mother did right before she left, according to Grandmother.

Now I am the one forced to obey Grandmother's whims. Like go on this date, even though we both know my time would be better served working on my latest acquisitions deal or washing my hair.

"Got it. I'm Ben—"

"Loving. I know." I flip open the menu, my eyes quickly scanning the offerings and landing on something suitable. Normally when Grandmother forces me to go on one of these tedious missions, I at least get a nice meal out of it. But this supposedly charming café was Ben's choice and I didn't have the energy to push back. I gesture to a woman standing nearby, wearing an apron and holding a notepad. "Hi, can we order?"

The woman rushes over to the table. She looks to be well into her sixties, the kind of woman who is wearing her age like no woman in my family would, not a lick of Botox to be found on her pale, wrinkled face. Her face is kind, though, her hair a mass of gray curls, and she smiles as she reaches our table. "Good evening, lovebirds. My name is Mimi, and I have the pleasure of taking care of you tonight."

I flash her a tight smile, deciding it's not worth it to correct her assumptions about me and this man I just met, a man who I will never see again once I walk out the door in approximately thirty-eight minutes, give or take. "Thanks, Mimi. I'll have the Cobb salad, no bleu cheese, dressing on the side, and a glass of chardonnay." I hand her my menu and pull my phone from my bag so I can check my emails while Ben orders.

"Oh, um, I hadn't quite decided yet, actually," Ben stammers when it's his turn. "But I guess I'll just have the spaghetti. And a glass of red."

"Fantastic! I'll be right back with your drinks." Mimi

looks between the two of us as if she's missing something before toddling away.

"So . . ."

I sigh, setting down my phone and turning my attention to my so-called date. "Look, Ben, I'm sure you're a very nice guy, obviously smart given the whole doctor thing, and relatively handsome, but let me just be up-front with you here. I'm only on this date to appease my grandmother so she doesn't write me out of the will and leave our flourishing law firm in the hands of my incompetent asshat of a cousin. I'm not sure how you got roped into this blind date, but I can guarantee you my grandmother only cares about your good genes, which are only important if I were to plan on having kids, which I'm definitely not. So, we don't really need to do the whole getting to know you song and dance. Let's just eat our meals in peace and be on our way."

Ben blinks at me for a second, before the corner of his mouth tilts up in a smile. "Wow. Can't say I've ever been rejected before drinks have even arrived."

I shrug, itching to turn back to my phone and respond to the messages overflowing my inbox. I have a huge meeting tomorrow morning, one that could secure the firm a billionaire client, so it's not like these responses can wait long. "I just see no point in wasting either of our time."

He folds his arms, leaning on the table. "We do have to eat. Is it such a terrible prospect to have a conversation while we share a meal?"

"Or, alternate plan, we can both eat, and I can answer emails while you do whatever it is you need to do for your job."

His eyebrows raise. "I'm a pediatric surgeon."

Ugh, Grandmother, really? A pediatric surgeon? So much

for that whole *don't have kids if you really don't want to* line she's always trying to feed me. She's becoming more obvious in her old age.

"Great, well, I don't know what kind of workload you bring home with you every night, but whatever it is, feel free to take care of it." I swipe open my phone.

"I don't bring work with me on dates."

"Your loss." One of the first lessons Grandmother instilled in me was to be ready to work at any possible moment, lest any free time be wasted.

Mimi arrives back at our table just as my need for wine is hitting its highest level. "Here we are." She gently sets down our glasses in front of us and then instead of returning to her job, decides to stick around. "I just have to say, the two of you make an absolutely gorgeous couple. Truly. You look like you were made for each other!"

I pull my gaze from my phone so I can grimace. I open my mouth to—politely—ask her to bug off, but Ben beats me to it.

"Thank you so much, Mimi. That's so kind of you." He flashes her a brilliant smile that, while obnoxious in its warmth, has the desired effect of sending Mimi on her merry little way. Ben takes a large swig of his wine and then, thankfully, lapses into silence.

I take full advantage, firing off responses to ten emails in the time it takes for our food to be prepared and delivered. Mimi lingers, hovering over us and asking if we need anything despite us both saying no the first two times she asked.

When she finally slinks away after neither of us engage, I set my phone to the side.

"Are you going to bless me with your presence?" Ben takes a huge bite of his pasta and meets my gaze head-on.

"I don't know what you mean, I've been here the whole time."

He finishes chewing and sips from his wineglass. "I guess in the physical sense, sure."

I stab a tomato with my fork. "I thought I had made my intentions clear."

"You don't intend for this to go anywhere. You weren't exactly subtle."

"So then where's the miscommunication?"

He twirls his fork in his bowl of spaghetti. "I don't understand why we can't have a conversation if we're going to be sitting here anyway."

"Because I have work to do."

"Do you always have work to do?"

"Yes."

"When do you take time for yourself?"

"I don't."

"That doesn't seem very healthy."

"I'm fit as a fiddle, Dr. Loving." I gesture to his pasta with my fork, lettuce speared on the tip of it. "Dare I say, I might be healthier than you."

"There's more to health than the difference between pasta and a salad." He chugs the last of his wine. "When was the last time you took a vacation?"

"I'll take a vacation when I retire."

"I literally save children's lives for a living and even I take vacations."

"Some of us are just born with a strong work ethic, I guess." Though I don't think I was born this way. So much of my drive can likely be attributed to my burning need to be nothing like my mother, but that is a sentiment I don't share with anyone, let alone handsome strangers.

Ben sits back in his seat. "I think I've lost my appetite."

"Great." I raise my hand for the check. I'll be home earlier than I thought, giving me more time to prep for my meeting tomorrow. It's essential that we bag this client if we really want to take things to the next level at Andrews & Associates. And by we, I really mean I, as I am the one who has orchestrated this whole deal, and I will be the one to take full credit when it's solidified, basically guaranteeing the firm will go to me should my grandmother ever decide to retire.

"Leaving so soon?" Mimi gestures to the plates of half-uneaten food. "You haven't even finished your dinners."

"Sometimes it's best just to cut your losses, I suppose." Ben holds out his hand to accept the check.

Something about his statement feels like a rejection and it sort of stings. Which is ridiculous because clearly I didn't want to be here in the first place.

Ben studies the check, one of those old-fashioned-looking ones where the server has to write each item in by hand.

I snatch it from his grasp. "Please. Let me." I pull my wallet from my purse, credit card at the ready, when I realize there's no total at the bottom of the bill.

Instead, there's a note.

Tonight, your meal is on me, with the hopes that during the next one you share together, you'll choose to be present and accept the love that surrounds you.
XO, Mimi

I snort-laugh, looking around the restaurant for Mimi so I can tell her I would rather just pay for my meal than endure her passive aggression. But the little gray-haired lady is nowhere to be found, and to be frank, I don't care enough to waste any more of my time.

I toss the piece of paper back on the table, throw down a fifty-dollar bill, and give a half wave. "I'd say nice to meet you, but I don't think you'd want to return the sentiment."

Ben looks at me, his eyes boring into mine like they see way too much. He takes the bill from the table, folds it in half, and slips it into the inner pocket of his blazer. There's an enamel pin in the shape of a giraffe on the lapel and I wonder if he just came from work too, if—despite his protests—the line between work and home blurs for him as much as it does for me.

But none of that matters because this is the first and only time I will be in the presence of Dr. Ben Loving. I should have known this date was doomed from the moment Grandmother told me his ridiculously on-the-nose name.

Pushing back his chair, Ben stands and gestures for me to exit the restaurant in front of him. His hand finds the small of my back as we make our way through the tables, and I should really hate how my body instinctively leans into the warmth of it.

The moment we step outside, I put as much space as possible between us. "Well, this has been an experience. See you around, I suppose."

"Take care, Cam."

I feel his eyes on my back as I walk away, feel the heat of his gaze until the moment I turn the corner, hailing a cab and escaping into the safety of the back seat.

I hardly get any work done for my big meeting that night. I'm distracted by the whole blind date of it all, running the lackluster conversation through my mind on repeat for no discernible reason other than I can't seem to get Ben out of my head. I fall asleep way earlier than I normally would. The last thing I see in my mind before I drift off is a pair of warm brown eyes and that stupid giraffe pin.

2

I know from the moment my eyes pop open that something must be seriously, terribly, god-awfully wrong.

First, I'm tucked in a bed while streams of sunlight pour in through a window. My alarm is supposed to ring long before the sun rises—I squeeze in my prework workout when it's still dark outside. Even on the rare day I allow myself to sleep past six, my blackout curtains keep out all hints of light. But I'm in a bed dressed with a butter yellow comforter, and that blasted sunlight is streaming through curtains made of a delicate white lace. I'm tucked in bed and everything feels warm and . . . cozy.

It's gross.

"Where the fuck am I?" I mutter as I toss aside the offensively cheery blanket. "What the fuck?"

Ridding myself of the confines of the not so unpleasant warmth has exposed something even worse. I'm wearing pajamas. Pink polka-dotted pajamas. The old-fashioned kind, with buttons down the front and an adorable little collar. Well, it would be adorable if I were five. Or lived in the '50s. Where is my black silk slip nightgown? Today is the biggest meeting of my already stellar career—I don't have time for whatever the hell this is.

The hair on the back of my neck begins to rise.

As I swing my feet to the floor, more details of the room—the jail cell? the torture chamber?—crystalize.

The painting above the bed, a girl riding a mint green bicycle, a bouquet of brightly colored flowers sitting in the basket.

The furniture, all coordinated and—gag—made of white wicker.

The plush armchair wrapped in a floral fabric any grandmother other than mine would covet.

"Maybe I died," I muse out loud, still talking only to myself. "This must be my own personal version of hell." Can't say I'm too surprised that's where I ended up.

I open the closet, which is lacking my standard lineup of designer suits and structured separates. They seem to have been replaced by dresses. Lots and lots of dresses, in soft pastels with masses of ruffles, nothing like the LBDs I don on the rare occasion I actually go out for something other than a business meeting. I pull out what looks like the least offensive one, a sky blue concoction. At least, it's the least offensive until I catch a glimpse of the strawberries embroidered all along the front of the bodice.

I drop the offending garment on the plush white carpet.

I spin in a slow circle, trying to absorb all of the pastel-colored nightmares surrounding me. Except it all blurs together like I'm on a carousel from hell.

And then I catch a glimpse of myself in the mirror hanging over the dresser.

And I scream.

My platinum, ice blond, took multiple bleachings and even more conditioning hair treatments to achieve, perfectly sharp bob is gone. Instead, I have honey blond hair that hangs past my boobs, highlighted and barrel curled like I'm some fucking cheerleader.

And my face. My face is perfectly made up, my skin airbrushed and blemish free. Which means I slept in my makeup, which as Grandmother taught me at the ripe old age of ten, is one of life's greatest sins. I press said face closer to the mirror, trying to spot any hint of a breakout, but all I see are rosy cheeks in a shade brighter than I would ever dare to wear and lashes that look fake but somehow seem to be real.

I think I'm going to hurl.

Sprinting toward the bedroom door, I throw it open, not knowing what I expect to see, or even want to see, on the other side. I'm sort of hoping the door will open into the fiery pits of the inferno and I can just leap in and put myself out of my misery.

But no flames swirl on the other side.

It's just your standard living room, complete with a cushy sofa that looks to be covered in blue and white gingham and a million throw pillows, many of which appear to be crocheted.

I force my feet to move, crossing through the living area into a kitchen that I can't even digest. Suffice to say the KitchenAid mixer is color-coordinated with the cushions on the chairs surrounding the farm-style dining room table.

It's the little ties that do me in. The cute little bows keeping those motherfucking cushions in place.

I sink down onto the couch—it practically swallows me whole, it's so plush and overstuffed. I know enough to know I need to drop my head between my knees and try to steady my breathing, but both are easier said than done. Bending in half is hard when I'm fighting against the quicksand of this sofa and breathing is even harder when I realize I must have lost my damned mind.

Either that or I died in my sleep and am currently in the underworld. And honestly, I'm not sure which is preferable at this point.

The last thing I remember is sitting at my desk in my home office, trying to get some work done. Not exactly a singular memory.

I force my lungs to fill with air.

I was irritated, annoyed. Someone had done something to piss me off.

Again, not exactly an unusual set of circumstances.

I'd been on a date right before. Another one of Grandmother's setups. This one was cute, but not cute enough to distract me from the work I should have been doing instead.

We said our goodbyes and headed home. I went through my normal nightly routine, slipped in between my five-thousand-thread-count sheets, and fell asleep.

And after that, everything goes blank.

I cautiously raise my head, pretty sure I'm not going to pass out.

Examining the facts always helps, so I review them in my mind once again. I was annoyed by my date, went home, tried to work, went to bed. And then?

And then I woke up in the bedroom of some '90s teen sitcom.

"Phone. I need my phone."

I rush back into the bedroom, surprised it's taken me this long. Most days I wake up already reaching for my cell.

Nothing sits on either of the nightstands. I frantically search the floor surrounding the bed, under the pillows, in the crack between the mattress and the headboard.

Nothing.

There isn't even a charger plugged into the wall, waiting patiently for its companion.

I dash back into the kitchen. Surely a place like this has a landline. This kitchen screams for a yellow phone attached to the wall, the kind with the long curly cord and the spinner thing instead of buttons.

But there's no phone there either.

No brick-sized cordless phone rests in a station in the living room. Another cursory search reveals no home computer. No laptop. The only piece of technology seems to be the large flat-screen TV, evidence I haven't gone back in time to the dark ages. I quickly find the remote and turn it on, desperate for some kind of connection with the outside world. But no Netflix or Hulu icon appears. There's no guide directing me to more than a thousand different channel options. There's one channel, playing a movie with a dog and a preacher and a woman in a knee-length swirl of a skirt.

I shove my feet into a pair of fluffy bunny slippers and race to the front door. The outside of my prison is just as prettily pristine as the inside, a green lawn that must take buckets of water to keep alive and flower beds filled with blooms that are actually blooming—something I would never be able to manage in real life.

I turn my head first to the right, then to the left, only to find rows of matching houses on either side, as far as the eye can see.

Pushing open the white picket gate—of course there's a white picket fence—I cross the street, heading toward what looks like signs of civilization. A block away is a street lined with shops best described as "intentionally charming." Striped awnings and hand-lettered signs and café patios with tiny tables and matching chairs and umbrellas.

I stop the first person I see, a woman in her midthirties with the same cheerleader curls I now have hanging down my back—someone should tell her she is too old to pull off that hair, but then again, so am I. "Hi, yes, excuse me. Who is in charge here, please?" I don't normally go full "Karen let me speak to the manager" the moment I encounter a problem, but desperate times and all that jazz.

"Well, hi there!" The woman beams, her voice lilting with the barest hint of a Southern accent. "You must be new in town! Welcome to Heart Springs!"

My mind quickly scans a mental Google map, but I know well enough to know I've never heard of any place with such a ridiculous name. "Heart Springs? Is that upstate?"

"Upstate?" Her laugh tinkles pleasantly. "That's too funny!"

"Is it?" Although this whole thing certainly does feel like a sick joke. "I'm sorry, it is very nice to meet you or whatever, but I really do need to speak with whoever is in charge."

"You mean the mayor?"

"Sure. Yes. The mayor. Where can I find them?"

"She works in the coffee shop, right over there." The woman points to the nearest building.

Without stopping to question why the mayor works in the coffee shop, I about-face and rush to the door.

"So nice to meet you!" the woman calls from behind me. "Hope you enjoy your stay!"

Not likely, I think, but don't bother to say. I wave over my shoulder as I push open the door of the shop, a tinkling bell accompanying my entrance. A flyer for an annual Apricot Faire is posted in the window. Just the thought makes my stomach turn, but I push on, needing answers more than I need a dirty martini after a sixteen-hour workday.

The smell inside the cozy café instantly reminds me that I haven't yet inhaled my standard double espresso. Maybe the lack of caffeine is responsible for the complete collapse of my brain?

An older white woman zips back and forth behind the counter, humming merrily while she preps for the day.

I wait a whole five seconds for her to notice me. When she doesn't, I march right up to the counter. "Excuse me?" I keep my voice as measured and polite as possible given the circumstances. So, you know, not very.

The woman startles, her gray cloud of hair bobbing as she jumps. "Oh my! I'm so sorry, I didn't see you there."

I manage to lift one corner of my lips in a tight smile. "No problem. I need a double shot of espresso and some information."

She putters around behind the counter, bringing a pair of reading glasses from the top of her head to her eyes. "A double shot of espresso? Wouldn't you rather have a vanilla latte or a caramel macchiato? Our special drink of the month is a lavender honey latte and we have pumpkin spice all year round!"

"God no." My eyes narrow on her as she starts fiddling with the espresso machine, my faith in her abilities to pull me the burst of caffeine I need dwindling. "How about that information while you're working on that?"

She laughs and it tinkles just like the door chime. I find both sounds equally irritating. "I'm not sure what kind of information I can provide, but fire away."

"First question is an easy one. Where the hell am I?" I lean both hands on the counter, tempted to vault over the stupidly pink thing and make my own damn espresso.

The woman pulls a tiny mug down from a shelf. "Well, I don't think there's any need for that kind of language."

I wait for her to answer my question, but apparently my use of the word *hell* has rendered her speechless. I sigh, my thumb and forefinger pinching the bridge of my nose. "So sorry. Could you tell me where I am? Please."

"Heart Springs, of course!" She packs the ground espresso into its pod, and we finally might be getting somewhere.

"Right. That much I've already established. But where *exactly* am I?"

"Where are any of us, really?"

"That is, in fact, what I'm trying to figure out."

Her laugh titters once again. "You're too funny, Miss . . ."

"Andrews. Campbell Andrews. And it's Ms." And I'm really not all that funny. I don't have time for jokes.

The espresso machine roars to life and for a second, all I do is listen to the glorious sound of the rich brew dripping into its cup.

Then the woman turns around, handing me the mug,

and for the first time I get a good look at her face. And her nametag.

I almost drop my cup. "Mimi! You were our waitress last night! You left us that passive-aggressive bullshit note on our check!" I look frantically to the corners of the coffee shop, looking for hidden cameras because clearly *Punk'd* is being revived and I somehow ended up as the first victim. "Seriously, what the fuck is going on here?"

"I have never seen you before in my life, Ms. Andrews." Mimi's hands land on her hips. "And I told you there's no need for that kind of language, young lady."

I snort. "I'm neither young nor a lady. And excuse the profanity but I'm freaking the fuck out here. I woke up this morning . . ." I hear the words as they come out of my mouth.

And there's the answer, staring me right in the face.

Duh.

I haven't actually woken up yet. Clearly this is all some kind of elaborate dream, the meaning of which I will not be examining further once I do actually stir myself from this nightmare.

"Of course, this is all just a dream. It's all in my head." I chug the espresso because I'm not one to leave good coffee behind, even if this is all just my subconscious being a royal prick. "Sorry to disturb you, Mimi, won't happen again. Though I still think your little note from last night was shitty!"

"See you again tomorrow, Ms. Andrews!"

"You definitely won't!" I push out the front door of the café, this time enjoying a casual stroll back to the kind of house I would live in only in some obscure alternate reality where I believed in love and marriage and happily ever after and "settling down."

Since I won't be in this fairy land for much longer, I take in the sights. The wide expanse of green lawn, the picturesque white gazebo, the sunshine that legitimately warms my shoulders. This dream is in high def and I, for one, appreciate my imagination for putting in the work. I can't remember the last time I had a dream this vivid. Normally the only thing running through my mind whether asleep or awake is obscure case law.

The row of houses I escaped from are all painted in pastel colors with coordinating trim. Mine is pink with a yellow front door, because of course it is.

I'm approaching that beacon of sunshine I left wide open, ready to tuck my apparently beyond exhausted ass back into bed so this dream can come to an end, when the front door of the house to the left of mine bursts open.

A man, white, tall, brown hair, dressed in a matching plaid pajama set I've never seen on a real-life human before, runs down the front steps to his white picket fence, his head turning frantically back and forth, much as mine did just a few minutes before.

And that's when I stop in my tracks because despite the messy hair and stubbled jaw, he's immediately recognizable.

"Ben?"

His eyes narrow as he takes me in, approaching me slowly like I'm some kind of monster from under the bed and he needs to proceed with caution. I don't think I was that much of a bitch last night, but whatever.

I am surprised to see him in my dream, though. I didn't realize he'd left that big of an impression on me.

"Cam?" His voice is hoarse, still thick with sleep. "Where are we? What's going on? What's happening?"

I cross the few final steps separating us, patting his arm like it might bestow some comfort. Hmm. Not a bad bulge of biceps he's got going on there. "Don't worry. This is all just a dream."

"A dream?" He breathes a sigh of relief. "Thank god."

"I know, right? I'm going straight back to bed in the hopes of waking up immediately. Props to you though, not many men make it past date one, and you made it all the way into my subconscious!" I start to head back toward the little pink dollhouse.

"Wait, but if this is your dream, then how am I seeing it too?"

I wave at him over my shoulder. "That's totally something Dream Ben would say."

Not that I know him well enough to know what Dream Ben would say, but who cares? This is my dream and I'm putting an end to it right now.

I march up the stairs leading to my front door and right back into the bedroom. I tuck myself into those cozy ass sheets, pulling the comforter up to my chin.

I've been "awake" for only about an hour, but sleep pulls me under quickly, my brain confident I'll be for real waking up in my own bed, my own apartment, and my own life soon.

3

I cautiously open one eye, though I don't even need to do that much to know that somehow, even after what must be hours of extra sleep, I still have not awoken from my dream.

Sunlight once again shines through the lace curtains (what is even the point of lace curtains?). As I climb warily from the bed, I look down to see the same polka-dotted pajamas, and a quick glance in the mirror shows me I'm hair and makeup ready. At least, hair and makeup ready were I rushing a sorority.

I pinch my arm. It stings, and though my nails are short and painted a pale pink, they leave a mark on my skin.

My stomach spins.

Pinching is supposed to be the test, right? If every piece of media ever written abides by the "pinch me" rule, then Dream Me shouldn't be able to leave a physical mark.

Something has gone seriously wrong.

"I need to get the fuck out of here."

I rush toward the closet, rifling through until I find a

pair of yoga pants and a matching top that I swear weren't there before. They're a disgusting Pepto-Bismol pink, but beggars can't be choosers. Quickly discarding my stupidly adorable pajamas, I yank on my new clothes. There's a pair of pristine white sneakers in the shoe bin by the front door; I shove my feet in them and am in the front yard less than ten minutes after "waking up."

I check the yard to my right, but there's no sign of Ben. I can't let myself worry about him right now—it's every woman for herself. I march down the street, prepared to walk however long it takes to get my mind to shake off this dream. I spend an hour every morning on my Peloton and I live in New York; whatever this tiny speck of a dream town has in store for me can't compete with the step counts I rack up at home.

I don't let myself think of the alternative—that this isn't a dream at all. Surely there is no other explanation. There's no possible way any of this is real. How could any of this be real?

But if it is, if by some slim margin of chance, I've somehow found myself transported through a rip in the multiverse, then I am going to find my way out right now. I'm going to walk myself right back to New York City if that's what it takes.

I need to get back home. Not just to New York, but to my office. I haven't missed a day of work in years and I'm not about to start.

My stomach sinks as I realize I already missed a day of work, and not just any day—the day with the biggest meeting of my career.

Grandmother is going to kill me. And then fire me. Not sure which is worse.

But there is no way I'm taking this lying down. I will make my way back home and fix this. I'm resolute and determined. Heart Springs or whatever the fuck it's called didn't realize what they were signing up for when they took on Campbell Andrews, but they're about to find out. I have a goal, and I will achieve it. I don't know how to do anything else.

And yeah, the walk starts to get exhausting. And yes, it seems like despite the straight path, I'm really traveling in a circle. I suppose that's to be expected when all the houses here look exactly the same. Surely I'm making progress because the slight ache in my thighs means I've been walking for a while.

But the road in front of me looks exactly the same as the road behind.

I wish I knew how much time had passed, but in reality, it doesn't matter. I haven't reached my destination, and therefore, I have to keep going.

Finally, who knows how many hours later, I spot a sign of life in the form of the mailman. He's walking down the sidewalk toward me, and it's like he appeared out of thin air, whistling a jaunty tune as he tucks envelopes into each mailbox.

But I'm so desperate, I don't even care where he came from or how he got there. I rush to his side. "Hi, excuse me, could you point me in the direction of New York City? I need to get there as soon as possible, it's kind of an emergency."

"New York City?" the man exclaims, a wide grin on his face. "Well, I can't say I've ever had the fortune of traveling to the big city, ma'am."

"Yes, yes, I can't imagine you would. But surely you know the general direction? Am I at least going the right way?"

"Well now, young lady, I don't think it would be safe for you to venture out to a place like New York City all by yourself. You should probably turn around and head right back home." He pats me on the shoulder and moves along the sidewalk, heading in the direction I came from.

"Yeah, see, the whole thing is, I'm trying to get back home. New York City is my home!" I call to his back. He doesn't turn around, his whistling tune fading the farther he gets from me.

I spin back around and may or may not stomp my foot in frustration before I continue on my way.

Eventually, the sun starts to sink, so if nothing else, time does still seem to function here, wherever here might be. I don't want to admit it, but the more I walk, the less likely it seems that this might be all in my head. Why haven't I woken up by now?

I pause for a moment, which is a big mistake. Once my muscles are no longer in motion, they seize up.

"Shit," I mutter, bending over to stretch.

I need to keep going.

But even I can see this has turned into a fruitless mission. I've been walking all day and I'm still in practically the same location I was this morning.

My hands fall to my knees, my head drooping. "Fuck."

I pull myself up straight, pushing back my aching shoulders.

And I turn around, ready to make the long walk back to what I guess is my new home, down but definitely not out.

Only to see said home is a mere ten feet ahead of me. It's like I've been on a treadmill all day, racking up the step count but making zero actual progress.

I trudge the remaining distance and walk back through the gate I never bothered to close.

"I don't think this is a dream," a deep voice says.

I turn to face my neighbor's house and find Ben sitting on the front porch of his matching home, though his is blue, and I'm really not digging the gendered color scheme here. He's kicked back in a wooden rocking chair like some kind of little old man, his legs stretched out in front of him and crossed at the ankle like this is just another normal day.

"What brought you to that conclusion?" I've been thinking the same thing, but I want to hear his reasons too, in case they're easy for me to refute.

"I saw Mimi." He gives me a small smile that is possibly meant to be comforting but isn't really, given the state of everything around us.

I cross to the fence separating our yards. "What did she say?"

He leans forward, elbows resting on his knees. "That's between me and Mimi. But you should go talk to her."

"No thanks." My legs are begging me to sit down, and I know I need to get inside before they can physically hold me no longer. "I'm still ninety-nine percent sure this is all just a terrible nightmare. Therefore, I'm going back to bed and fully planning on waking up in my own apartment."

"Good luck with that, sweetheart." He waves me off with a cocky grin, like he has all the answers and I have none. "See you tomorrow."

Where was all this swagger on our date? If he'd shown even an ounce of this attitude then, I might have at least taken him home for the night and then maybe none of this would even be happening.

I flip him off as I push through my front door. "See you never."

SUNSHINE WARMS MY FACE AGAIN THE NEXT MORNING. I don't need much more than that to know nothing has changed.

I'm still in Heart Springs.

For the third morning in a row, I'm waking up in a bed that's not my own, in a place I've never even heard of. I haven't been able to check my email in seventy-two hours, which is seventy-one and a half hours longer than I've ever gone before. My grandmother has no idea where I am, and though I know she won't be fretting about my safety, she sure as hell is going to be pissed at me for screwing up a billion-dollar deal. I'm trapped here, with no way of getting home and no way of calling for help, loathe though I am to admit I need it.

We've gone beyond something being not quite right and I've been pushed over the edge into an unfamiliar emotion: hopelessness.

I throw off the covers and trudge into the living room. Everything looks just as pristine as it did the day before, and the day before that. My dragging feet carry me to the kitchen, where, luckily, I find an espresso machine waiting.

Espresso you make for yourself is never as good as when someone else makes it for you, but if my only other option is another face-to-face meeting with Mimi, who claims not to know me, then I'll deal with subpar coffee.

After I knock back the shot, I open the door to the pantry. I don't think I've even eaten anything since being here, and though I didn't feel hungry before, my stomach is suddenly rumbling. And the pantry is full of my favorite snacks, all the junk food I only let myself indulge in on the rare occasions when I lose a case.

I scoop a bag of Doritos and a sleeve of Oreos into my arms, bringing the goods back with me to the couch. I sink—quite literally—into the cushy sofa, flicking on the TV as I open the cookies.

A woman's face fills the screen as the TV comes to life. She wears a frilly pastel sundress, much like the ones hanging in the closet in my room. Her makeup is simple and natural, her hair curled and hanging over her shoulders.

I try to change the channel, but despite pushing the buttons on the remote and the TV itself, no other choices pop up.

"Whatever," I grumble through a mouthful of cookie crumbs.

If I'm going to be stuck here in pastel purgatory, I may as well enjoy the break. When was the last time I let myself sit on the couch and just veg? Probably junior high, but even then, I was busting my ass to make straight As and win every speech and debate competition I could find. My mom would always encourage me to take it easy, enjoy time with my friends and not worry so much about silly things like grades and trophies. Which is how she ended up on the other side of the country working for pennies, tapping out on raising me before I even reached high school, leaving me in the care of my grandmother, who got a chance to fix the mistakes she made with her own daughter. Grandmother isn't one to make the same mistakes twice, which is how I ended up a partner in our family's law firm. I've never regretted not taking my mother's advice.

But today, I let myself go with it. Minutes bleed into

hours. The only time I move from the sofa is to get more snacks. Luckily the pantry keeps a full stock of options and I sample a little bit of everything.

When the first movie—a story about a brunette PR exec who goes back to her small hometown and falls in love with a bakery owner—ends with the woman giving up her dreams to stay in the small town, I throw a Twinkie at the TV.

Fortunately, I have terrible aim.

Unfortunately, as soon as that movie ends, another one begins.

This one is about a blond talent agent who follows her client to a small-town inn where she gets snowed in and falls in love with the owner.

At the end, she quits her agency—the one she founded—to move in and work with her new husband.

By the time the fourth film wraps, a horrifying realization has dawned on me. The towns in these movies, they look alarmingly like Heart Springs. Everything is bright and colorful and clean. The people sound like they're in a sitcom from the 1950s. All the conflicts resolve in exactly one hour and forty-two minutes.

And I am the big-city girl—brash and "unlikeable" and with a high-powered job that, according to these movies, is making me miserable and sucking away my chance at true love.

I'm a big-city girl and I'm trapped in a small town.

I sit up straight—or as straight as the cushions will allow me to.

I'm a big-city girl and I'm trapped in a small town.

The opening of this story might be familiar, but I refuse

to be the kind of woman who abandons her dreams for the love of a small-town man.

Fuck that.

I wipe the crumbs and cheese dust from my hands. And from the fabric of the pajamas I've been wearing all day. And from the couch cushions.

I head into the kitchen with new determination. Ignoring the pantry, I find the junk drawer—every kitchen has one. And this one holds exactly what I need: a notepad and a pen.

I take my tools back to the living room and turn my full attention to the TV.

I spend the rest of the afternoon taking notes, paying attention to the hidden nuances of the stories on the screen, the familiar plot points and recurring characters, the common ways the conflicts resolve. Then I use the rest of the night to make my plan.

4

The pink cotton dress has little yellow flowers embroidered along the edge of the sleeves and the bottom hem. It's something I wouldn't even have picked out for a niece, if I had any, but combined with my fresh rosy cheeks and blond barrel curls, it creates the perfect look.

I take a deep breath before opening my front door, not sure what to expect from the other side, but knowing I have to greet it with a smile.

I don't look to my right as I march down the front path and to the white picket gate. I haven't seen Ben since my failed escape attempt, and for some reason, I almost dread seeing him again more than I do Mimi. He's the only one here who saw a glimpse of the real me, the only one who might be able to blow my cover. The cover I'll have to don convincingly if I have any hope of making my way home.

I plaster a grin on my face before I push open the door of the café, the bell tinkling joyfully, mocking me and my total lack of joy. The jingling shouldn't bother me so much, but it's an audible reminder of where I am and what I'm about to face.

Mimi is once again behind the butcher-block counter, and once again, there's no one else here in the shop, the few scattered tables sitting waiting for patrons. The chalkboard menu details the day's specials, the kinds of coffee drinks with multiple ingredients and more sugar than coffee. Mimi doesn't look up from her work, studiously ignoring me.

But this time, I know just what she's looking for. "Mimi! It's so good to see you again!"

Her eyes narrow briefly as she takes me in from head to toe, my perfect pink dress and wide smile. There may be a hint of approval in her scrutinizing gaze, but that could be wishful thinking. "Good morning, Cam. I'm happy to see you."

I approach the counter warily, never losing my false façade. "I would love to try one of those honey lavender lattes you mentioned, if you don't mind."

"Of course." Her hands immediately begin prepping ingredients, but her eyes never leave me, even as I sashay away, fluffing my skirt before sliding onto one of the distressed pastel chairs. Mimi finishes my drink and brings it over to the table, setting the mug in front of me before taking the chair opposite.

I look down at the coffee, a heart in the foam to match the sprig of lavender resting on the saucer. "I wanted to come in and apologize for my behavior the other day. I have to admit I was a little thrown when I arrived here!" I chuckle, though there isn't an ounce of humor in it, and I can't help but feel like I'm blowing this already. I really should have paid more attention in that theater arts elective I was forced to take in high school.

"And now?" Mimi brings her own mug to her lips, her eyes never straying from my face.

"And now I feel so blessed to be here!" I barely hold back the cringe, but I think I successfully turn my frown upside down.

"You do?"

"Yes, of course. I had been saying how much I was in need of a break, and now here I am, in the perfect place for a little mental recharge." Never once have any of those words passed through my lips before, but she couldn't possibly know that. Could she?

Mimi sips from her coffee without saying a word.

But she doesn't need to, because it's clear she isn't buying what I'm selling. I don't know why I thought I would be able to keep this up. I am the brash big-city girl, and maybe I just need to embrace my roots, lean into it. After all, this whole thing is supposed to be some kind of journey, right?

I sigh and settle back in my chair. "Can I be real with you, Meem?"

"Please do." She waves her hand for me to continue.

"On the one hand, I get what's happening here. I even get who you are in the whole grand scheme of things." In more than one of the movies I imbibed the day before, there was a wise older person—usually Santa, but not always—who was there to guide the heroine on her new journey to a totally boring life. Given Mimi's presence at the restaurant the night before this whole thing, she has to be that person for me. A sort of fairy godmother, but the opposite.

Mimi raises one eyebrow as if daring me to continue.

"I'm the big-city girl. I'm loud and opinionated and make no apologies for putting my career first." I hesitate for a second, but she doesn't interrupt me. "I was rude to Ben on our date, and I plan to apologize to him for that as soon as we're done here." I didn't actually plan to do that because I don't know that I really owe him an apology, but something tells me it's what Mimi wants from me.

"And what do you want to happen after that, Cam?"

"Truthfully? I want to go home." I need to go home, need to get back to work, but I know my audience, and I know that's not how to win over Mimi. So instead I play up another angle. "My grandmother and the rest of my family, they need me." It's not exactly a lie, though I certainly don't mean it in the way she's probably taking it.

"Why do you think you're here?" Mimi settles back in her seat, mirroring my position.

"Because I put my career first?" Because I apparently pissed off somebody powerful big time and am paying for it now? Karma is a bitch and all.

Mimi nods, like the answer is correct, but not nearly complete. "And why do you want to go home?"

A million possible answers float through my brain, but I didn't make partner at thirty-four by blurting out the first thing that comes into my head when questioned. "I want to be there for my grandmother." Another not-lie that certainly doesn't tell the whole truth.

It's not hard to tell that Mimi is not being won over. She crosses her arms over her chest. "Okay then."

The breath catches in my chest. That was almost too easy. A wide smile spreads across my face and I clap my hands together. "Amazing! What do I need to do? Click my heels together three times and whisper *there's no place like home*? Let me know what I need to do, and we can get this done today, right now, the sooner the better!"

Mimi's tinkling laugh echoes through the café. "Oh, dear. No. There's no way you're going anywhere today."

I freeze in my seat. I'd been about to leap from the chair and rush out of the coffee shop, ready to put this madness behind me. "What do you mean?"

"Exactly what I said. You're not going anywhere today."

If I'm not mistaken, her tone is verging on threatening and one thing I do not take well is threats. "Look, Mimi, I don't know who died and made you old lady Jesus, but if you think you can just trap me here in this hell hole, you've got another think coming." I slap down my palm on the bright yellow table. "Do you know who my grandmother is? She has taken down adversaries way more formidable than the freaking mayor of Heart Bumfuck Nowhere Springs and she will sue your ass and take you for everything you've got."

Mimi sits quietly for a minute, not at all cowed by my tirade. "Are you done?"

The unfamiliar feeling of shame heats my cheeks, but I don't let it rattle my voice, don't let it shake my resolve. "I just want to go home. Tell me what I need to do to get home."

Mimi's lips curl up in what can only be described as a smirk, and my, how the tables have turned. "It's only three things, really."

"Three things? Easy. Spell it out for me and I can knock out this shit and be back home for a tasty takeout dinner."

"Number one: you must find a career you are passionate about."

I sit back in my chair, crossing my arms over my chest.

"Done. No one could say I'm not passionate about my career." I think we have well established it's my only passion.

Mimi purses her lips. "Let me clarify. I don't just mean a career you are good at, one you are successful in, or thrive at. I mean a career you really, truly care about. One that brings you joy and fulfillment."

"I made partner at thirty-four. I'm fulfilled as fuck."

She raises her eyebrows in a hint of a challenge. "Number two: you must become a valued member of the community."

"I take on at least one pro bono case a year. That has community value." The statement sounds defensive and weak, even to my own ears, but really, how much time can I be expected to devote to helping others when my job demands my full and complete attention? "Okay, fine. I can bust out some community service." Or throw some money at the problem and make it quicker and easier for all involved. "What's the last thing? Hit me with your worst."

The grin that spreads across her face is nothing short of gleeful and I know whatever is coming next is not good. "You need to experience true love."

The second her words sink in, I burst out laughing. The laughter overwhelms me, consumes me; I bend over at the force of it, clutching my sides.

When I finally get a hold of myself, I sit up straight in my seat and level Mimi with a glare. "Yeah, that's not going to happen." One would presumably need to believe in love in order to fall into it.

Based on the sheer mass of media I consumed yesterday, this demand shouldn't come as a surprise—it's one of the themes that linked all the movies I watched. But really, no one in their right mind can expect me to give up my whole life for a man. I don't like to think of there being anything in the world—real or imagined—that I can't do, but falling in love might be the one thing on the list. I've seen firsthand the results of "true love"—it's how my mom ended up a single mother who never lived up to her full potential.

Mimi gives me a helpless shrug. "I guess you're going to be in Heart Springs for quite some time then." Her smile is calm, totally pleasant, never once dropping even as I give her my best stare down.

Am I one to back down from a fight? No.

Do I fully understand where I am or how I got here or what even this place really is other than my own personal ninth circle? No.

Do I see any way out of this mess that doesn't involve pushing straight through? Also no.

Sure, I could go back to my house and march in the opposite direction from the one I took two days ago. I could walk until my thighs officially turn to jelly and I collapse on the pristine sidewalk. I could burrow down underneath a comforter that has no business being as cozy and temperature controlled as it is (somehow I managed to stay both pleasantly cool and cuddly warm) and refuse to come out of the house until I'm magically reunited with my blackout curtains and designer wardrobe.

But something tells me neither of those options are going to yield me the results I'm looking for.

And so, the decision is really a simple one. If I must go along with these wholesome, heartfelt shenanigans in order to get back to where I belong, then that's what I'm going to do. How hard can it be to fool a bunch of not-real people into believing I'm buying into their small-town Hallmark bullshit? I'll just put on a happy face, find a career I "love," whip up a couple of pies for the school bake sale, and convince one of the bumpkins the town is sure to throw at me that I'm totally into him.

"Okay." I manage not to choke on the single word controlling the fate of my entire existence.

Maybe I do have a flair for the dramatic after all.

"I'm glad to see you've had a change of heart. And so quickly too! It takes most people longer to move on to the acceptance phase." This smile from Mimi seems genuine, though she still watches me with an all too knowing gaze that will be haunting my dreams for years to come, I'm sure.

"I think you'll come to find I'm not like most people," I say as sweetly as I can manage.

"Hmmm. You might be right about that." She finishes her coffee and takes both of our mugs over to the counter. "Have you thought about what you would like to do first?"

"Let's go with the career thing." I know my strengths.

"I think that sounds like a wonderful idea." She pulls a notebook from the pocket of her apron. Flipping through the pages, her brow furrows until she seems to find what she's looking for. "Ah. Here it is. Okay, so for careers, there are three possible openings. Number one is running the bookstore. Number two is working at the bakery. And number three is becoming a wedding planner."

My nose wrinkles before I can stop it. I hate literally all of those options. Novels are a waste of time. I haven't eaten carbs in at least five years. And marriage is a farce, which probably makes me a bit more cynical than your average wedding planner. "I was really hoping I could put some of my already developed and well-practiced skills to good use. Is there a town law office?"

Mimi makes a note in her little book. "Now, now, the whole point is for you to do something new, not fall back on the career you already know."

"But it's a career I'm very good at. And very passionate about. Didn't you say I needed to be passionate about it?"

"Yes, but there's a difference between passion and obsession."

I cross my arms over my chest. "I am not obsessed with my job."

"So you work standard weekly hours?"

"For a lawyer, yes, I do." The standard for partners being at least eighty hours a week, but I didn't make the rules.

"And you have hobbies outside of work?"

"Yes," I lie.

"And friends who are not affiliated with your job in any way, shape, or form?"

My cheeks heat as the lies continue. "Yes."

"Hmmm." She makes another note in her blasted book.

"Okay fine. I guess I'll try the bookstore first. How hard can it be?"

"Fabulous. One thing to keep in mind—the citizens of Heart Springs think you have willingly moved to our beloved town and are looking for a job and ways to meet people. They are content here, living the kind of lives that truly make them happy. Don't do anything to ruin that for them. Be at the bookstore first thing tomorrow." She tucks her notebook into the apron pocket and turns to wipe down the counters. I suppose I am dismissed.

I push back my chair, smoothing down my skirt. "Can't wait." I don't bother hiding the sarcasm. I've already agreed to her ridiculous plan; no more need to pretend.

"And Cam?" Mimi calls just as I'm shoving the front door open.

I pause just long enough to catch her parting words.

"I encourage you to approach everything and everyone in Heart Springs with an open mind and an open heart. It's the only way you'll truly find your way home."

I turn my head so she doesn't see my eyes roll.

The walk back to my house feels as long and tedious as client depositions. My mood does not improve when I approach the front walk and see Ben sitting on the porch next door.

Why the fuck isn't he out finding himself or whatever? If he talked to Mimi two days ago, shouldn't he be busy finding his life's passion?

I borderline slam the gate of his yard open, stomp up the front walk, and collapse in the chair next to his.

"Hard day?"

I don't need to look at him to see the smirk. I reach across the small space separating us and swipe the beer out of his hand, taking a long swig and practically draining it. "I don't think this is a dream."

"Pretty sure you're right about that much, sweetheart."

"So what is this place? Tell me your theories." I hand him back his almost empty beer bottle, but he gestures for me to keep it. Two more fresh ones have appeared on the table between us. Or maybe they were there all along.

"A rip in the space-time continuum? The multiverse? I don't know if we'll ever really know. Some things are just beyond explaining, I think."

I take another swig. "How can you be so calm about this?"

He shrugs. "In my line of work, you often have to deal with the unexpected. Getting ruffled by every little thing doesn't help anyone."

"I don't think this is some little thing," I mumble, picking at the label on the beer bottle. It doesn't have a brand name on it, just "beer" written in bubbly white letters.

He hesitates for a second, but then continues speaking. "I've also seen some things, at work mostly, but in life too, that are just beyond explanation. Maybe this is one of those things."

Hmm. I don't buy it, but I don't have it in me to shoot down his argument, at least not at the moment.

Maybe having Ben here will turn out to be a good thing. I get to have a partner in crime, someone else to suffer through this unique torture we've been exposed to.

"So did Mimi give you your tasks?" I ask.

Ben's eyes stray from mine, dancing across the front yard in avoidance. "She did."

"Do you also have to find a career you're passionate about, help the community, and find true love?" My nose wrinkles as I repeat my list of assignments, as I think about how impossible they all seem.

"Not exactly." He shrugs again, though this one is stiffer, like he's forcing himself to be casual. "I already have a career I'm passionate about, and I already help the community. So I mostly get to keep doing those things."

That doesn't seem quite fair. When I told Mimi I was passionate about my career, she shot me down, but Ben somehow gets to keep his? Sounds like some patriarchy bullshit to me.

"Do you at least have to try to fall in love in the process?" I study the side of his face, making note of the slight blush pinkening the tops of his ears and his cheekbones.

"Something like that."

"Wow, Ben, we just met. No need to dump your entire life story on me all at once."

He makes direct eye contact and I like that he doesn't flinch from my sarcasm. "I wasn't aware you were interested in the details of my life. I seem to recall you telling me we didn't need to do the whole getting to know each other song and dance."

"Yeah, well that was before we got trapped in Pleasantville with no internet access."

A half smile tugs on the corner of his lips. "How are you faring not being able to check your email?"

"I've been better, Doc." I study that smirk, wondering what might lie beneath it. "How are you faring? Being away from whatever it is that's important to you?"

The smirk fades. "I'm not going to pretend I'm not worried, about my patients in particular, but I know what I need to do to get back to them and I've never been one to back down from a challenge."

At least that's something we have in common. I hold out my beer bottle. "Cheers then, I guess. To finding a way home."

He clinks his bottle against mine. "To finding what we need."

5

I don't bother looking in the mirror when I wake up the next morning, knowing full well what's going to greet me in the reflection. There are probably lots of people in the world who would love to wake up with their hair and makeup done each morning, but something about it doesn't sit right with me. Possibly because it's neither the hair nor the makeup I would choose for myself.

Speaking of choices, it's time for my least favorite one of the day.

I stand in front of the closet, my hand on the doorknob. "I don't suppose today you could give me something to wear that actually suits my personality." I twist the knob, but don't open the door just yet. "Please," I add, for good measure.

Despite my very good manners, all I see when I open the door is pastels and floral prints.

I close it again with a sigh. "Look, I get what you're trying to do here, but I'm going to work in a bookstore today. I don't think a frilly dress is going to cut it."

I open the closet once again, not expecting my pleas to have any sort of impact.

Everything inside is still pastel. Of course.

But once I start rifling through the clothes, I realize my pleas might not have gone totally unheard. Yeah, baby pink isn't exactly my color, but I'll take a cardigan over a dress with poofy sleeves any day of the week.

I even find a pencil skirt hidden in the depths. It's made of denim, so not a complete victory, but I pair it with a white T-shirt and a soft lavender sweater—and I don't totally hate the look as a whole. I figure working in a bookstore means I have permission to wear sneakers, and my feet are not missing my standard four-inch heels.

When I push through the door of the tiny—and fine, I'll admit, adorable—bookstore a few minutes and a short walk later, I expect to be greeted by some kind of person in charge. Someone who will tell me exactly what needs doing and how to do it.

But of course, when Mimi said run the bookstore, she literally meant for me to run the bookstore. There's no one in the building except for me and a bright orange cat, who brushes against my legs and immediately causes me to sneeze.

"Great. Just fucking great."

Well, first things first, I manage to find the light switch, hidden behind, you guessed it, a huge stack of books. The overhead lights are dim, providing just enough illumination to be able to see, and very much adding to the whole cozy and mysterious atmosphere.

There's an ancient-looking cash register sitting on top of the worn wooden counter, tucked away in the front corner of the store. The rest of the space is filled with bookshelves, mismatched colors and sizes of spines squeezed into every available inch. In the back of the room, I find a small, squishy-looking armchair that the cat has claimed. I'm tempted to join him—or her, can't really tell—but if I want to make this store my life's passion, I might need to figure out how to actually operate it.

"Come on, Cam. You graduated magna cum laude from Columbia. I'm pretty sure you can manage one tiny bookstore."

I do a lap around the cluttered space, getting my bearings before I try to decide where to start. If I let myself get too caught up in the big picture—the one where I have no idea what I'm doing—I'll probably just collapse in that armchair and accomplish nothing. But that is not the Campbell Andrews way. I take another lap, this one slower and more methodical, familiarizing myself with the needs-to-be-completely-redone organizational system.

I'm acquainting myself with the different sections (labeled with faded, barely legible stickers) when a bell chimes to alert me to a customer. Just what I need. Another blasted bell, and an interruption just as I'm starting to figure things out.

But I slap on that fake smile that's almost becoming second nature now and head back to the front of the store. "Hi!" I say in a voice many a salesperson has tried on me. "Welcome!"

The woman, who looks to be in her midfifties, flashes me a bright smile. "Well, hello! You must be the new girl everyone's talking about!"

I fight to keep my smile from morphing into a grimace. "That's me! Word sure does travel fast around here."

She looks me over from head to toe, giving me the full

assessment, her smile never faltering. "It sure does. How are you settling in?"

"About as well as anyone who's had their whole world turned upside down might be?" I shrug in a way she hopefully finds sheepish and charming. I take Mimi's words of warning about the citizens of Heart Springs and assume it's best to keep things vague. "Moving can be so tough!"

She chuckles. "Fair enough. Relocating to a new town can be so overwhelming, but we're so happy you're here! I just came in to pick up the new Nora Roberts. Have you put it out yet?"

"Um. Hmm. That's a good question! I just got here and was trying to familiarize myself with the shop when you walked in." I stride over to the counter, hoping to find some kind of organization system or a working computer with software cataloging all the books the store has in stock, but all I find is the register and some old bookmarks. I let out a puff of breath. "Well, I'm sure I can find it for you. You said the author is Norma Robins?"

The woman looks at me like I've suddenly sprouted an extra head. "Nora Roberts, silly!"

"Right. And what genre does she write?"

Her eyes widen. "You work in a bookstore and you don't know who Nora Roberts is?"

"Well, to be fair, I didn't exactly pick this job. I mean, I did, but from a very limited list of possibilities. There weren't a ton of openings, but I'm not a big reader, honestly. I never really saw the appeal." I know the moment the words are out that they are the exact wrong thing to say. "But I'm excited to learn! I mean, I can definitely read all these books in no time, I'm sure." I gesture helplessly to the thousands of books lining the shelves. Even with my law school–honed speed-reading skills, it would take me months of nothing but reading to put even a dent in them.

"I think I'll just find the book for myself, thanks." The woman's friendly demeanor has completely faded and by the time I manage to ring up her book on what must be the original store cash register, she looks like she wants to murder me.

The second the door closes behind her, I'm tempted to lock it and turn out the lights, but it's only been an hour and there's no way in hell I'm giving up already.

I roll my shoulders back, tilting my neck from side to side like Rocky gearing up for a fight. I can do this. I can absolutely, one hundred percent, totally manage to run this store. And find a way to become passionate about books.

"Books are great," I mutter as I begin to alphabetize the mystery section, not that I'm going to recognize any of the titles or authors or, god forbid, be able to provide customers with any recommendations.

After a few minutes, I head back to the front of the shop, searching the counter for any supplies that could possibly help. I find a worn notebook and a stub of a pencil and bring both with me as I return to perusing the shelves. I start two lists: one of things to do around the shop, like make new labels and dust, and one of titles that look interesting. Maybe, if I have a few go-to books I can suggest to inquiring customers, it might buy me some time to actually read some of them.

And so the day goes.

I send off an eight-year-old girl holding a book with a smiling clown on the cover, sell a religious romance by

Sierra Simone to the town preacher's teenage daughter, and even manage to find a book about clocks for a doddering old man who told me he likes to "tinker" with old machines.

By the time the sun is setting, I've managed not only to keep the bookstore standing but to actually sell some books. I even checked a few items off my to-do list.

As I lock the door on my way out, making sure to shut off the lights and fill the cat's water and food bowls before I leave, I can't help but feel pretty damn proud of myself. I might not be the biggest fan of reading, but maybe there's a chance this whole bookseller gig will turn out to be my passion. Maybe my success today is a sign of some sort of inherent book-recommending magic I never knew I had in me.

My steps are jaunty as I make the short walk from the store back to my little cottage of a house. I knew it wouldn't take me long to knock these tasks off one by one, but even I can admit that I didn't expect it to come together in one day.

I'm not even annoyed by the sight of Ben, once again in his rocking chair, once again sipping on a beer, like he hasn't been forced to spend his whole day doing something completely out of his comfort zone.

He gives me the smuggest of smiles as I approach and maybe there is a tad bit of annoyance after all.

"What are you so happy about?" I pause in front of his gate, even though I know I shouldn't be bothered. I should head right through my own front door and not give that cocky smile a lick of my time.

"How was your first day at work?" He asks the question in a tone that makes it clear he already knows the answer. So much for the sort of camaraderie I thought we had established yesterday.

I cross my arms over my chest. "It was fabulous, actually. I think it's safe to say that I nailed it."

Ben purses his lips. "Nailed it, huh?"

His look is all too knowing and a rock of foreboding sinks my stomach. "Yes," I respond with rapidly draining confidence.

Ben leans forward, his elbows resting on his knees, beer bottle dangling from his fingers. "You sold an eight-year-old *It*."

"The clown book?" My brow furrows. Of all the possible missteps I've been running over in my mind, that wasn't one of them.

Ben doesn't hold back, throwing back his head and letting loose a guffaw. "The clown book? Seriously? How have you never heard of *It*?"

"I don't read much, okay?" I say defensively.

"It was written by Stephen King!" His laughter continues, wiggling under my skin.

Now that he says it, the author's name does ring a bell. I knew it was familiar when I was ringing up the purchase, but I couldn't quite place my finger on why.

I glare at him, refusing to give him the satisfaction of seeing me cowed. "Okay fine, I made one mistake. It was my first fucking day. Give me a break!"

Ben's eyebrows shoot up. "One mistake? Sweetheart, you also sent the preacher's daughter home with erotica and sold Old Man Tate *A Clockwork Orange*."

"He was looking for a book about clocks! It's right there in the title." I plant my hands on my hips. "And I will not apologize for that erotica bit. Everyone deserves the chance to explore their fantasies." Though maybe I should have skipped the one with all the religious overtones.

Ben's body finally stops shaking with laughter and his gaze turns to pure pity. "You really had no idea, did you?"

I bristle, pulling myself up to my full height, dropping my arms from their defensive position. "I don't know what you're talking about."

"You actually thought you had done a good job today."

My cheeks heat, and I don't know why the idea of Ben seeing me fail irritates me so much. Maybe because the idea of failing at all irritates me so much, let alone having it happen in front of my annoyance of a neighbor/former blind date/only person in this town who I thought might understand how it feels to be stuck here.

"Oh yeah, well if it's so easy, how was your first day? Did you even work or have you been sitting here all day waiting for the opportunity to judge me?"

Ben's smile fades. "I'm not judging you."

I shrug off his words, like the lie paired with the judgment doesn't sting even worse. "Whatever." I turn to march the few feet over to my front gate.

"Wait. Do you want a beer or a glass of wine? Seems like you might need one." His smile is back, but this one lacks the teasing glint from before.

"Sure. Why the hell not." I trudge up his front path, collapsing into the chair next to his and accepting the proffered wine. "So how did you know about all the mistakes I made?"

Ben extends his long legs in front of him, crossing them at the ankles. "Despite your assumptions, I did work today. Took over for the town doctor, who's on an extended vacation. People in small towns love to gossip, especially about the new kid."

"Of course you get to keep your normal job. I find it hard to believe no one in this town has use for a lawyer, and yet I'm out here trying to run a freaking bookshop," I grumble.

He chuckles, but it doesn't sound totally genuine. "I wouldn't say this is keeping my normal job. The most daunting thing I did today was pull a LEGO minifigure from a kid's nose."

The image brings a slight smile to my face, but I do my best to hide it. "Not something you deal with on a regular basis?"

"Not quite."

I nudge his elbow. "Go ahead, brag. You know I'm not one to be offended by a show of ego."

Ben shrugs. "I'm a surgeon, of course I've got a bit of an ego." He hesitates for barely a second before continuing. "I specialize in cardiothoracic surgery, kids who have heart issues and need major intervention."

I don't even have to feign being impressed. "Seems like you're a pretty big deal, Dr. Loving." It's not hard to imagine him, all competent business in the operating room, all calming bedside manner when dealing with nervous kids and their more anxious parents.

"I do the best I can." This time Ben is the one nudging my elbow with his. "It will get easier, it was just the first day."

I swallow a gulp of wine, relishing the warmth that spreads through my chest. "I think we both know I'm not cut out to run a bookstore, Doc."

"I think the important thing to note is that you tried something new and you gave it your best."

I snort. "I'm not a kindergartener. There're no adulthood points for effort. Either you succeed or you fail. Safe to say, today I failed." The words taste sour in my mouth, even after another swig of wine.

Ben picks at the label of his beer bottle, the same generic one from the night before. "I don't think life works like that. It's not all so black and white."

"It is in my family."

Ben doesn't say anything for a minute, but I can feel his eyes on me, like he's x-ray visioning into my brain and learning things no one should really know.

And that's my cue to leave. I've already shared more than I would normally, and I don't like the sort of warm feeling in my chest that comes with Ben trying to offer me comfort and companionship. I chug the rest of the wine and set down the glass on the small table in between the two chairs. "Thanks for the wine. I guess I'll see you tomorrow."

"Have a good night." He gives me a lingering look.

I ignore the shiver it sends down my spine. "Yeah, you too."

I force a determined smile across my face as I push open the tinkling door of the café the next morning. I'm dressed in a mint green sundress and a small part of me is hoping if I look the part of the angelic, reformed former big-city girl who now fully embraces smalltown life, I might be better equipped to finish my tasks and get my ass home. "Good morning, Mimi." Maybe if I pretend like yesterday never happened, she will too.

She greets me with a soft smile and piteous eyes. "Good morning, Cam. I'm sorry you had such a rough day yesterday."

It irks only because, all things considered, it didn't actually feel like such a rough day. At least, not until the very end. "It's okay. I had a feeling I wasn't cut out for bookselling, but I'm ready and willing to move on to the next." Cam Andrews doesn't stay down for long.

Mimi studies me for a minute, as if she's trying to determine whether I mean what I say. I must pass the test because she turns to start fixing me a latte, and even though

I'd rather just have an espresso, I let her make me one of her frothy specialties.

I head over to our usual table while she makes my coffee, sinking into the chair and doing my best not to let myself sink into a full-on pit of doom. Accepting Mimi's proffered mug gratefully, I take a sip before steeling myself to ask the dreaded question: "So, what do you think I should try next?"

Mimi taps her nails along the pink ceramic of her own mug. "I know there's a wedding this weekend, and Kate could probably use some help, so that might be the next best bet."

"Kate?" If there is someone else actually in charge, wedding planning already sounds easier than running the bookstore. I can take direction if nothing else.

"Yes, Kate is Heart Springs's resident event planner. She takes care of all the weddings and town events."

Given that I have so far only met like five people in the entire town, it seems like Kate might have a pretty easy job. How many weddings can there be among such a tiny population? This wedding gig seems like it probably involves a lot of scrolling through Pinterest. You know, if they actually had phones and social media. And while I am not one who enjoys sitting back and doing nothing, it might be easier to be passionate about that than stocking bookshelves or measuring flour.

"Okay, great. Well, I guess when I'm done here, I'll head over and meet Kate and let her know she has an extra set of hands for the big day." I'm trying really hard not to get my hopes up because honestly, this job sounds too good to be true. I thought bookselling was going to be a piece of cake and it turned out to be a total nightmare, and I don't want to make the same mistake with this whole wedding gig. Most likely, the only part of this one that will be a piece of cake is the actual cake.

But when I stride out of the coffee shop a few minutes later, I'm cautiously optimistic, emphasis on the cautious. Mimi told me to turn left and keep walking and I'd come to Kate's shop; since it's my first real stroll through the main part of town, I take my time.

The town really is idyllic, if you're into the whole small-town romance vibe. The pastel rainbow color scheme is consistent throughout, the sun shines brightly but not too hot, and for the first time since I arrived, I find myself among other people. People besides Ben and Mimi and the few customers I met at the bookstore. And of course, every single one of them greets me with a smile and a hello and seems genuinely happy to see me.

It's a foreign feeling. Despite working with family on a daily basis back at home, none of them ever seem excited to see me. Even when I'm closing deals and bringing in huge accounts. I don't have any siblings—at least my mom was smart enough to quit while she was ahead—and my relationship with my cousins has always been more competitive than friendly (it's not my fault Grandmother picked me to be her successor at the ripe age of nine—what was I supposed to do, be less awesome?). I can't even think what my reception will be like when I finally make it back home, having been out of the office for who knows how long, and missing the biggest meeting of my career so far.

Hmm. Maybe I should take my time here in Heart Springs, delay the inevitable familial disappointment for as long as possible.

I land in front of Kate's shop and quickly change my mind about that.

The awning over the front window is a soft baby pink, as is the trim around the window and the door to the shop. The words "Best Day Ever" are painted in a gold, flowing script across the glass, behind which are three of the biggest, poofiest wedding dresses I have ever seen.

When I push open the door, the first few bars of the Wedding March chime throughout the room, carpeted in pink and overflowing with flowers, linens, invitations, and sample table decor. I've never had claustrophobia until this moment, but it hits me hard.

"Hello?" I call out into the empty and yet stuffed to the brim room.

A stunningly gorgeous Southeast Asian woman flurries into the room, her arms laden with binders, one pen in her mouth, another holding up her messy bun. She wears a pink sheath dress and pink ballet flats and it should look ridiculous but somehow she manages to look something bordering on chic.

"Hi, I'm Cam." I catch one of the binders as it topples from her pile, tucking it under my arm and taking a few more from her stack before they fall.

Kate lets the rest of them slide onto one of the tables—set with various sample place settings—and removes the pen from her mouth, revealing a wide smile. "Hi, Cam. Mimi told me to expect you."

I still have yet to see a single phone in this town and somehow everyone always knows what's going on everywhere at all times.

"I'm sorry to interrupt while you're clearly so busy."

"Nonsense. I could use the help." Kate gives me a quick

once-over. "I take it you don't have any experience with weddings?"

"Can't say that *I do*." Pun intended.

"Well, that's no problem. If you just listen carefully to instructions, I'm sure you'll do just fine." She starts flipping through one of her binders (it's, you guessed it, pink). "The main thing to remember is that you are always wrong and they are always right."

"I'm sorry?" The reason I have built such a successful career is because of my ability to be right, which I am. Pretty much always. Truly. Always.

"If the bride tells you she really wanted pink flowers even though you know she said white, you have a signed contract saying white, and you have her mood board without a drop of color on it, you obviously ordered the wrong flowers and will correct your mistake immediately."

I start to slowly back toward the door, hoping she's so busy she won't notice if I disappear and run for the hills because I've definitely made a terrible mistake.

She pins me in place with a pointed look. "Don't worry. Most of the ire will be directed at me, not you."

"Do you receive a lot of ire?" It could be my total lack of wedding knowledge, but I would think people would be pretty kind on what's supposed to be the happiest day of their lives.

Maybe they all know deep down that marriage and lifelong love are a crock of shit.

Kate laughs, and despite the subject at hand, it seems genuine. "Oh yes, of course. Weddings are emotional, and when emotions are running high, people get nervous. And I tend to be the one they take those nerves out on."

I wrinkle my nose. "That doesn't seem fair."

She shrugs. "If it means they get to enjoy their day, then I don't mind."

"You are a better person than I, Kate."

"It's all worth it in the end, you'll see."

This is probably my last chance to run from the shop screaming, but instead I pull my shoulders back and stand tall, taking on my favorite pose of determined strength. I need to get home, and if bearing the brunt of some mother of the bride's stress gets me there, then I can handle it. Surely a couple of anxious moms aren't any tougher than my usual clients.

I SHOULD REALLY STOP MAKING SUCH RIDICULOUS DECLArations, I think as I gently pry the mother of the groom's fingers from my forearm, where she is gripping so tight, I'll probably have bruises tomorrow.

"The pocket fold on these napkins is all wrong!" She finally drops my arm, but only so she can grab a stack of neatly folded napkins, completely destroying the precious pleats.

"Ma'am, until about an hour ago, I had no idea what a pocket fold even was." I back away from her slowly, so as not to startle her with my sudden movements. "Let me go find Kate, and I'm sure she can figure this out."

"You rang?" Kate gently pushes me out of the way and within sixty seconds has the momzilla calmed down and even smiling. She ushers the mom out of the reception hall and instructs the servers to fix the mangled napkins. And she does it all with a smile on her face.

"I thought the brides were supposed to be the difficult ones."

Kate laughs. "Oh gosh no. Moms are the worst, second only to the rare but horrendous groomzillas."

"You should be nominated for sainthood," I mumble, brushing a stray thread off one of the tables.

"It just takes a little patience." She adjusts one of the centerpieces, turning it a millimeter at a time until she's satisfied with its placement. "You're doing very well for your first time, especially considering I only had a day to prep you before throwing you into the action."

I don't mean to relish in this small bit of praise, but I haven't felt anything even close to competent since I woke up in this candy-colored hellscape and it feels nice. "Thanks," I say, and I mean it.

Maybe I can do this after all. Maybe Kate can teach me how to smile and nod while a stranger berates me. I mean, if anything, my family might have perfectly prepared me for this job. The next time someone gives me attitude, I'll just pretend I'm dealing with Grandmother when she's on one of her tirades—keep the eyes engaged but shut down my emotions. I've been doing that my whole life.

What I'm not prepared to handle is a bride with cold feet. And when today's bride, Emily, grips my arm in a hold not unlike her future mother-in-law's, her eyes wide with fear, I don't know what to do. Honestly, Kate should be the one in the bridal suite, fluffing the dress and fixing the train as we get Emily ready to take the long walk down the aisle, but she's off wrangling the wedding party.

"I don't know if I can do this," Emily whispers, her French manicured nails digging into my skin.

I try desperately to channel Kate or Mimi, fuck even Ben could probably handle this better than I can. "What do you mean?" I'm stalling, hoping and praying Kate will push through the door and work her magic.

"I don't know if I can do this."

"*This* meaning . . . ?"

She looks at me like I'm an idiot. "Walk down that aisle and get married."

"Pledging your entire life to one person is a pretty bonkers concept when you think about it." The words slip out before I can stop them. I fake laugh as if it can cover my mistake.

"Exactly. Like am I really going to commit the whole rest of my existence to a man who doesn't even know how to load a dishwasher?"

"Yes?" Hopefully, because if not, I think I can probably say goodbye to my chances of getting home. Something tells me a career as a successful wedding planner doesn't start with your first wedding ending in, well, zero marrying. "I mean, that's just one little flaw. Everyone has flaws. Certainly he has other good qualities to make up for it?"

She snorts. "Like how he leaves every single light on and every single cupboard open?"

"Charming personality quirks!" My voice rises unnaturally high. "Emily, it's normal to be nervous before making such a huge, life-altering decision, but you and Tim love each other." The words burn my throat because I know love is never enough, but I'm selfish enough to keep pushing this woman if it means I don't have to completely botch another career path.

Emily tosses her bouquet on the couch. "I don't think I should do this."

I grab the flowers before they can get crushed and shove

them back in her hands. "Emily, you've gotten this far, babe, think about how disappointed everyone will be if you call it off now." My stomach turns because why the hell should she care how disappointed *everyone else* will be? This is her life and her decision to make.

She sinks down onto the couch, her head falling into her hands. "I don't think he really loves me. And I don't think I love him either."

Fuck it. I sit down next to her. "Then let's get the fuck out of here."

She turns her head to meet my gaze, her eyes wide. "Are you serious?"

"Fuck yeah, I'm serious. If you don't love him, why the hell would you marry him?"

"We were high school sweethearts. Our families are best friends. It was just expected, you know? And I do care about him, but maybe that isn't enough." Tears start to fill her eyes.

I hand her a tissue. "Just because it's expected doesn't mean it's right. Have you talked to Tim about this at all?"

She shakes her head. "He's my best friend. I didn't want to hurt him."

"If he really cares about you, then he'll want you to be happy." I pat her on the knee in a way I hope is comforting. "Besides, why are you more worried about his feelings than you are about yours? That's how women end up in untenable situations with the garbage bags we call men. Do you really want to end up alone and miserable in a year or two, saddled with Tim's kid and unable to make a life for yourself?"

Blowing her nose loudly, she looks at me with wet eyes. "You really think that's what could happen?"

I may have imparted too much personal info there, but I don't let it slow me down. "It's a real possibility, Em. I've seen it happen." I push to my feet. "Let me go get Kate."

Before I have the chance to leave and go find out what the hell to do now, Kate pushes into the room, a bright yet harried smile on her face. "Everything okay in here?"

"Emily doesn't want to get married," I say with an almost proud smile on my face.

Kate's face drains of all color. "I'm sorry, what?"

"We've been talking, and Emily decided she doesn't want to go through with the wedding."

"You've been talking?" Kate yanks on my elbow, pulling me aside into a corner of the room. "What did you say to her?"

"She told me she didn't think she could do this and so we talked, and it turns out she isn't sure about marrying Tim." I know this creates a lot more problems for Kate, but shouldn't she be happy that I've helped this woman avoid a major life-ruining mistake?

Kate closes her eyes and her nostrils flare with the deep breath she sucks in. "So my bride told you she was a little nervous and you somehow convinced her she doesn't want to get married?"

"I think that's oversimplifying things a bit." I cross my arms over my chest.

"Get out," Kate instructs. "Get out and do not talk to another person involved in this wedding."

"But I—"

Kate halts my protests with a single look.

I sneak a peek at Emily, who's still sitting on the couch, still crying, and somehow looking a lot less resolute than she was just a few minutes ago. I don't say another word, pushing out of the room and away from another self-induced disaster.

The town's one event space is located in the center of the main square, and I stomp all along Main Street until I'm back in front of my gate. I know without even looking that Ben is sitting on his porch, judging me.

I march a few steps down the sidewalk and throw open his little white gate instead of mine. Plopping into the rocking chair next to his, I gesture to the beer wrapped in his hand. "Got any more of those?"

He raises a single eyebrow, but doesn't say anything, reaching behind the small table and pulling out two already opened beer bottles like well-timed magic. "Cheers?" He reaches across the gap with his beer.

I tap mine against his.

"Bad day at work, sweetheart?" Can you hear a smirk because I'm pretty sure I do when he uses that "term of endearment."

"What are the chances we can just not talk about it?" I swig from the bottle and lean my head back against the cushioned chair.

"Your first wedding and you made the bride cry?"

Curse this town and its ridiculously fast traveling gossip.

"To be fair, I didn't *make* her cry. She was sort of already crying." I push down a very inappropriate giggle because really, nothing about this situation is funny. Not one bit. "I just didn't exactly help the situation."

Ben smirks—a visible one—though he attempts to hide it with a sip from his bottle. And fails miserably. "Safe to say Kate won't be asking for your help again in the future?"

"I think that's a pretty sure bet."

We sit in a comfortable silence for a minute.

"Did she end up going through with it?"

Ben knows exactly who I mean, and somehow, though I just left the venue, he already has the answer. "Yes. Emily and Tim managed to make it down the aisle and through the entire ceremony, relationship intact."

I should probably be happy that I somehow managed to not completely ruin the day, but I can't make myself smile. "Poor fool."

Ben leans back and turns his head in my direction. "Let me guess, you don't believe in love?"

I scoff into my beer. "Of course I don't believe in love. Relying on one person, committing yourself to them for the rest of your life? Assuming that because you found someone dumb enough to pledge themselves to you that you somehow get to escape the worst of the world's problems? Tying your self-worth to the approval of someone you can never really know? Giving up your independence for the sake of having one more person's expectations to live up to?"

Ben doesn't say anything for an awkwardly long time. "That might be the saddest thing I've ever heard."

My laughter rings hollow. "Why, because it's true?"

"No. Because you've never truly experienced what it means to be loved, by anyone, I'm guessing."

His stark words knock the wind out of me. I've never hid the fact that relationships are not my thing. I don't date, and it's certainly no secret that I'm not exactly looking for love.

But the insinuation behind his declaration—that I've

never been loved by anyone—hurts more than I'd like to admit. Partly because, in a lot of ways, I think it might be true. Sure, my grandmother cares for me. I think she does, deep down, want what's best for me. But I still often wonder how much of that is because of me, and how much of it is because she's trying to fix her own regrets.

My mom might have loved me once, back before she decided to put her own happiness first. Then again, maybe she always knew I would be better off with Grandmother. Maybe I wouldn't be where I am now if she had stuck around. I don't have the emotional bandwidth to question if her decision was worth it.

"If you're such an ardent admirer of true love, then where's yours?" I throw the words at him as if my barbs can erase the impact of his.

He shrugs, taking another casual sip from his beer. "I just haven't found the right person yet."

"What makes you so sure they exist? Or that you'll ever find them?" I mean the questions to convey my skepticism, but that doesn't stop me from wanting to hear his answers. That want catches me off guard—it's not like me to be interested in someone else's opinions. But something about Ben makes me want to know him. I study his profile, for the first time appreciating the strong line of his jaw and the chocolate brown of his eyes.

He meets my gaze, holding the eye contact for longer than is wholly comfortable. "I've seen enough true love to know it exists. And I don't know that I'll find it for myself, I just have faith that she'll come to me when she's meant to."

"That sounds like a lot of poetic bullshit to me, neighbor." I chug the remainder of my beer.

He flashes me a small smile. "I have a feeling you might end up changing your mind."

Because if I don't, I'll be stuck here forever. Neither of us says it out loud.

Ben clears his throat. "If you want to take a break from the carousel of failed careers, you could start working on one of your other tasks." He catches the look I throw him. "Not the love one, don't worry."

"What did you have in mind?"

"I'm organizing a fundraiser for the children's hospital, because despite the fact that no one here really seems to get sick or injured, there's always a children's hospital in need of funding."

Of course there is. So people like Ben can volunteer and raise money for them. It's like the man was sent here specifically to make me look bad.

"It's a carnival," he continues, "so there'll be games and food and rides. It's a lot to manage and I could use some help." He nudges my elbow with his. "I imagine someone who volunteers might soon find themselves to be a valued member of the community."

"Yes, but at what cost?" I mean it to come out as a joke, but the words sound cutting, even to me.

"Spending time working with me sounds that horrible, huh?" He both lets me off the hook and doesn't accept my bullshit, a rare trait.

"I suppose if I'm going to get through this whole disaster, I might need to make at least one friend."

"Am I the lucky winner?" Ben's eyebrows shoot up in mock surprise. "Whatever did I do to deserve to be blessed with the friendship of Campbell Andrews?"

I throw him a false grin. "Proximity."

He places a hand over his heart. "You are too kind to me, sweetheart."

"I'm sure I won't stack up to your actual friends since I don't exactly have a lot of practice, but beggars can't be choosers." It sounds like I'm fishing for information, and I might be.

"To be honest, I wouldn't say I have a ton of close friends. My colleagues and I are close just due to the circumstances that bring us together, but I've always been a bit of a loner."

"Yeah, me too." Though Ben's lonerhood seems to be a choice, whereas mine sometimes feels like people just don't want to be around me.

But I probably bring that on myself.

"So what do you say, ready to lend a helping hand?"

My fake smile morphs into a real glare. "I guess if I have to prove myself useful, this carnival thing doesn't sound like the worst idea ever."

"Praise be!"

"If nothing else, you might be the only other person in Heart Springs who knows what sarcasm is."

"It is a gift."

A small laugh escapes me. "Well then, I guess that officially makes us friends, Dr. Loving. I can't say I've had too many of those in my life."

He nudges my arm with his elbow, the bare skin of his arm brushing against mine and making me shiver. "Happy to be your first, sweetheart."

7

I creep into Mimi's coffee shop the next morning, not knowing quite what to expect. Will she be mad at me for totally screwing up career number two? Do I actually care if she is? Is she going to pull the not-mad-just-disappointed card my grandmother is so fond of? Because I can handle a lot, but that's the one thing that kills me every time.

Of course, I needn't have worried. Mimi greets me with a smile and immediately pulls me a shot of espresso, not even trying to force a flavored latte with foamy flowers on me.

I accept the tiny cup gratefully. "To be fair, I did warn you that none of your proffered careers were going to work for me."

Mimi tilts her head and smiles at me like I'm a petulant child she's choosing to indulge. "Part of the goal is for you to try something new, dear. For you to push outside of your norm."

"But why should I do that?" I swig my espresso and hand

back the mug in a silent plea for another. "My life back home is perfectly fine. I'm good at my job. I'm successful and fulfilled. Maybe my life doesn't look exactly like everyone else's, but who wants that?"

Mimi putters around behind the counter for a minute before handing me a second shot. "But are you happy?"

"Is anyone really happy these days?"

She plates a muffin and slides it across the counter. "I am."

"No offense, Meem, but you live in literal fantasy world. Of course you're happy." I consider leaving the muffin behind, but it smells too damn good to let it go to waste. Taking the plate, I head over to what's become my table and wait for Mimi to join me as she always does.

For the first time I notice I seem to always be Mimi's only customer. Despite now knowing at least a hundred people live in the town of Heart Springs—based on the guest count of the wedding that almost wasn't—I still seem to only regularly encounter Mimi and Ben. Which is odd.

But my attention quickly slides back to Mimi herself, when she slips into the seat across from me and gives me a leveling look. I shove a bite of blueberry muffin in my mouth to avoid her gaze. The top is all crumbly and crusted with sugar and it's fucking perfect.

"Look, Cam. There's a lot of things you're going to have to figure out for yourself."

"What does that even mean?" I ask around a mouthful of delicious pastry. "What kind of things? Like what's the meaning of life? Why are we here? Is anything even real?"

"Perhaps we should start with some questions that are a little more grounded."

"It's all bullshit if you ask me." I take a tiny sip of espresso, figuring I should probably pace myself with this one.

"What I will tell you is this." Mimi reaches across the table and gently pats my arm. It's such a foreign move of pure comfort that it makes my breath stick in my chest. "If you're here, it's for a reason."

"Yeah, I already knew that. I just need to know the reason so I can figure out how to be *not* here." I wave my hand, gesturing to the cheery colors of the café.

Mimi shakes her head with a sad smile. "That's not what I mean, Cam. I mean, you wouldn't have ended up here if you were truly happy back at home, if there wasn't something missing from your life. I've never had anyone blow through two careers in two days and not make any sort of progress."

"I think that says more about the careers than it does about me," I mumble, shoveling in more bites of muffin.

"Does it though?" She raises her eyebrows in a way that is somehow not judgmental, which is really quite impressive.

"Well, I'll have you know I'm going to switch gears for a bit. Put the career thing on hold and focus on the other tasks."

Her eyes light up. "Does that mean you're ready to move on to the love portion of the program? Because I have your suitors all ready." She claps her hands in excitement.

"I'm going to be volunteering for the dumb kids' hospital carnival thing." I rush the words out and it takes a second for Mimi's declaration to process. "Wait a minute. Did you say you have my suitors ready? Is this going to be like the job thing? I have a set number of dudes to pick from?" The muffin turns sour in my stomach.

"Well, yes, that's how it works. I pick the men for you—your file said men, that's what you prefer, yes?"

I nod, too stunned to do much else.

"Great. I set you up on dates and you figure out which one is going to be the one for you."

I pinch the bridge of my nose between my thumb and forefinger. "Let me get this straight, I couldn't even manage a day at the jobs you picked for me and now I'm supposed to fall in love with one of the men you've picked for me? Why do I not feel great about my chances?"

"Probably because you have a terrible attitude."

"Wow. That was harsh, Meem." I throw back the rest of my espresso, which has gone as cold as my shriveled heart.

She sighs. "Believe it or not, I have your best interests at heart, Campbell Marie." Ouch. And of course she knows my middle name. "You'll just have to trust in the process."

"Yeah, see, if there's a real process, I'd like to see it laid out for me, step by step. Seeing is believing and all that."

"Would I lie to you?"

I laugh, and despite the total unfunnyness of the situation, it's a real one. "Would you lie to me? I barely know you. Why wouldn't you lie to me?"

"Because I only want the best for you."

"Yeah, well in my experience, people really only want the best for themselves." I push back my chair deliberately hard, so it creates that awful scraping sound. "If you'll excuse me, I've got to go pretend to care about some kids I've never met to try to suck up to a community I'm trying desperately to escape."

She mumbles something under her breath, but I've already shoved open the door, knocking into Ben as I come barreling out of the shop.

"Howdy, neighbor!"

I close my eyes and take in a steadying breath. "You did not actually just say that."

Ben grins and it lights up his eyes. "Rough morning?"

"As rough as any of the rest of them, I suppose." I fidget with the hem of my skirt, realizing how rare it is for me to not constantly have my phone in my hands. And yet in just a few days here, I've gotten used to not checking it every five seconds.

"Excited for your first day of volunteering?" That damn smile of his is all too knowing.

"Oh boy, am I!" I exclaim with completely false enthusiasm.

He chuckles and gestures to the café. "I'm just picking up my morning coffee and then we can walk over to the school. We're using the gym as the staging grounds for the carnival." Pulling open the door to the damned tinkle of the damned bell, he glances over his shoulder. "Want anything?"

I've already had two shots of espresso, but what's a few more. "I'll take a latte. Hold the flower foam art."

"I don't think that's how it works." He lets the door shut behind him, and I plop down at one of the outdoor tables to wait.

The main street of shops circles a large grassy expanse, the site of the upcoming carnival and this past weekend's Apricot Faire, which I luckily arrived just in time to miss. Today the pristine lawn is dotted with people, picnicking and enjoying the absolutely picture-perfect weather. The sky is a shade of blue rarely seen in the city, with cotton ball clouds scattered artfully. The sun shines brightly, but there's never even a drop of humidity. The breeze does amazing things for my hair, but doesn't ever turn into a true wind. It's perfect, if you're into that sort of a thing.

In these few minutes of silence, my brain starts to wander, which honestly, has never been a good thing. I wonder how much time has passed back home. How many meetings I've missed. I shudder as I consider how many unread emails I'm going to come back to. Assuming I have a job to come back to. My grandmother might have been grooming me to take over the firm since I was nine, but that doesn't mean she gives me any real leeway. Not showing up for work for days on end and missing the biggest meeting of my career so far is surely grounds for both firing and removal from her will.

I might turn out just like my mother after all.

Ben emerges from the café, handing me a reusable to-go cup. "There's no waste here, so you can just bring this back to Mimi on your way home."

"Of course. Wouldn't want to create fake waste in this fake town that's not real."

Ben takes my grumbling in stride, starting to walk down the absurdly clean sidewalk, away from the café and our houses. We pass by a number of shops, including the bookstore and Kate's wedding planning office, both of which I studiously avoid, lest anyone catch a glimpse of me and my shame.

We come to a stop in front of an old-timey bright red schoolhouse. I don't know why I was expecting a modern concrete monstrosity, because of course the kids of Heart Springs go to school in a building that looks like it's straight out of *Little House on the Prairie.*

Ben leads me around to the back, where there's a gymnasium that looks somewhat closer to what I'd expected, with a basketball court and bleachers, and right now, tons and tons of carnival stuff. Games and prizes and all the wooden pieces that will come together to form booths, signs and tickets and costumes and so many boxes. The floor of the gym is entirely covered.

I stop shortly inside the door. "Exactly how long have you been working on putting this carnival together?"

We've only been in Heart Springs for a few days; there's no way all of this came together since then.

"A lot of the plans were already in motion, I just sort of stepped in and took control."

"Why?"

"Because I enjoy helping people?" He doesn't include *dumbass* at the end of his statement, but it's implied. "And since everyone here is absurdly healthy, I need something to do with my days."

"Like work on tasks you don't seem to have been assigned?" My unoccupied hand flies to my hip as I survey the massive amount of stuff. "Please tell me you have some kind of advanced organizational system at work here."

Ben rolls his eyes, tossing his bag onto one of the bleacher seats. "Of course I do."

I take a long swig of my coffee. "And what exactly is the plan for today?"

"Tomorrow we're going to start setting up out in the town square, so today is all about making sure everything is ready to go. We've got boxes to unpack and a lot of stuff to organize and sort so it's ready to be moved."

"Sounds like there is going to be manual labor involved in this job." I started paying people for manual labor a long time ago and have never had any intentions of going back.

Ben crosses his arms over his chest, the movement

making the fabric of his gray T-shirt pull tightly across his biceps. "Mimi mentioned she had your suitors all picked out and ready to go. You're welcome to head back to the café and arrange some dates instead."

I clap my hands together and force a smile across my face. "Who doesn't love a little manual labor?"

Ben leads me over to one of the huge stacks of boxes and leaves me with instructions to unpack stuffed animals and sort them into various bags for the game booths. It's boring, menial work, but at least the stuffed animals aren't heavy. After watching me for a few minutes to make sure I don't screw up this very simple task, Ben heads to the opposite side of the gym, leaving me with quiet that doesn't feel all that peaceful.

Mimi's earlier comments start to play over in my mind even though I know nothing good can come from dwelling on them. Who cares if I wasn't happy in my real life? I can't think of a single person I know back in the real world who I would consider to be truly happy. I think that's just how it's supposed to work. You're born, your parents screw you up to varying degrees, you find a job that pays the bills and start living to work, and then you die.

Sure, there are probably a few people out there who actually like their spouse and enjoy spending time with their kids, but I haven't met anyone who could truthfully claim so; certainly no one in my family could pretend to enjoy one another's company.

So yeah, despite Mimi's good intentions, her little come-to-Jesus moment isn't going to lead me toward any sort of radical *my life is changed, I'm going to quit my job and live for the people* bullshit.

Though maybe if I pretend to go along with her little plan now that I've had some time here in Heart Springs, it might put me one step closer to getting the fuck out of here. Will Mimi buy that I've changed in such a short amount of time? Hmm. The next time I see her, I'll have to try it out.

"How's it going over here?" Ben interrupts my musings, and I realize I haven't exactly been moving at top pace while I've been contemplating the best way to fake enlightenment.

"Great!" I gesture to the still mostly full boxes around me. "Should be done in no time."

"Right." Ben sets down his clipboard and opens the next box in my pile.

Back to the quiet of it all, only this time it somehow manages to actually feel peaceful.

When the peace becomes a little too comfortable, I clear my throat. "So Mimi told you she wants me to start working on the whole falling in love bit?"

"She told me she had your suitors lined up and ready to go." His brow furrows as if he is contemplating some serious question, which seems incongruous with the stuffed panda he holds in one hand and the stuffed penguin he holds in the other. It shouldn't be cute, and yet . . .

"Did she give you any details about these so-called suitors?" I toss a pink unicorn into a bag and turn to open the next box, hoping to get some info on the men in question before I have to come face-to-face with them.

"She did."

I wait a few beats. "Are you going to fill me in?"

"No." He shoots me one of his playful grins. "Sorry, sweetheart, but I can't break the code."

I blow a stray strand of hair out of my eyes. "Well, what can you tell me? Are they all terrible? Are they going to expect me to fall all over myself trying to be the perfect little wife? Am I going to have to give up my career?"

He stares at me like he's never seen a human woman before, the force of his brown eyes seeing so much more than I want them to. "Is that what you think relationships look like? You giving up yourself to make someone else happy?"

I shrug, turning my attention back to the boxes at my feet because it's easier than getting lost in the depths of his gaze. "I've never seen any evidence to support the contrary."

"Is that why you would barely even look at me on our date?"

I sigh loudly and dramatically as if that might deter this line of questioning. "I don't want a relationship, so I didn't see any point in delaying the inevitable." The inevitable being a total crash and burn, which is exactly what happened when my mother fell in love with my father. "I still don't think it's fair that I have to go on a bunch of dumb dates and you don't. How come someone out in the real world hasn't snatched you up already, anyway? You seem to buy into this love bullshit. What's the deal?"

"I've asked myself that a lot actually." Ben's voice is quiet, and if I didn't know any better, I might think there was a trace of pain in his words. "Even though I've managed to strike a better work-life balance than some people in this room, I think my job still makes it hard to get close to people."

I try to put myself in Ben's shoes for a minute, something I don't usually make the effort to do. "I imagine you see a lot of loss."

He goes still, his eyes finding a random spot on the floor and locking in. "Loss doesn't even begin to cover it."

I want to reach out and offer him some kind of comfort, but I don't really know how to do that, so instead my hands hang uselessly at my sides. "I'm sorry, Ben."

He shakes off the funk like a dog jumping out of a swimming pool, running a hand through his hair and flashing me a sheepish smile. "Anyway, I can understand why women aren't exactly lining up to be with me."

I take that smile as a signal that it's time to leave the emotions behind. "I find that hard to believe. I mean, your sense of humor leaves a lot to be desired, *sweetheart,* but you're cute and nice. You cure sick kids, for fuck's sake."

Ben shrugs again. "I go out on dates, but so far I haven't met someone I felt like I could truly open up to, you know?"

I don't know, because I have no desire to open up to anyone, but I nod anyway, as if I understand his frustration. "Have you gone out on a lot of blind dates?"

"A few."

For some reason, that thought sends a burst of some foreign feeling through my chest. I cover the lapse with a smile. "Bet none of them have been as awesome as me."

"None of them have been as *something* as you." There's a tad less sarcasm contained in his voice this time.

"Who set you up with me, anyway?" Normally Grandmother picks her candidates for me from a select pool of associates and I don't see how Ben could possibly have been on her list.

"My cousin, Sophie."

"Does she hate you or something?" I rack my brain, trying to think of anyone I might know named Sophie.

Ben doesn't laugh at my not-joke. Instead he meets my

gaze, waiting for me to make full eye contact before continuing. "She worked at your firm as a summer intern a couple of years ago. Told me that you were one of the smartest, fiercest women she'd ever seen. Said if there was anyone in New York who could handle me and my life, it would be you."

The words catch me so completely off guard, I almost fall over. Sophie, the summer intern. I vaguely remember telling her she would never make it in mergers and acquisitions if she allowed her emotions to run away with her. I thought she hated me. I assume most of our interns hate me.

"Oh," I finally manage to say when the silence becomes unbearable. "Is she doing well?" It's deflection, but I find myself really wanting to know.

Ben smiles one of his genuine smiles. "She's doing great. Decided to go into immigration law. It's tough on her, but she loves it."

I nod. It's the perfect job for someone like her. "Tell her I said hello."

"I will." Neither of us acknowledges what has to happen before he can follow through with that.

I toy with the mane on a stuffed pony. "Do you think I can actually do this, Ben? Can I find a way to get out of here?"

He takes the pony, and our hands brush the slightest bit. "I think there probably hasn't been much in your life that you've set out to accomplish and haven't. So if you really want to get out of here, I think you'll find a way."

It's the kindest thing anyone has said to me in a really long time and it stops the breath in my lungs for just a second. I choke a little when the air starts flowing again and I busy myself with opening another box in the hopes he hasn't noticed. "Thank you, Ben. That means a lot."

Ben clears his throat, already shuffling away from me. "I'm just going to go finish up what I was working on. Let's say we'll head out in about an hour?"

He doesn't wait for me to respond before he turns and scurries off to the other side of the gym. I should have known better than to do something as foolish as show even a hint of emotion. Ben doesn't care about me or my feelings, he's just like everyone else in my life. Here to push me to get the job done by whatever means necessary. My feelings haven't ever mattered before, and they certainly don't matter here.

I turn my attention back to the job at hand and sort the remaining stuffed animals like my life depends on it. This, at least, is something I know I won't fail.

8

Two days later, the School's Out for the Summer carnival has somehow almost miraculously managed to erect itself in the middle of the town square. I left the gym chock full of supplies and building materials and woke up the next day to a legit freaking carnival—the only thing missing being the guests.

When I arrive, everything appears to be firmly under control. Ben is striding around the outdoor space, clipboard in hand, answering questions before they're even asked, directing the group of volunteers with his patented calm and ease.

I approach one of the food vendors and request a churro, which comes out piping hot and smelling like a cinnamon swirl of heaven. I hand over one of my volunteer food coupons in exchange.

I stride in Ben's direction, taking the time to appreciate the hard work that must have occurred to get all of this set up. Hard work I luckily didn't have to participate in much beyond sorting a few stuffed animals. Hard work that he took on willingly, because he isn't a soul suck of a person.

"Here." I thrust the warm churro at Ben. "You look like you need a sugar break."

He studies the treat warily for a half a second before grabbing it and tearing off half in one bite. "Thanks."

"Everything looks great, Ben. I can't believe you put this all together in a matter of days. I think it's time to let guests in and start making some money." I gesture toward the entrance, where a few people are already milling about.

He checks his watch and nods. "Yes, we open in a few minutes. Which means it's time for you to get to your post."

"My post? I thought I was mostly here to eat fried foods and offer moral support."

Ben blinks a lot but doesn't say anything. He heads down one of the rows of games, expecting me to follow.

And I do. What choice do I have?

Ben stops in front of one of the booths.

A target and a large vat of water, a little plank hovering over the pool.

The dunk tank.

"Okay, what do I need to do? Take tickets?" I guess I can manage that, though it will require interacting with a large number of people. Normally that doesn't bother me, but here in Heart Springs, nothing ever seems to work out as simple as planned.

Ben smiles, and it's slightly condescending, but in sort of a nice way. "No. I don't need you to take tickets, sweetheart."

I cross my arms over my chest, flattening the ruffles lining the bodice of my lavender dress. "Okay, then what do you need me to do?"

"I need you to climb up in there and prepare to get dunked."

I laugh out loud. A real genuine laugh, one that causes me to double over. "You have got to be high as a goddamned kite if you think I'm getting anywhere near that thing."

Ben takes a step closer to me, crowding into my space and causing me to step back toward the ladder. Damn. Has he always smelled this good? "I thought you wanted to become a valuable member of the community. Don't you want to help the children of Heart Springs?"

"To be fair, I never really said I wanted to help the children, I just didn't think I had a whole lot of say in the matter." I attempt to inch my way away from the water-filled monstrosity, but Ben keeps managing to corral me closer and closer to the dastardly steps. The woodsy scent of him invades my nose and a warmth spreads through my chest when his fingers brush against mine.

"You know, all three of your potential suitors will be coming to the carnival. I'm sure nothing would make Mimi happier than a carnival meet cute."

"At this point, I think I might prefer three terrible, godawful dates." Lunging in the opposite direction of the tank, I try to make a break for it.

Ben catches me, his hands latching loosely around my wrists, our bodies almost flush.

My heart stutters in my chest and for a second, I wonder if I'm suffering from some sort of heart condition. But then Ben drops his hands as if it's physically painful to make contact with me. My heart trips once, but then returns to its regularly scheduled programming.

He steps away. "If you're not able to help out, I guess I can let Mimi know you're ready for introductions." He runs a hand through his hair. "It's a shame. I have a feeling you would've brought in enough money to meet our entire fundraising goal."

"The people of Heart Springs hate me that much, huh?" It shouldn't bother me. It does.

He flashes me a small smile. "Well, you did traumatize an eight-year-old and almost ruin a wedding."

"Fair enough." I give the dunk tank a thorough once-over. If I'm dumb enough to climb up that ladder and take a seat on the flimsy platform, I'm sure to be plunged into the water. Repeatedly. Of course, my other option is to find out which dashing gentlemen of Heart Springs Mimi is planning to foist upon me.

Honestly, both options sound equally terrible.

But only one option helps Ben, one of the few people who has actually taken the time to get to know me and support me since I woke up in my own personal hell.

"Okay fine. I'll do it."

Ben grins like he knew I was going to cave the entire time. "Fantastic." He holds out his hand.

Despite my trepidation about what comes next, I don't hesitate to place my hand in his. His palm is warm and his strong fingers grip mine in a way that makes me feel totally secure. I revel in that feeling for a half a second before Ben helps me climb up the ladder next to the tank.

"I hope you know there's not another person on this planet I would even consider doing this for." The plank jutting out over the water is not at all stable and I have to grip it with both hands to keep from plunging in before we've even started. I mourn the loss of Ben's hand the minute I have to let it go.

"I'm truly honored, sweetheart."

I glare at him from my perch, but there's not a hint of sarcasm in his eyes. "You owe me big."

"Happy to cash in anytime." Ben throws an honest to god wink over his shoulder as he turns and strides down the aisle. "We're opening the gates now. Good luck, sweetheart!"

"I hate you!" I call to his retreating back.

By the time I get myself fully situated on the plank that will undoubtedly be dropping me into the hopefully not freezing cold water below, a crowd of people has already formed around the booth.

A woman steps up first. I don't recognize her, but it becomes clear who she is after just a few seconds.

"My daughter used to love clowns. In fact, she even requested a clown theme for her birthday party next month. I bought clown plates and clown cups and clown goody bags. I even hired a clown." The woman winds her arm back. "And now my daughter is terrified of clowns." She lets her ball fly.

It misses, but not by much.

"Eight is a little past clown party age if you ask me," I mumble under my breath.

"My daughter can't sleep at night, and I'm out hundreds of dollars." The woman lets another ball fly.

This one connects.

The board folds underneath me and I'm plunged into the water. It's lukewarm, thank baby Jesus, but when I climb out of the tank and settle back on my seat, the slight early summer breeze is chilly on my wet skin. My dress is drenched and sticking to every part of me and, really, I should have been provided with a wetsuit upon agreeing to this farce.

I recognize the man who steps up next.

He tosses the ball from one hand to the other. "I think you know why I'm here."

"I was only trying to help, Tim. Your wife is the one who was having doubts." I'm not about to apologize for potentially saving a woman from going through the heartache and financial devastation of inevitable divorce.

He chucks the ball with perfect aim.

And I go in again.

Tim still has another ball to throw, but he passes it off to Emily, his now wife, who luckily doesn't have his arm strength.

But Kate does. She knocks me into the water not once, but twice. I think she missed her calling. She should probably quit wedding planning and try out for the local baseball team.

By the time I hoist myself out of the water for the fourth time, I'm shivering. And on top of that my hair is plastered to my head and I'm sure my makeup has completely abandoned ship. I wrap my arms around myself, trying to latch on to even the slightest bit of body heat, but there is none to be found.

I take two more unwilling plunges into the depths of the dunk tank before Ben comes to my rescue.

"All right, folks. I think Cam has had enough for now. Go explore the rest of the carnival and spend lots of money. Remember, it's for a good cause!" Ben shoos away the crowd. They mumble and grumble a bit, but it doesn't take them long to find other games to play that don't involve torturing poor, semi-innocent souls.

I wearily climb down the rungs of the ladder, my skin covered in goose bumps.

Ben hands me a towel, his eyes lingering on the bodice of my dress, which is now practically see through and clinging to my breasts.

"Thanks," I manage through chattering teeth.

"Oh come on, it's not that bad. I made sure the water was heated."

"How very kind of you." I burrow myself into the towel. "Unfortunately, you didn't account for the oh so important detail of wet clothes plus cool air equals fucking freezing."

His brow furrows. "I don't suppose you brought something to change into?"

I glare at him. "Seeing as I didn't know water torture was on the menu for this children's carnival, no I did not."

He chuckles, but he slips out of his sweatshirt while he laughs at me. "Take this. Why don't you run home and change into dry clothes, and then when you get back, I'll find a job for you on land instead of at sea."

"You're not funny." I tug the sweatshirt over my head and fold myself into its warmth. "And what makes you think I'll be coming back?"

"Because you know it's important to me and you don't want to let me down?"

I blink at him.

"Okay. How about, you know you need to do this if you want to find a way out of here?" He reaches up and tucks a dripping strand of hair behind my ear.

"I hate you." My breath catches as his fingers graze my cheek.

His voice softens, so I have to lean in closer to hear him. "The feeling's mutual, sweetheart."

The real annoying part is that neither of us means it.

9

I take my time wandering through the carnival, making my way toward the exit. There are more people here than I've seen at any one time since landing in Heart Springs, and they're all laughing and playing games and eating funnel cake and seemingly having a marvelous time. It's not the kind of scene I ever would have longed to be a part of, but something about seeing it all here in front of me, well, that might be a jolt of loneliness piercing my heart.

I search the crowd for any signs of potential suitors, but all I can see are couples and families, which is a bit of a relief. I don't know if I'm ready to come face-to-face with the kinds of men Mimi thinks are right for me. When even Ben's sweatshirt can't keep me warm enough, I hurry for the exit and make the short walk back to my little cottage. I'm tempted to hop in a hot shower, and lord knows I've earned one, but I promised Ben I would come back quickly, and it probably won't help my case with the community if I abandon a children's hospital fundraiser. And since finding a spot among the community somehow seems like it might be the only task I actually have a hope of accomplishing, I don't think I can afford to fuck this one up.

So I change into a pair of jeans and a dry T-shirt and slip Ben's sweatshirt back over my head. Only because there don't seem to be any hoodies hiding in my frill-filled closet and I need something to keep me warm. Nothing to do with the fresh woodsy scent lingering on the fabric. After running a brush through my hair, I tie it up in a bun and wipe the remains of my makeup from my face.

Ben is waiting for me at the entrance when I make my way back to the carnival. I know the instant he spots me because his eyes take me in from head to toe, and I'm too far away to be sure, but something like appreciation lingers in his gaze.

But I must be hallucinating because by the time I cross through the gate, he's back to all business.

"That was quite a long break, but glad to have you back." He steers me, hand on my back, down one of the many aisles before depositing me at the bakery booth. "This is Emma, help her with whatever she needs." He lingers there, hand still on my lower back for a half a second.

"Ben! We're out of tickets at the ring toss booth!" a faceless voice in the crowd calls.

"Duty calls," he tells me, his hand skimming my waist as it drops back to his side. "You okay here?"

I nod, words sticking in my throat.

"See you later, sweetheart." Ben strides down the aisle.

I do not watch him walk away, not even for a half a second.

I take in a steadying breath before turning to face Emma,

a beautiful Black woman who looks to be in her early thirties, who no doubt has heard all kinds of terrible things about me and would really rather have anyone else here in her booth to assist. She's wearing a bright yellow dress and a jean jacket, the kind of outfit I would scorn in New York, but here in Heart Springs, I can appreciate the pop of color and how comfortable Emma seems in her own skin.

Emma greets me with a warm smile that lights up her whole face. "Hi there! I've been looking forward to meeting you!"

"You have?" The words slip out before I can stop them.

Emma laughs, and it's kindhearted without even a hint of teasing. "Of course! Mimi mentioned that you might be interested in working at the bakery and I've been looking forward to the help."

I take the pale yellow striped apron she offers me, tying the strings around my waist. "I don't know if you've heard, but so far I appear to be the opposite of helpful."

She shrugs, handing a customer change and a perfect-looking pie in a pretty lavender box. "That just means you haven't found the right job yet. Maybe baking is going to turn out to be your one true passion."

"I doubt it." I eye the various baked goods artfully arranged on the yellow gingham covered tables. Everything looks like it could be photographed for *Martha Stewart Living*, and if the smells are any indication, they taste as good as they look. "I don't think I've ever baked anything in my life."

"Well, you never know until you try!" Emma handles another customer before turning her attention solely to me. "Would you rather take orders or box up the goodies?"

"Taking orders means dealing with people, so I'll do the boxing."

Another kind smile lights up her warm brown eyes. "You got it! I'll point things out as needed, but everything is labeled, and the boxes are under the table."

"Great." I try to infuse the simple declaration with an exclamation point, but it probably comes out more strangled than enthusiastic.

Yet despite my trepidation, my time in Emma's bakery booth goes relatively smoothly. It takes me a minute to figure out where all the items live, but we quickly develop a rhythm, Emma taking orders for cupcakes and cookies and the most heavenly looking cinnamon rolls, and me boxing them up. I'm tempted to swipe my finger through each treat piled high with frosting, but I show some self-control and before long, all of the baked goods have been sold.

Emma releases a huge breath and claps her hands as we send the final customer off on their way. "Oh my. Thank you so much for coming to help me, I don't think I would've survived that on my own!" She wraps me up in an impromptu hug, and I can't help but hug her back.

"No problem. It feels nice to actually be useful for a change." I've experienced more failure in the past few days than the previous few decades combined and I didn't quite realize how much it was bringing me down until this minute. "Thank you for being patient with me and showing me the ropes."

"My pleasure!" Emma bustles around the booth, packing up the remaining boxes and the various display platters. Until she spots something and stands up with an "Oh!" She immediately begins fiddling with her hair, patting and twisting the halo of curls surrounding her gorgeous face.

I look around for the cause of her sudden interest in beauty maintenance, but only see Mimi, striding toward the booth with a purpose. It's the first time since being here that I've seen her outside of the café and as I take in her relaxed jeans and baby blue twin set cardigan, topped with a simple string of pearls, my interpretation of her as the classic grandmother figure is cemented.

"Fantastic. You're still here." She doesn't actually sound all that happy to see me, which sort of stings a bit. "And you met Emma." Mimi nods to her, though Emma isn't paying attention, her gaze focused on the man standing behind Mimi.

He's a tall and lanky East Asian man with bright eyes and brown hair that's disheveled in a not on purpose way.

Mimi grabs him by the arm and brings him forward, practically shoving him into my face. "This is Ethan."

A lot of things happen at once after that.

Ethan stammers out a hello.

Emma lets out a sound that's suspiciously whimper-like.

I groan. Audibly.

Mimi rolls her eyes.

And Ben comes charging down the aisle, stepping between me and Ethan, clearing a space between us.

"Cam, I need you to come assist with cleanup," Ben says, breaking the absurdly awkward tension.

"I think she can stay and chat with Ethan for a few minutes," Mimi insists.

I'm already backing away from whatever this hot mess is. "Sorry, Meem, but I should make sure I'm working hard for the betterment of the community. Nice to meet you, Ethan, maybe you could stay and chat with Emma for a few minutes?" I link my arm through Ben's. "Emma, I'll plan on being at the bakery tomorrow morning for my first shift?"

I don't wait for an answer, tugging Ben along in the direction of anywhere but here.

Once we're away from the crowd, I pull Ben to a stop. "Please tell me Ethan is not one of my suitors." Nothing against the guy, he just has *not my type* stamped all over him. I don't do nice guys. Literally or metaphorically.

"Unfortunately, Ethan is one of your suitors." Ben's jaw tenses, and I think it's the first time I've seen him visibly upset before.

"*Unfortunately* because in spite of his unassuming looks he's really a total jackass?"

"*Unfortunately* because Ethan is one of the nicest guys in Heart Springs." Ben turns away from me.

I let the words sink in without questioning how Ben knows enough about him to make such a statement, and totally lie to myself about how much those words sting. "And the worst thing that could happen to a nice guy would be being matched with someone terrible like me, right?" Even though I'd already mentally written off Ethan, I can't deny the prick of Ben's disapproval.

He sighs and runs a hand through his hair. "I didn't mean it like that."

"Sure." I yank on the sleeves of Ben's sweatshirt, pulling it over my head and shoving it into his chest. "Well, you don't have to worry about Ethan. I'm not going to date him."

Ben barely catches the hoodie, looking for a second like

he wants to shove it right back at me. "I'm afraid it doesn't work like that, sweetheart. If Ethan is one of your suitors, then you have to go out at least once."

I shrug. "I'll have a cup of coffee with the guy, but I'm not going to be pursuing anything with him."

"Too good for a nice guy like Ethan?" Ben's words are cutting, and I'm wondering where the hell the sudden attitude is coming from.

"Emma is clearly into him."

"I wouldn't think that would stop you."

"Fuck, Ben, did someone piss in your Cheerios this morning? What the hell happened over the course of the last hour? I know no one in this town actually likes me, but I didn't realize you hated me as much as everyone else." I spin on my heel and march toward the exit, completely done with this bullshit. For an hour or so there, working in the booth with Emma, it seemed like things might be going okay. I wasn't fucking up everything, and it actually felt good.

And now the one person I thought might be sort of on my side has completely turned on me.

Whatever. I won't allow Ben's words to affect me. It's not like I really believed we were becoming friends.

As soon as I get back to the cottage, I'm losing myself in a hot bath and a glass of wine.

"Cam, wait!" Ben's voice catches me as I'm turning down the sidewalk in front of our houses.

I don't stop, continuing to stomp my way along until I can throw open my front gate.

He catches me just before I can slam the front door in his face. "I'm sorry." He sucks in a long breath, winded from chasing after me. Which is his own damn fault. I push on the door.

Ben holds up a hand, but he doesn't make contact with the yellow-painted wood. "Please. Just give me a second."

I shouldn't, but there's something in the deep brown of his eyes that causes me to open the door back up, just the slightest bit.

"I'm sorry. I shouldn't have said that. I was upset about something else and I took it out on you."

I cross my arms over my chest. "What were you upset about?"

His eyes flutter closed for a second while he gathers himself. "I can't tell you. I wish I could, but I can't."

"Why?"

His brow furrows. "What do you mean?"

"What happens if you tell me? Does Zeus come down and strike you with a lightning bolt? Does the Great and Powerful Oz send you hurtling back to Kansas?"

"I just can't." He holds up a hand to stave off the protest he knows is coming. "Please just believe me when I say I'm trying to look out for you. But sometimes that's not the easiest thing to do here. You just have to trust me."

I scoff. "I don't trust anyone, Ben. I'd think you'd know enough about me by now to realize that."

He flashes me a soft smile. "I do. I know what I'm asking, and I'm asking it anyway."

I study him for a second, looking for the usual signs someone is blowing smoke up my ass. But all I see is Ben, the first, and by default, best friend I've ever had. "Fine. But don't take your anger out on me again, got it?"

He gives me a mock salute. "Sure thing, sweetheart."

"Well, have a good night, I guess."

"Yeah, you too."

I close the door behind him and peek out the front curtain to watch him head back to the carnival. For a second, I feel guilty for abandoning my cleanup duties, but the feeling doesn't last long. Between the dunk tank and Mimi's emotional warfare, I think I more than fulfilled my obligations to the community.

And something tells me that tomorrow, going into the bakery and facing Emma and dealing with the whole Ethan situation is going to be the pinnacle of awkward.

And so into that long, hot bath I go.

10

Emma greets me with a warm, genuine smile when I push through the door of the bakery the morning after the carnival. Like everywhere else, the shop is done up in pastels, lots of lavender and soft yellow, but somehow it works, creating an environment of homey comfort. Helped along, no doubt, by the completely intoxicating smells seeping from every corner of the space. I return her smile, tentatively, low-key waiting for her to bite my head off. Because it would be totally justified given that I'm being set up with the guy she clearly likes.

Instead she waves and offers me a mug of coffee like the goddess she is. "Good morning, I hope you don't mind, but I asked Mimi about your coffee order and she told me you liked lattes, extra pumpkin spice." She spins back toward the counter, the skirt of her lavender sundress twirling.

I grit my teeth, not wanting Emma to suffer for Mimi's transgressions. "Did she now? Well, that was very sweet of her." I take a sip, bracing myself for the worst, but I don't know if it's Emma's magic or if this town is finally getting to me, but it's fucking delicious. "Goddamn, that's good."

Emma's light brown cheeks color, either at the compliment or my choice words. "I'm glad you like it."

I set the mug on the counter so I can tie the polka-dotted apron she hands me around my waist. "Emma, I just wanted to apologize for last night. I shouldn't have walked out on you like that, I just don't really deal with awkward situations all that well."

She waves me off, turning her attention to a large tray of cupcakes. "It's not a problem, we were pretty much done anyway."

I duck into her line of vision so she has to meet my eyes. I want her to see the sincerity with which I'm going to deliver my next words, because it doesn't happen often, and I need her to believe me. "And I want you to know that whatever dumb hoops I have to jump through to appease Mimi's little matchmaking mission, I'm not interested in Ethan. He's definitely not the man for me, and I won't be going out with him more than the obligatory one time."

Emma purses her lips and turns away from me once again. "Well, don't feel like you need to do that on my account."

Reaching for my coffee, I try to discern just how much I can push this woman I barely know. ". . . Clearly you're interested in him."

She shrugs, artfully tossing some sprinkles on each of the cupcakes. "What makes you say that?"

I take another sip of coffee. "Emma. It was pretty obvious from the moment he walked up to the booth last night."

She pauses her sprinkling and a look of horror overtakes her face. "Do you think he noticed?"

"He's a man, so probably not." Cocking my head, I continue to study my newest boss. "Why haven't you ever said anything to him? By all accounts, Ethan is a nice guy. Even if he's not interested—and he'd be a fool not to be, considering you're a total smoke show who bakes for a living—I'm sure he would be cool about it."

Emma hefts the tray of cupcakes over to the display case and neatly arranges the baked goods on the lavender shelves. "I could never make the first move! That's the man's job."

I roll my eyes. "In what world? Maybe I'll use my so-called date to fill him in on all your amazing attributes."

Emma's eyes widen. "You can't do that!"

"Why not?" I lean my butt against the counter. I should probably offer to help or do something productive, but the caffeine hasn't fully sunk in yet and I'd much rather expend my energy figuring out how to bring Heart Springs out of the 1900s. The early part.

"Because you just can't. If he's interested, he'll make the first move."

"What if he's too shy? What if he thinks you aren't interested? Seriously, Emma, there's nothing wrong with seeing what you want and going for it. Where I'm from, women make the first move all the time." I swig the last of my coffee and place the empty mug in a tub stacked with other dishes needing to be washed.

Emma's eyes tighten in something looking suspiciously glarelike. "You can take those to the back. Sponges and dish soap are under the sink."

Man, I know no one likes being pushed out of their comfort zone, but dishwashing duty seems kind of a harsh punishment from someone I thought I was getting along with.

But Emma turns her back, and if I don't want to completely blow my final job opportunity, I probably shouldn't irritate her any more than I already have. I hoist up the tub and barely manage to make it to the kitchen without dropping the whole damn thing.

Not only do I have this huge stack of dishes to wash, but the sink is already filled with all the pans and bowls and measuring cups Emma must have used to bake this morning's muffins and croissants and pastries.

"Fan-fucking-tastic."

This is my chance to prove I'm not a total waste of space when it comes to demanding careers. Sure, I'm used to the demands coming from angry clients and my overbearing family members, but if I can handle my grandmother belittling me in front of the entire firm, I can manage a few dishes.

An hour and a half later, I'm finally drying the last set of bowls. My back is throbbing. My hands are pruney. And my feet feel like I've been walking the streets of Manhattan in six-inch stilettos. For ten hours.

I toss the towel on the counter and bend over to stretch out my back, groaning as my muscles pull and ache in all kinds of unfamiliar ways.

The door to the kitchen swings open.

"Peace offering?" Emma hands me a plate with a perfectly decorated cupcake.

"For what?" I question, even as I accept the plate and rip the wrapper away from the cake.

"I was flustered by your questions, about me and about Ethan, and I shouldn't have given you dish duty just because I was upset." Emma moves to the fridge, pulling out a carton of eggs before crossing to the giant shelves housing all the dry ingredients.

"Emma, you're my boss, you can make me wash dishes whenever you want. Or whenever you need." I break off the bottom half of the cupcake and smush it down on top of the frosting.

Emma watches me curiously.

I hold up my creation. "Perfect frosting to cake ratio and it means I don't get a face full of buttercream when I bite into it." Which I do, taking down half the cake in one chomp. "Fuck me, this is amazing," I mumble around my mouthful of red velvet deliciousness.

Emma grins, sifting flour into a large bowl. "Thank you. And thank you for what you said, about Ethan."

I swallow the remainder of my cupcake. "I meant it, you know. I know I don't exactly have the best reputation around here, but if there's one thing I'm never going to do, it's go after someone else's man."

She cracks an egg with one hand, effortlessly adding it to her batter. "He's not really my man, and you could certainly do a lot worse."

I watch as she mixes all the ingredients together. "I'm sure I could. But it's still not happening." I rinse my hands in the sink. "Now, what would you like me to work on next? Assuming you haven't already decided to fire me."

She pushes a muffin tin my way. "You haven't done anything that would warrant a firing."

I flash her a sweet smile. "The day is young, Emma dear."

"You're not nearly as scary as you want everyone to think you are, you know." She hands me a stick of butter. "Now grease those pans so we can get these muffins in the oven before the next rush."

"Yes, boss." I give her a mock salute, and we share a laugh. And it feels good.

....

I DON'T BOTHER OPENING THE GATE IN FRONT OF MY house when I've finally made it home after my shift at the bakery. I push right through Ben's gate instead, but I don't find him waiting on the porch. I think about leaving, but I kind of want to tell him about my day. About how, even though I got off to a rocky start, it didn't turn out too terribly.

So I knock on the door. I almost leave when he doesn't immediately answer, but then the door swings open and I find I can't breathe.

Ben stands in the doorway, dressed in jeans that hug his hips and a tight T-shirt. A pair of thick gloves hide his hands and a pair of plastic work goggles sit on top of his head, pushing his hair out of his face and highlighting his perfect cheekbones and square jaw. "Hey, sweetheart. Didn't expect to see you today."

"Sorry for stopping by unannounced. Clearly you're in the middle of something." I gesture to the goggles. "I can come back later."

"Come on in, I was just doing some work in the garage."

"Garage?" I do a mental scan of my own identical home, knowing there's no garage attached.

Ben leads me through his house, which, though the layout is the same as mine, couldn't be more different. There's lots of dark woods and navy blues and bottle greens. It's like our homes are stereotypical his and hers versions of the same place.

He pushes open a door at the back, gesturing for me to step into a brightly lit space.

"Holy shit." I don't know what I expected to find on the other side, but it wasn't this.

The space is filled with wood furniture in various stages of completion. A large oak dining table takes up one corner, and chairs are scattered throughout, some with missing legs, some looking like they need a coat of paint.

"Did you make all of this?" I run a finger along the smooth edge of a bookcase. "How did you get all of this done in only a couple of days?"

Ben takes off his gloves, opens a small fridge, and pulls out two beers. "It's really strange. Yesterday when I got home from the doctor's office, I was just thinking about how much I was missing my woodworking." He pops the top on one bottle and hands it to me. "This door appeared almost as if out of nowhere and when I came inside, all of my old projects were here waiting for me."

"Well, I guess we know who Heart Springs's favorite child is." It sure as fuck isn't me, not that that's any big surprise. He gestures to a chair with four legs, and I sit. "How do you find time to do all of this while working as a surgeon?"

He drags over another chair, sitting across from me. "Hobbies are important. And, some days, I find I really need a way to decompress."

I can only imagine. The amount of guilt I feel when I mess up a deal—even if it does happen rarely—can be overwhelming. When Ben has a bad day at the office, children's lives are on the line.

I trace the intricately carved pattern on the arm of the chair. "You do beautiful work."

Ben's cheeks flush, and he tries to hide it with a sip of

beer. "Thanks. I imagine that's a high compliment coming from you."

I let my hands rest on the arms of the chair, feeling an appreciation for the curves of the wood, as if knowing Ben's hands shaped the chair suddenly make it more comforting. "It is."

Ben smirks, but it's teasing, and if I'm being honest, kind of cute. "I take it you don't have many hobbies."

I twist my beer bottle in my hands. "I don't have time for hobbies."

"Seems like you don't make time for much." His words might sting if it weren't for their underlying truth.

I look for something to throw at him, but since the only thing within range is a glass beer bottle, I figure I should abstain. "Yeah, yeah."

"How did it go at the bakery today?"

I shrug, swigging the last of my beer. "It was mostly good, I think. Emma is basically the nicest person I've ever met so she should be an easy boss to work for. Can't say baking is going to suddenly be my new life's passion, but I think of all the options so far, it's the least painful."

"Maybe you just need to give it some time. You might surprise yourself."

I roll my eyes. "Easy for you to say. You're the golden boy who somehow managed to escape all of this with no tasks involved."

Ben sets down his beer. "I have a task."

It's a good thing I'm out of beer, because I would have choked on it. "I'm sorry, what?"

Ben sighs, rubbing his hands down the thighs of his jeans, drawing my attention to the toned muscles of his legs. "I have a task, I just haven't told you about it."

I stand, crossing to the fridge and grabbing two more beers. "Wait a minute, so you mean to tell me while I've been sitting here every night letting you see how badly I've been failing at everything I try, you've been working on your own tasks and not giving me the details?"

Ben takes both beers, popping the lids before handing one back to me. "Seems so."

"Rude." I wait an appropriate amount of time to let him give me the info I obviously need. "This is the part where you tell me about whatever it is Mimi's making you do."

"No can do, sweetheart."

I study him as he very purposefully avoids my gaze. "Hmm. Well, I know it has nothing to do with your job. Does it have to do with your love life? You did willingly go on a blind date, so you might actually be looking for a real relationship."

"It's not love related." His answer is a little too quick. I bookmark that response to examine further later.

"Family related, then?" I realize then that I know nothing about Ben's family, probably because I've never taken the time to ask.

He shrugs. "Nope."

"Of course not. You probably have one of those families where you all like one another and get along and enjoy being together."

"I don't think that's as rare as you think it is, sweetheart." He taps his fingers on his beer bottle. "But yeah, mine are pretty great. One sister, two parents who are still in love and happily married. I got pretty lucky in that department."

I wonder what that must be like. "Sometimes I wish for a family like that."

"You might make it easier to have one like that if you talked to yours, told them how you really feel about things."

"I've never been good at making things easier for myself." I sip from the bottle of beer and lean back in my chair.

Ben leans back too, though this time his eyes stay firmly trained on me. "Why is that, do you think?"

"Uh oh, did Mimi send you to psychoanalyze me? Is this your task? Get inside my head and figure out why the fuck I can't just find a way to be happy with this prescribed little life?"

Ben doesn't say anything. Damn him for being able to sit quietly, a trait I've never been able to master.

I chug half the beer before spewing out my story. "My family is a lot. My grandmother was one of the first women to graduate from Harvard Law School." I shoot him a side-eyed glance, watching for his reaction, though he doesn't give me much of one. "She started this law firm in New York and basically turned it into one of the biggest and most successful in the country. We specialize in mergers and acquisitions." Raising my eyebrows, I throw Ben a questioning look.

"I've heard of it from Sophie, but don't really know what it entails."

"Basically, we help big businesses buy other businesses."

Ben purses his lips. "I'm assuming by that you mean you help greedy corporations acquire struggling independent companies?"

I ignore the judgment in his nonquestion. "Yup. And we do it well. I do it well. I knew by the time I was five years old that I was going to be a lawyer, just like Grandmother. I knew by the time I was ten I was going to be the best lawyer, just like Grandmother. And I knew by the time I was twenty I was going to run the firm one day, just like Grandmother."

"Did anyone ever stop to ask you if that's what you wanted?" Ben asks the question softly, but it still feels like a punch to the solar plexus.

"That's not a thing we do in our family. You fall in line, you exceed ridiculously high expectations, or you get out."

"Who got out?"

"My mom." I shrug like it's no big deal, as if being abandoned by your mother could ever be anything other than a big deal. "She was supposed to be the successor. My grandmother's firstborn, her only daughter. She was groomed to take over the firm when she was young, but she basically revolted. She fell in love with my dad and got knocked up. He left before I was born. Grandmother was still willing to give her a chance—pay for childcare while my mom went to law school—but my mom refused. Said the firm was a crime against humanity and she wanted no part of it. When I was twelve, she moved to California and became an art teacher, and we haven't heard from her since." I didn't know much when I was little, other than I wanted to do everything in my power to not fail like she did, to not continually disappoint my grandmother the way she did. The intense desire for success only grew as I got older, as I became even more determined to prove I was not the weak kind of woman my mother was.

"I'm sorry."

It's a simple statement, but one I haven't heard in a very long time. At least not regarding something like this. My associates at the firm apologized to me constantly, but that's probably because they were messing up constantly. Is it my fault I pushed them all to succeed and most of them couldn't hack it?

I set my beer bottle on a nearby stool, still half full. If I don't stop drinking now, the pity party is going to turn ugly, and I refuse to fall apart in front of Ben. "I should get to bed. Gotta be at the bakery early again tomorrow." I push up from my chair.

Ben reaches out a hand but stops short of making physical contact. "Thank you for telling me all that, I'm sure it's not easy to talk about."

"You can pay me back by not using it against me."

Ben stands, bringing the two of us level, with only a few inches of space separating us. "I wouldn't do that, Cam."

It's stupid, but I think I actually believe him. I nod and turn to leave.

This time he does make contact, his hand wrapping around my wrist. The brush of his skin on mine is heady, the woodsy scent of him filling my nose.

He hesitates long enough that I know he's not happy about whatever it is that comes next.

"Just say it, Ben. I'm a big girl, I can take it."

"Mimi wanted me to tell you your date with Ethan is tomorrow. He'll pick you up at three o'clock." He drops my hand and takes a step back.

I nod again, words lodged in my throat. This time when I turn to leave, Ben lets me go. But that doesn't stop me from looking back at him as I stroll from the room.

11

There's a knock on my door promptly at three o'clock. I answer it, plastering a fake smile on my face because I think Ethan and I both know how this date is going to go down.

"You look nice," he says, visibly struggling to choke out the compliment. He hands me a bouquet of yellow daisies.

"Thanks. Let me just put these in water." I gesture to the kitchen and move toward it without inviting him in. I return a second later, having unceremoniously stashed the flowers in a mug.

"Shall we?" Ethan holds out his arm.

It would be the height of rude not to take it, and I'm tempted, but I have a strong feeling Ethan doesn't want to be here any more than I do, so we might as well try to get along for the afternoon. I slip my hand into the curve of his elbow. The brush of skin on skin stirs absolutely zero feelings, and when I lean closer to take a subtle whiff of him, I get nothing in return. The man smells like nothing. I think that pretty much immediately eliminates him as romance hero material.

The silence between us grows painful until I finally break it. "Where are we headed?"

"We're going out to the strawberry fields to pick some berries and have a picnic. The Strawberry Festival starts tomorrow."

My nose wrinkles before I can control it. I've never understood the fascination with picking berries or apples or whatever as some sort of activity. I can go to the market and buy a bushel for a fraction of the cost, without having to get sweaty and dirty. And what kind of town needs two fruit festivals and a carnival in less than two weeks?

Ethan's eyes meet mine. "Somehow I don't think this is going to be your kind of date."

"Picnics are fun, I guess." If you like bugs crawling all over the food and drowning in perfectly good glasses of wine.

We walk for a few more silent minutes before we reach a sign for the berry farm. It tells us to wait for the wagon to come pick us up. A wagon. This date is getting worse by the minute.

Neither of us even makes an attempt at conversation in the two minutes it takes the wagon to come rambling down the dirt road. Ethan offers me a hand to help me climb up into the back and I take it. Once again, there's nary a hint of a spark.

Ethan settles on the bench seat next to me, leaving at least a foot of space between us.

The wagon lurches into motion, and I fall practically into Ethan's lap, moving quickly to push myself upright before my hands come into contact with any particular places that they absolutely should not.

"Sorry." I brush my hair out of my eyes and smooth down the skirt of my yellow sundress. Grandmother always told me blondes should never wear yellow because it washes us out, and I definitely factored that tidbit into my wardrobe decision for the afternoon.

"No problem," Ethan mumbles.

"Look, Ethan, I can think of few things worse in life than trying to have any sort of meaningful conversation in the back of a fucking wagon, but in the interest of preserving both of our sanity, let me just make it clear that I have no intention of pursuing a relationship with you."

The relief that washes over his face should be insulting.

It *is* a little insulting, if I'm being totally honest. So I don't know why I rush to justify my declaration. "You seem like a really nice guy, and I'm sure there are lots of women out there who would love to date you." I can think of one in particular, but I keep that to myself for now. "But you're not the one for me, I'm afraid."

Ethan scrubs his hands over his thighs, covered in jeans that accentuate his lanky frame. "Please don't take this the wrong way, but I'm so glad you said that."

"Gee, how could I take that the wrong way?" I slide a little farther away on the bench.

Ethan moves a couple of inches closer to me but keeps his hands where I can see them. "I just meant that there is someone else out there . . . for me, I mean . . . and I don't think I could give you the full attention you deserve and I would really hate to hurt you. You do seem like a nice person."

"Do I, though?"

"Well, Emma seems to like you, so you can't be all bad."

Ethan hesitates for a second. "I know that it might not be appropriate to ask this, considering we're supposed to be on a date . . ."

I raise one eyebrow, but don't interrupt him.

"But there might be someone else who's caught my attention. I'm just not sure if she's interested in me."

I smile because he really is adorable. "Interesting. I have a friend—a work associate who's becoming a friend, really—who is going through a similar situation."

For a second, a spark lights his eyes, but it fades as soon as it comes. "I'm sure whoever your friend is, she's far more impressive than me. I'm sure anyone in town would be lucky to have her."

"You're right about that." I steady myself after another jolting lurch of the wagon. "But she's got her heart set on one person in particular."

Ethan's head falls. "I could never be worthy of her, can't really provide her with the kind of life she deserves. I'm just a schoolteacher, and I'm not sure how it works where you're from, but here in Heart Springs, there isn't a lot of money in teaching."

"I think that's a universal truth, my friend." I brush my hands, clearing away some straw and potential splinters. I'm very much over this whole Heart Springs 1950s notion of gender roles and vow to do what I can to quash it. "But Emma isn't the kind of person to judge you based on your income. Besides, the bakery seems to be doing just fine, she doesn't exactly need your money."

Ethan's eyes widen at my use of her name, but I'm spared his response as the wagon finally comes to a halting stop. I once again take his hand as he helps me down but drop it the second my feet hit solid ground.

"So, Ethan, now that we know we are not going to be riding off into the sunset together—literally or figuratively—can we skip the whole manual labor part of this date and go right to the eating and drinking part?" I wouldn't want to pick strawberries with a man I wanted to bang, I sure as hell don't plan on wasting my energy on this farce with Ethan.

He shrugs and leads me over to a table positioned under the shade of a huge tree. "I don't see why not."

I try—unsuccessfully—throughout the course of our picnic to convince Ethan that he needs to just ask Emma out already, but he continues to insist she needs a man who can "provide for her." Our picnic comes to a screeching halt when I lose my patience and tell him he doesn't deserve her if he isn't going to grow a pair and ask her out.

When I get home from my "date," Ben's front porch is empty.

Which is fine. It's not like I have a whole lot to report anyway. And I certainly haven't gotten used to our daily hangouts. And he probably isn't going to be too happy with me when he hears about what a disaster the date was.

So really, it's better that I don't have to see him.

I am very good at my job—my real-world one, that is—and can convince just about anyone of just about anything. But somehow I fail to convince myself that it doesn't bother me that Ben isn't waiting for me. I fail to convince myself that I don't actually miss him.

EMMA'S SMILE THE MORNING AFTER MY NONDATE IS slightly more strained than usual.

"Ethan is a very nice guy, but I have zero interest in him

whatsoever," I declare the moment I walk through the door. I know I already told her I wouldn't be pursuing him, but clearly the message didn't sink in the first time.

Hence her huge sigh of relief. "Oh, I'm so sorry to hear that," she lies after she catches herself, still grinning widely.

"Emma, this is ridiculous. Ask the man out on a date." I wash my hands and tie an apron around my waist.

"Cam, I appreciate what you're trying to do, and I honestly mean that, but please just trust me when I say it's not that easy. Things have always been done a certain way around here and I don't want to be the one to rock the boat." She buries her attention in the pantry, stacking ingredients on the long butcher-block counter.

I let out a sigh of my own. "Fine." I grab the eggs from the fridge, already well-versed in Emma's routine, even after just a few days working in the bakery.

We complete the rest of the morning setup, Emma doing most of the baking, me unloading trays and filling the display case, in near silence, but it's not awkward and stilted like it was with Ethan. Aside from Ben, Emma is the only person in Heart Springs who really seems to get me—and who seems to have any interest in getting to know the real me. And since Ben ditched me last night, she might now be the only one who legitimately cares about me, so I won't push her. I'll just do my best to make her life easier. And maybe continue to subtly encourage her to pursue Ethan and smash the patriarchy and all that.

Mimi pushes through the door of the bakery right after the morning rush, not even trying to hide her scowl.

I hold up my hands. "I told you trying to make me fall in love was a terrible idea."

"Ethan is a kind, successful, intelligent young man." Her hands land on her hips and for a moment she almost reminds me of my grandmother.

I shudder. "I never would say otherwise. Ethan is all those things, he's just not the man for me."

"You will not get out of here if you don't play by the rules, Cam."

I check behind me, but Emma is safely tucked away in the back kitchen, oblivious to this conversation. "You don't scare me, Meem." She does scare me, a little bit, but I sure as hell am not giving her the satisfaction of knowing that. "I can take you."

Ignoring my very weak threat, she crosses her arms over her chest and smiles, but it's smug. "Lucky for you, I have two more men waiting in the wings."

"Can't fucking wait." *To hate them too* is implied.

Mimi nods her head and the next thing I know, the door is swinging open again like she has telekinesis or just really good timing.

But my attention is quickly pulled away from my fairy torture mother. It lands squarely on the man who strides through the door, and it stays there.

Because holy hell.

He's hotter than Chris Hemsworth and Sebastian Stan. Combined. Tall and broad with arms that could totally rip a tree trunk in half. Golden brown hair and bright green eyes and a smile that could quite literally drop panties. My frilly pink ones might have just burned right up.

Okay, Mimi. You win this round.

"This is Jason," she says, her smirk growing even smirkier. "He's bachelor number two."

Jason sticks out his hand, and I daintily place mine in his huge paw. His fingers completely dwarf mine, and as he brings my hand to his lips, I don't even roll my eyes at the ridiculous gesture.

"Pleasure to meet you," I say in the sweetest voice I've managed since landing in this war zone.

"Same." Jason's voice is gravelly and rough and sexy as fuck.

Smiling coyly, I lean over the bakery counter, glad I chose a dress with a lower neckline this morning. "I'm looking forward to getting to know you better."

"Same."

Okay, so the man doesn't exactly have a way with words. The date I have in mind won't really require anything more than one-word responses anyway. Words like "yes" and "more" and "fuck me harder."

Mimi steps in front of Jason. "You'll be accompanying Jason to the End of Summer concert in the park in two days."

"End of Summer?" My brow furrows and I know I'm going to need extra Botox by the time I break free of this place. "Didn't summer just start like a few days ago?"

"Eventually you'll realize things work a little differently around here." Mimi hooks her arm in Jason's and drags him to the door.

"Nice meeting you!" I call to his retreating broad, broad back.

He waves in response, following along as Mimi tugs him down the sidewalk.

I bite my lip, holding back a grin.

Emma smiles, shooting me a knowing glance. I was so

distracted by Jason's pecs, I didn't even see her approach. "Feeling better about this blind date?"

"I'm feeling better about something." Like the way I'm totally going to get laid in just a couple days' time.

Sex is something I've never invested a ton of time and energy in, but that doesn't stop me from wanting—and needing and getting—it on the regular. Men in New York are easy and uncomplicated when all you want from them is one night—no sleepovers allowed. And Jason is just my type, big and tall and not too chatty. Maybe one night in his bed is exactly what I need to get my head on straight.

Ben's face flashes in my mind, for a mere second, putting the slightest of dampers on my fantasies of Jason and what he can do with those biceps. But I'm not going to let Ben ruin my good time.

Emma laughs before nudging me out of my sex haze. "Back to work, hot stuff, lunch rush will be here before you know it."

I nudge her right back, but then jump into helping prep a batch of savory pastries, for the first time in a long time looking forward to what's to come.

12

I come home from a long day at the bakery and head directly to the bath. I've got full body prep to do—exfoliating, shaving, moisturizing—before my date with Jason if I want to be sexy time ready. I dump a whole bottle of lavender bubble bath into the tub in the hopes it will drown out the smell of vanilla, which now seems to be permanently embedded in my skin.

Rifling through my closet postbath, I sigh in frustration. Nothing hanging here is even remotely sexy. Not a single one of these damn dresses is form-fitting, and most of them don't do much for me in the cleavage department either.

I close the closet door and shut my eyes, visualizing the kind of short, tight dress I want to wear on my date. Something bordering on scandalous, something that leaves little to the imagination and gives lots of hints as to what's to come.

But when I open the door, I'm greeted with the same selection as before. I grunt in frustration and continue my digging. Finally, I decide to forgo the dresses altogether, pulling on the tightest pair of jeans I can find and pairing them with one of the camisoles that's meant to be pajamas. It's lacy and revealing and will let Jason know exactly what I'm expecting from this evening.

I haven't seen Ben since before my date with Ethan, and given our proximity, I'm assuming that's entirely purposeful on his part. Given how the other day I saw him peeking out his curtains as I walked up his front path only to hide behind them when I knocked on the door, I don't really have to assume. I don't know what the man wants from me. He didn't want me to hurt Ethan, and I let him down as gently as humanly possible. And the feeling was mutual.

So I'm not sure what the holdout is.

And I'm not sure why I really care.

Other than I kind of miss having my friend around.

Because I thought we were becoming friends. I actually opened up to Ben and told him things. I thought he was on my side.

"Apparently not," I mutter to myself as I close my front door, noting the empty porch next door.

"Apparently not what?" a familiar voice asks.

I spin around to find my phantom neighbor, waiting for me just outside my gate.

His eyes widen as they first meet mine and then travel south. His gaze rakes me over, from the loose waves of my honey-colored hair to my chest and all the way down. And I feel every inch of it. My face flushes and my breath quickens, and surely none of that is because of a simple look.

Ben clears his throat, yanking his eyes back up to mine. "You look nice."

"Thanks." I stride past him out the gate, making my way toward the town square, where the concert will be held.

"Hot date?"

"Pretty sure you know the answer to that."

Ben falls in step next to me. "You seem a little more excited about this one." If I didn't know better, I might think there was some kind of green-tinted emotion hiding in those seemingly innocuous words.

"Jason is much more my type than Ethan. This one might actually have some possibilities."

"I thought you didn't believe in love."

I consider pretending for a second, but this whole *love* song and dance with Ben is getting a little tiring. "I believe in lust, Ben. Pure, unadulterated, let's fuck on the first date lust."

We reach the wide-open grass, where people are already starting to converge, laying down blankets and setting up chairs.

Ben halts near the outskirts. "Cam, I don't think Jason is going to . . ."

"Sorry, Ben. I see my date. Catch ya later." I don't wait around to hear about what he doesn't think, I make my way over to Jason, who's spread a blanket on the grass (seriously, another fucking picnic?) and is waiting for me with a wide grin on his face.

"You look hot," he says, pulling me in for a quick hug.

I try to make the hug linger, pressing myself shamelessly against him, but he doesn't hold on for nearly as long as I'd like him to. Especially considering I can still feel Ben's eyes burning into my back. "You don't look so bad yourself."

A man like Jason can't look bad. He's dressed simply, in jeans and a dark gray T-shirt, but everything he wears is hugging his broad shoulders and thick thighs in all the right places.

We fold ourselves onto the soft blanket, and Jason gestures to the picnic basket resting on the corner. "I didn't know what you liked so I packed a little of everything."

I open the basket, pulling out a bucket of fried chicken and containers of potato salad and macaroni and cheese. There's also baked beans and biscuits and all the way at the bottom, a container of fruit. Maybe not my first choice of meals before a hookup, but it all smells delicious at least.

Jason opens all the food containers and hands me a plate. He scoops heaping piles of each dish onto his own plate before I get the chance to serve myself, which is fine, until I'm scraping the edges of the mac and cheese bowl to get half a serving.

"So, Jason, what do you do?" We've both settled into eating our dinners, though scarfing might be a more apt description for how Jason is inhaling his food.

"I'm in construction." He barely pauses to answer the question, continuing to spoon heaping forkfuls into his mouth while he talks. Which is, you know, super charming.

"Ah. Makes sense." I gesture to his hulking biceps when he shoots me a questioning look.

"Oh, these mostly come from the gym." He gazes lovingly at his arms, and I get it, they're gorgeous, but the man hasn't looked at my cleavage with nearly half as much admiration and I'm wearing straight-up lingerie to a public concert.

"How often do you work out?"

"Usually three times."

"A week?"

"A day." Jason's fork scrapes his plate as he finishes the last of his meal.

I wait for him to lick it, but luckily he refrains. I'm still only halfway through my much smaller portions when he hops up from the blanket, declaring he needs to go find a snack.

"I thought I was going to be the snack," I mutter to his retreating backside.

Not mad at the view of him walking away though.

"Having fun?" Ben gracefully fills Jason's empty seat a second later, leaning over to steal half of my biscuit.

I half-heartedly slap his hand away from my food, even though I fought hard for that biscuit. For some reason, I don't mind sharing with Ben, especially if it keeps him here. "Things are going very well, I'll have you know."

"You're a terrible liar."

"You're a terrible friend." I blurt the words before I think them through. The guilt instantly swarms me when Ben's eyebrows shoot up.

He doesn't say anything for a second, just continues to stare at me until I can't stand it any longer.

"I didn't mean that." I pop the remaining biscuit bite in my mouth. Maybe it will keep me from sticking my foot in it. "You've been a very good friend to me, Ben."

"Have I?" he asks the question quietly, like he doesn't expect an answer.

I punch him lightly on the shoulder. "Yes, you have. I don't think I would've survived being here if it weren't for you."

His look is searing. "You would have."

"You have a lot more faith in me than I have in myself."

"You should work on that."

"Maybe." I find myself leaning in Ben's direction, closing the gap separating us, moving my arm just a fraction of an inch so it brushes up against his.

He doesn't move away. If I didn't know better, I'd almost say he leans in just a tad farther.

I meet his gaze, opening my mouth to say something, anything, if it will keep us here in this bubble for a second longer.

"Hey, Doc, thanks for keeping my date company." Jason's voice is booming, and he sounds genuinely thankful and not at all jealous, which I find only slightly offensive.

Ben shoots me a look I can't quite interpret before standing. "Happy to be of service."

Jason claps him on the shoulder, the force of it causing Ben to stumble forward. "Enjoy the show."

"Yeah, see you guys later." Without a look back, Ben strides off across the lawn.

Jason retakes his seat, an overloaded plate of Mexican food in his hand.

I'm already full, which is good since Jason offers me nary a taco. Luckily the concert starts shortly after he sits back down, and I can pretend our lack of conversation is out of respect for the music.

The band is good, I guess, if you're into country songs about trucks and girls and dogs and 'Murica, which Jason seems to be. I let my focus wander, using the time to people-watch instead of paying attention to the show. Mimi is nowhere to be found, but I spot Emma and Ethan, sitting on two separate blankets just close enough together that they can sneak glances at each other, far enough away that no one else would notice. I wonder what would happen if I were to go over there and physically force their faces together like little girls make their Barbie and Ken dolls kiss. Not that I would ever really do that, but it is kind of fun to think about. And it might be the only way to get them together—if someone else makes the first move. Hmm . . . I'll have to think on that.

It isn't until my eyes land on him on the opposite side of the grassy expanse that I realize I've been looking for Ben. He's sitting in a low chair, surrounded by people, yet somehow totally separate from the crowd. It's been easy to assume Ben has assimilated into the town in an effortless way I never could, but maybe he hasn't made as many connections as I'd thought. Maybe Ben is struggling just as much as I am, just in a different way.

He meets my gaze almost the second my eyes land on him, a soft smile curving his lips.

And there's more of those weird chest spasms that should act as a reminder to go get a checkup when I get back home. It does something to me, that smile.

It forces me to turn to Jason and whisper, "You wanna get out of here? We can go back to my place."

For a hot second he looks like he wants to protest, but then he changes his mind and jumps to his feet. Throwing the blanket over his shoulder, he takes my hand and leads me out of the park.

I don't know if Ben's eyes are still on me and I force myself not to care.

The second we clear the steps on my front stoop, I shove Jason against the front door. The man is a beast, and I physically couldn't move him without his permission, but he doesn't make the first move. Or the second move, really, since I guess throwing someone up against a door and pressing my tits into his chest probably counts as the first move.

When Jason continues to remain statue still, I thread

my fingers through the hair at the nape of his neck and rise on my tiptoes, leaning in for a kiss. He immediately pulls away, putting a foot of space between us.

"Whoa." He chuckles. "No need to rush things there, Cam."

My eyes widen, likely to the point of ridiculousness. "Are you serious right now?"

Jason removes my hands from his hair and tucks them in his big paws, effectively ending our non-makeout sesh. "I really want to get to know you. Let's save the physical part of our relationship for a time when it will really be special, you know?"

"No, I don't know. How do you propose to get to know me better when you didn't ask me one fucking question our entire date?" I yank my hands from his and cross my arms beneath my boobs, hoping a glimpse of my fantastic cleavage will entice him to change his mind.

He has the nerve to look sheepish. "I'm just really shy, and it's hard for me to open up to people."

I roll my eyes. "Look, Jason, no offense, but I thought we were on the same page about what this is. Or what this was supposed to be."

"A chance at true love?"

I snort. "A good fuck."

Now his eyes widen.

But I don't have the patience for this anymore. "Clearly that's not going to happen, so I think we should probably just call it a night."

"Can I take you out again sometime?" The hope shining from his eyes seems genuine and it makes me feel like even more of an asshole than I usually do.

I sigh and give his hand a quick squeeze before dropping it so he doesn't get the wrong impression. "I don't think that's a good idea, Jason. We're not right for each other, and I would hate to waste your time." I don't even complain about the complete waste of time this date has been, which might be what they call personal growth.

After a final sad, pitiful smile, Jason waves and heads down the walk and out my front gate.

I wait on my porch for a few minutes, expecting Ben to pop up with an inevitable "I told you so." I suppose it would be well within his rights.

But when he does appear on his own porch, on the other side of the fence, seemingly from nowhere, he doesn't offer me the sharp words I probably deserve.

"I just opened a bottle of Pinot Noir before the concert, if you want a glass."

I want to take him up on the offer, and not just because I would kill for a good glass of wine right now. But something pulls me away from Ben. Maybe it's the way he smiled at me during the concert, or the way I subconsciously drifted toward him while we were sitting side by side on the blanket. Or maybe it's because I can't bear for him to continually see me in this foreign state of complete and utter failure.

Whatever it is, it has me shaking my head sadly. "I think I'm going to go drown my sorrows in a long bath." I push open my front door. "Not literally, of course."

He flashes me a sad smile and it hits me right in the chest once again. "Okay. Maybe we could catch up soon?"

His kindness makes my lungs ache, but I don't have the willpower to say no twice. "That would be nice."

"Have a good night, sweetheart."

"Yeah, you too."

13

The funk follows me into the next few days. I wake up every morning, hair perfectly coiffed, makeup flawlessly applied. I dress in a rainbow of frills and walk to the bakery, smiling and nodding at everyone I pass along the way. I help Emma with whatever tasks need to be completed at the bakery. And I still can't seem to get out of my head.

I'm refusing to believe that Jason turning down my offer of clear, available, no-strings-attached sex is responsible for my lingering bad mood because there is no way that man deserves to hold such power over me. His biceps aren't *that* big. Of course, sending him home empty-handed at the end of the night effectively crossed off two of my three falling-in-love options. No word yet as to who my remaining mystery bachelor might be, but I'm not feeling super hopeful about our odds. Maybe Mimi is really just setting me up to fail.

Things seem to be going okay on the career front, though I'd be lying if I said I suddenly found myself with an undying passion for baking. I like working with Emma, and she certainly tolerates me better than most bosses would. But while I'm a competent assistant, I don't ever see myself being more than that when it comes to working at the bakery. I don't have the passion for it that Emma does. I'm not dreaming up recipes in my off time or thinking of new flavor combinations as I spend hours perfecting a frosting design. I mostly only feel like I'm any good at it because Emma is such a patient teacher.

And as to finding myself a functioning member of the community, I'm beginning to wonder how one even gauges such a thing. Is it how many people wave at me in the morning? Do the smiles cancel out the trauma I inflicted during my stints as bookseller and wedding planner? Does the fact that I haven't done much else beyond the carnival mean I'm lacking in the community department?

I just don't know. And not knowing is not something I'm comfortable with. I always know exactly what the goal is and the steps to achieve it. As a kid it was making straight As and getting into an Ivy League, at Harvard it was being chosen as editor of the law review, as partner it was bringing in the most billable hours. In Heart Springs I constantly feel like I'm flying by the seat of my pants.

And if I'm being totally and completely honest with myself, the fact that, despite his offer to catch up soon, I haven't seen or heard from Ben over the last couple of days feels . . . bleh. I think I might miss him, which is why I try really hard not to have close friends, so I don't have to miss them when they inevitably abandon me.

Emma must notice my melancholy because she sends me home after the lunch rush with a warm hug and a box of baked goods, neither of which I feel like I truly deserve.

I decide to swing by Mimi's on my way back to the cottage since I haven't seen her in a few days. She's been suspiciously absent, especially considering how majorly I managed to fuck things up with both Ethan and Jason. I'm on my final job and down to my final man, and yet I've received zero guilt trips from the HBIC in recent days.

The bell tinkles as I push through the door, but the café is empty and no one is alerted to my presence. Mimi doesn't wait for me behind the counter, and as usual, no patrons sit among the distressed tables and chairs.

I slide into a seat to wait, assuming she must be fluttering around the back somewhere, making magic and steering the course of other people's lives.

I could really go for a coffee though.

Since working at the bakery, I've figured out (okay, fine, Emma taught me with an abundance of patience) how to pull my own espresso shots so they actually taste good, and I figure Mimi won't mind if I help myself. I mean, the woman has basically helped herself to control of my life and all I need in return is some caffeine, so I think it's a fair trade.

Heading behind the counter, I reach for the espresso and quickly freeze.

Mimi is in the back, I now know for sure, because I can hear her talking. Heatedly. Presumably to someone else.

When that someone else speaks and I recognize his voice immediately, I creep closer to the swinging door separating the kitchen from the café, shameless in my eavesdropping.

"I told you picking Jason was a mistake. She was never going to go for him." Ben, stating the obvious. "Not seriously, anyway."

"She was going for him just fine, Ben. The two of them were having a great date until you butted in." Mimi scolds Ben like she normally scolds me, and I'm not going to lie, it feels great to find out I'm not the only one who can get on her bad side.

"I didn't do anything! All I did was stop by and say hello to my friend, who I'm supposed to be keeping tabs on anyway." He sounds defensive, and what the fuck is all this business about keeping tabs? Is he only hanging out with me because Mimi told him to? My brain doesn't have time to fully digest that interesting tidbit before Ben continues on. "Cam isn't who you think she is, Mimi. I think you're going about this all wrong."

"I'm not wrong. I've never once been wrong and I'm not going to start now."

"She's different." Ben says the words with a hint of reverence, and I imagine his eyes softening and a soft smile playing on his lips.

My own lips curve up in a matching smile.

Mimi's voice is the one that audibly softens. "You need to be careful, Ben. You're getting too close."

"I don't know what you mean."

"I think you do. You know that your task is to help Cam complete hers. I don't want you to lose sight of that, or you might end up getting hurt."

"Why would I be hurt?"

"She needs to fall in love, Ben. And if you care about her—"

Ben starts to protest but is quickly cut off.

"If you care about her, you want her to experience true love. You want her to go back home. It's the only way you get back home too."

There's a long silence, and I wonder if their conversation has come to a close or if the emotions whirling around in my head are just blocking out their words. Ben's task is to help me complete my tasks? The only way he gets to go home is if I do too?

How could he not tell me something this major? I've told Ben things I haven't told anyone before, and he couldn't even tell me the truth about his task? I wait for anger to overtake me, but where there should be rage, there's nothing but an aching emptiness.

Ben speaks up once more, his voice hoarse and a bit choked, and I force myself to listen, to gather all the evidence of his double-crossing. "She needs someone smart. Someone who can keep up with her. Someone who will appreciate her work ethic, but also force her to take a break every once in a while. She needs someone who can make her laugh. Someone who listens. Someone who cares. Someone like . . ."

Ben.

A fist wraps around my lungs and squeezes until I'm gasping for breath. I clutch the counter, trying to keep myself upright, willing myself not to black out, until I realize the pain isn't actually physical.

There's only one person I can think of who fits all of Ben's requirements, and I thought that someone was my friend, though now I'm not so sure.

"How about Noah?" Mimi suggests.

I want to scream that that's clearly not the right answer. I wait for Ben's inevitable protest.

"I think he could make her happy," is what he says instead.

I don't hear the rest of the conversation, my brain too muddled to parse out individual words.

I do hear when the two of them move toward the door, and the sound sends me bolting for the exit. Pushing out of the café, the bell tinkling behind me, I race back to my cottage and slam the door.

First things first, I grab a bottle of chilled white wine, yank out the cork, and chug. Replaying the entire conversation in my head, I realize that everything I was feeling for Ben—warm friendship feelings and sparks and hints of something maybe possibly warmer than friendship—was all completely one-sided. Ben doesn't care for me. Not me as a person. He only cares about me completing my tasks. He only cares about getting back home.

My body aches like I've just endured a two-hour spin class and my brain is whirring as fast as the wheels.

Mimi's words loop in my mind, *you're getting too close.*

What does that even mean? How not close is Ben supposed to get when we freaking live next door to each other and he's apparently my own personal babysitter?

And why did hearing Ben describe the perfect man for me send me into a state of physical shock? Shouldn't I be grateful that this Noah character has Ben's stamp of approval? If he thinks Noah could be the one for me, he's already head and shoulders above Jason, who was mostly just shoulders.

Tucking the bottle of wine under my arm, I grab a pint of ice cream and head over to the couch. I flick on the TV and cover myself with the softest knitted blanket to ever inhabit the earth. The couple onscreen is declaring their love for each other and it should probably make me feel worse, but I mostly just feel numb.

....

I WAKE UP ON THE SOFA THE NEXT MORNING, AND DEspite the almost entire bottle of wine I drank, I don't seem to have even a lick of a hangover. And a quick glimpse in the mirror reveals my hair and makeup to be perfect, as usual. I frown, not because I'm unhappy with my appearance but because I'm starting to not hate these blasted loose curls cascading down my back like a contestant in a beauty pageant. So surely the apocalypse is nigh.

When I open my closet, I freeze in the doorframe. Gone are all my frilly dresses—there's not a hint of pastel hiding anywhere among the depths. Instead, I find earth tones and soft knits as far as the eye can see. It should be a relief, but mostly I'm just confused as to why the sudden change.

I tug on a pair of jeans and a camel-colored sweater, praying I don't sweat to death throughout the day. But I needn't have worried, because when I open my front door, I'm hit with a blast of chilly autumn air. The leaves of the tree in my front yard have turned red overnight, and bright orange pumpkins line the steps.

"What the actual fuck?"

"Happy fall, y'all," Ben's voice chimes from next door.

I glare at him. "Do not greet me with a pillow phrase ever again." He's already on thin ice after the conversation he doesn't know I overheard.

He crosses to the fence separating our yards, his hands tucked into the front pockets of his jeans. He's wearing a flannel shirt with the sleeves rolled up, which should make me nauseated but sends a small shiver through me. "What exactly is a pillow phrase?"

"You know, one of those cheesy sayings white women

have stitched on throw pillows. 'Live, laugh, love.' 'Home is wherever you are.' Bullshit like that." I take a few timid steps in his direction, not wanting to get too close. Forearms plus a whiff of his woodsy scent might be potent enough to send me hurtling through another rip in the space-time continuum.

He chuckles, but his smile doesn't reach his eyes. "Got it. I'll remember that for the future."

There's an awkwardly long pause during which I try not to stare directly at him while I also try to examine his face for any sort of clues as to how he might be feeling. Given how emphatic he was about me and this Noah guy, he's probably counting down the days until he's rid of me, until I fall in love with someone else and he gets to go home and never see me again.

"So we're officially in fall?" The question is clearly redundant, but it's all I've got. "Does this mean it's time for the pumpkin festival?"

Ben runs a hand through his hair, looking everywhere but at me. "I think it's the Harvest Festival, actually. But I imagine there will be lots of pumpkins involved."

"Of course." Another silence descends upon us. "Well, I should probably get to the bakery. Emma probably has a whole new store of pumpkin recipes for me to learn."

"Before you go—" Ben takes another step closer, running into the fence. He steps back with a sheepish smile. "Before you go, I just wanted to check in and see how you're doing?"

I study his deep brown eyes, hoping to discern what kind of response he wants. But they betray nothing, and so I decide to go for an honest one. "I'm feeling a little lost, honestly. I like working at the bakery, but there's no chance it's my passion in life. I don't feel like I'm actually contributing anything worthwhile to the community. And I've eliminated sixty-six percent of my love interests over the course of two dates." I keep my eyes locked on his during that last part, waiting for some kind of sign, but he doesn't even flinch.

I know I should yell at him for keeping the truth from me, berate him for pretending to be my friend when he's really only concerned about getting himself home.

But I can't make myself say the words, as if giving voice to them will make them true.

"Well, I'm going to be working on the Harvest Festival if you want to put in some more hours helping the community." His cheeks redden, and Mimi's warning not to get too close echoes in my mind once again.

"I would like that." And I would, I realize in that moment.

He holds my gaze like he's attempting to send me some kind of telepathic message, but whatever it is he's trying to impart, I don't get it.

"You should probably get to work," he prods after a few seconds. Apparently, the subliminal message was *go away*.

"Right. See ya later." I wave over my shoulder, pushing through my front gate and heading down the sidewalk without looking back.

Surprising no one but me, the entire town has undergone its fall transformation. Pumpkins are everywhere, fallen leaves crunch under my boots, even the air smells different. I breathe it in, and the slight chill feels refreshing in my lungs.

It takes me less than five minutes to reach the bakery,

and when I let myself in the back door to the kitchen, I'm surprised by the *lack* that greets me. No heavenly smells permeating the air. No sounds of bowls and spoons clanking together as Emma pours and mixes. And most noticeably, no Emma.

"Hello?" I call out, even though I can clearly see no one waits for me in the back. I stride through the swinging door to the front of the bakery.

Emma is on the floor behind the counter, knees pulled to her chest, head down.

"Oh shit, Emma, what happened?" I drop down next to her, checking for blood or visible signs of trauma, but nothing seems amiss. Other than the heaving sobs wracking her body.

She cries for a few solid minutes, never once lifting her head or stopping for breath. I rub what I hope are soothing circles on her back, whispering nonsense words of comfort hoping they will spur her into telling me what the hell is going on.

Finally, she manages to raise her head just enough so I can see her tear-filled eyes. Her cheeks are streaked with mascara, and I grab a napkin to wipe away the evidence of her distress.

"Thank you," she chokes out and somehow those two little words stir another bout of tears.

"Emma, you're freaking me out. What the fuck is going on?"

Wordlessly, she hands me a piece of paper that's been wedged in between her thighs. I open it up and read, my ire growing with each passing word.

"This is fucking bullshit." I'm tempted to crumple the

letter in a ball and light it on fire, but I have a feeling we'll need it. Or at least the information contained in it, because I intend to find the writer of this letter and rip him a new asshole.

"They're going to take my bakery, Cam." Emma sniffles, but she seems to be all cried out.

"We are not going to let that happen." I'm already on my feet, searching fruitlessly for a phone so I can set up a meeting with this dickwad lawyer as soon as humanly possible.

"I don't know what to do." Her head falls back to her knees.

I crouch down in front of her, forcing her to look at me. "Hey. None of that. I know receiving a letter like this can be terrifying." Satan knows I've sent my fair share of them, to people just like Emma. I've just never had to witness the reactions of the people receiving them. "But we are not going to roll over and let these guys win. We have a lot of legal options and lucky for you, I know them all. I am not going to let them take this bakery from you."

Emma wipes under her eyes. "I don't know if there's anything you can do to stop them."

"No way. Shit like this doesn't happen here. Heart Springs is this idyllic wonderland, right? So there's no way the jackass real estate developer succeeds in closing down the locally owned small business. That's not how these things work here." I run my eyes over the letter again, searching for the name of the person I am going to skewer and roast on a pit for threatening Emma like this. "Wait a second. Noah Crenshaw? Is there more than one Noah in this town?"

Emma shakes her head. "Not that I know of."

I collapse on the floor next to Emma.

"What's wrong?"

I open my mouth to tell her before I realize I'm not supposed to know about Noah yet. Neither Ben nor Mimi has filled me in on the details of my third bachelor, presumably because they know they've set me up with a total douche canoe.

Fuck.

They set me up with a total douche canoe because they think I am also a total douche canoe.

Not going to lie, that one stings.

Emma prods me with her elbow.

I clear my throat, determined to examine the implications of this discovery when I'm back at home in the peace and comfort of my bathtub. "Nothing's wrong. Why don't you close the bakery for today, take some time for yourself. Go home and relax, or maybe see if there's someone you can talk to. Ethan's probably available." Okay, it's not exactly subtle, but we're in a moment of distress here.

"Okay." She agrees, but it's reluctant.

I jump up before she can change her mind. I write a note on a blank piece of paper and tape it to the front window. Heading back behind the counter, I help Emma to her feet and hand her her coat and purse. "I'll do a quick cleanup and make sure the door is locked when I leave."

Before I can protest, Emma throws herself at me, arms wrapping tight around my torso. "Thank you, Cam. I don't know what I would've done without you here."

My arms are stiff by my sides, but after a second of being unable to breathe due to the strength of her grip, I manage to pat her on the back a few more times. "No problem."

She releases me, and tears are shining in her big brown eyes once again, only this time they are accompanied by a small smile. "You're a really good friend."

I don't have a response, and she doesn't seem to need one. She gives my hand a final squeeze and heads out through the kitchen.

No one has ever called me a good friend before.

I don't know that anyone has ever called me a friend before.

That thought wouldn't have bothered me a few days ago, but now I realize how depressing it is.

Well, Emma just might be my first real friend, and that means I can't let her down. I do a quick wipe down of all the counters and make sure the few ingredients Emma took out this morning get put away before I lock all the doors and head out to the main street on a mission.

14

I stop the first person I see. "Excuse me, could you please tell me where I can find the offices of Noah Crenshaw?"

"Sure! They're right over there." The woman points directly across the town square.

Of course, his office is right here because where else would it be?

I thank the woman and march across the grass. It's still green, despite the sudden change of seasons, though all the trees surrounding it are canopies of orange and red and yellow.

I barge through the door with a "Noah Crenshaw & Associates" sign hanging out front, not stopping it from smacking into the wall. "I need to speak with Noah Crenshaw. Immediately." Any trace of manners has fled the building because no one who works for scum like this guy deserves my politeness. I conveniently ignore that, in my world, I am the scum like Noah Crenshaw.

"Do you have an appointment?" the young, blond woman sitting at the reception desk asks sweetly.

"Nope. But I don't care. I need to speak with him. Now."

"I'm very sorry, ma'am, but without an appointment, that's just not going to be possible."

"It's okay, Celeste." A deep, rumbling voice travels down a hallway. "Send her in."

I don't wait for Celeste to acquiesce, brushing right past her desk and down the hall toward the voice. Stomping into Noah's office, I slam the door shut behind me. I spin around, ready to give this motherfucker a piece of my mind, except when I finally get a glimpse of him, I lose all power of speech.

If some magical wizard could conjure me up my dream man, he would look exactly like Noah Crenshaw. He's standing behind his desk, showing off his height and wide frame. He's not as muscley as Jason, but it's easy to see that his finely tailored suit covers well-defined arms and shoulders. His hair is dark and curly and his eyes are so bright blue they pierce me from across the room. His lips tilt up in a knowing smile, and the smirk only makes him hotter.

Fuck. Me.

"Can I help you with something, Ms. Andrews?" This close, that deep rumbling voice hits me in the belly and slides right on down.

"How do you know my name?"

He laughs, coming around to the front of his desk and leaning against it, his ankles crossed, showing off his thick thighs.

Ugh. Thick thighs are my one true weakness.

"Everyone in Heart Springs knows your name, Ms. Andrews. I would've thought you'd figured that out by now."

His voice drips with condescension, which helps pull me out of my lust-fueled haze.

"Right." I pull myself up to my full height and hold up Emma's letter. "I'm here on behalf of my client. I wanted to give you the courtesy of letting you know that we will be fighting this. In case you wanted to do the wise thing and back off now."

He crosses his arms over his chest and grins. "Why would I do that? My client wants that building. The owner of said building is willing to sell at a fair price. If your client is so invested in her business, she can purchase the building for herself."

"You cannot give a tenant thirty days' notice to vacate when she still has months left on her lease." I haven't actually looked at her lease, but I figure a small bluff or two never hurt anyone.

"You're not in the big city anymore, Ms. Andrews. Things work differently here."

I scoff. "So Heart Springs operates with no law and order?"

Noah shrugs. "I wouldn't put it like that."

"What kind of person would do that to a hardworking woman who owns her own business and is a valuable member of the community?" I don't know why I try appealing to his humanity—it has certainly never worked when it's been tried on me. But things are supposed to be different here.

He raises his eyebrows, his look response enough. He knows exactly who I am, exactly what I would do if I were in his shoes.

I tuck the letter in my back pocket. "Fine. Have it your way. But please believe me when I say you are not going to win this." I cross a step closer to him, getting a whiff of something musky and expensive. "I will destroy you."

He leans forward just slightly. "I welcome the challenge, Ms. Andrews."

I stomp toward the door.

He waits until my hand is on the doorknob before he calls after me. "I'll pick you up at seven tomorrow."

I spin around and hit him with my best glare. "Excuse me?"

That damned grin splits his face. "We have a date tomorrow. At seven. I'll pick you up." He chops his words into short sentences, like I'll have trouble comprehending otherwise.

"You cannot possibly think I will be going out on a date with you after all this."

"Think about how disappointed Mimi would be to hear you say that." He leans back on his hands, pulling the fabric of his shirt tighter over his stomach, displaying visible ridges. "She seems to think you and me might be destined to be together, Ms. Andrews. And when Mimi makes a match in this town, she's rarely wrong."

I don't respond, flinging the door open and ignoring the way his laughter echoes down the hall.

Striding purposefully along Main Street, I push past the few townspeople I encounter without even a hint of a hello. I'm back in front of my cottage within minutes, though it isn't my front gate I push open. I pound on Ben's door, not stopping until he flings it open, exasperation on his face.

He tries to school his features, but I catch the hint of fear when he sees me.

"Would you like to tell me what the hell you're thinking?" I demand, pushing past him into his living room.

Ben closes the door with a sigh, leaning up against it,

leaving a couple of feet of space in between us. "I don't know what you're talking about."

I yank Noah's letter out of my back pocket. "Like fuck you don't. It's not bad enough that I could possibly lose the one job that I don't totally suck at, you also have to set me up with the man willing to destroy my one and only friend?"

That last bit affects him, even though he tries to hide it. "I can't have this conversation with you, Cam."

I hate when he calls me by my actual name. "Why not? Because you don't want to admit you were never really my friend in the first place? That you're only hanging out with me because if I fail at my tasks, it means you're stuck here too?"

He doesn't seem surprised by my reveal, and I wonder if he knows that I overheard his and Mimi's conversation. "That's not true. I am your friend, and I genuinely want to help you." He takes a cautious step forward. "Yes, my task, my way out of here is to help you complete yours, but that doesn't mean I'm not your true friend."

I take my own step closer to him. "Then why are you setting me up with a douchebag like Noah Crenshaw?"

His brown eyes meet mine and it doesn't take a full minute of silence for me to understand the message they're trying to impart. Noah Crenshaw might be a douchebag, but he and I have a lot in common. On paper, it makes perfect sense why the two of us would be matched together.

"I'm not going to let him close the bakery, you know."

Ben shoves his hands in the front pockets of his jeans. "Good. I hope you find a way to save it. Life without Emma's cinnamon rolls would be a sad one."

"And it's going to be very difficult to fall in love with the man who is my opposition."

"We'll see."

"You think I'm just like him, don't you?" I ask the question softly, half-hoping he won't hear me.

His response is just as quiet. "I think there's no one else quite like you, sweetheart."

I suck in a breath, hoping the hit of oxygen will steady my racing heart. I brush past him on the way to the door, our fingers skimming in the merest of contact and yet it sends a shiver up my spine. I pause at the door. "Do you really want me to fall in love with him, Ben?"

It takes him a minute to consider. "I just want you to be happy."

"Sure you do." I force myself to open the door and march down his front steps before I do something stupid like throw myself in his arms and kiss him. Because that would be a really dumb thing to do. And it's not something I even really want to do, of course; the emotions of the situation are just messing with my head.

Besides, the last thing Ben would want is to kiss someone like me. In his eyes, I'm an unfeeling corporate monster with no friends and no one to love me. Who could ever, when I seem to be entirely unlovable.

The thought of Ben finding me unlovable hurts more than I'd like to admit.

And so I curl up on the couch, determined to find a way to move forward. I need to save the bakery. I need to find my place in this community. And apparently, I need to fall in love with Noah Crenshaw.

If that's what it's going to take to get me home, then that's what I'm going to have to do.

15

I need to see your lease," I say to Emma the moment I walk into the bakery the next morning. My determination to save the bakery and fall in love only intensified the more and more I thought on it last night. My desire to go home and put this whole experience behind me only intensified the more and more I thought about Ben last night. And so today, I'm putting my plan into action.

I spend the morning hours poring over every piece of paperwork Emma is able to dig up. Normally my associates and interns are tasked with highlighting and flagging and underlining, but today I do it all for myself, searching for the one clause that could possibly save this bakery from extinction.

Of course, the easiest way to save the bakery would be for Emma to buy the building herself, but one look at the business's finances and I know that's not happening.

My hours of searching bring me little hope. The lease—which Emma informed me she signed without consulting a lawyer of her own—seems to be entirely weighted in the owner's favor. We had a nice, calm discussion about signing things without understanding them and without legal representation and I'm fairly certain she'll never make that mistake again.

It does leave me scrambling, but I didn't make partner at thirty-four by staying down after a couple of solid punches. This fight is nowhere near knockout level just yet and by the end of the first fruitless day, I'm only more determined to find a way to win.

When I arrive back at my cottage after work, I don't even spare a glance in Ben's direction, even though I can feel his presence, sitting on the porch. He wants me to put all my focus and attention on completing my tasks and getting us both home, then that's what I'll do. No more fake friendship required.

I hop in the shower, spend some time doing my own hair and makeup for once, and carefully select a burgundy fitted sweater dress and knee-high brown boots. When there's a knock at the door at seven o'clock on the dot, I'm date-night ready.

Sucking in a long, calming breath, I remind myself that Noah Crenshaw is my last option. If I want to get out of here, I have to let myself fall in love. And I have to do it fast. I open the door with a smile on my face. "Hi."

Noah's eyes sweep me from head to toe, a slow grin spreading across his face. "Hello." He hands me a bottle of wine. "You look absolutely stunning."

The compliment brings a blush to my cheeks. "Thank you." I accept the wine, grateful he brought me something useful instead of flowers—the ones from my last date are dead and wilting and yet I can't be bothered to throw them away. "Did you want to open this now?"

Noah leans casually against the doorframe, posing like he's being photographed for *GQ*. He's in another sharp suit and I can't deny how good he looks. If we were back in the real world, I would've happily accepted his dinner invitation, though I don't know that we would've made it to the dinner, *wink wink*.

"We have a reservation, so maybe we should save the wine for after dinner," Noah says with an actual wink.

I roll my eyes like I don't find the move charming and stash the wine in the fridge to chill. "Shall we?"

Noah heads down the front path, opening the gate while I lock the door behind me. I turn to follow him, but my steps halt when my eyes find Ben's.

He's sitting in one of his gorgeous chairs, a beer in hand and a look on his face that makes me want to forget all my plans for the evening and wrap him in a big hug. The shift in seasons has brought on an early evening darkness, but Ben has hung strands of bistro lights on the patio, illuminating the space. He gives me a sad smile, but I don't know how to return it.

"We don't want to be late, Ms. Andrews," Noah reminds me, though his tone is gentle and not at all scolding.

I tear my gaze away from Ben and march down the front path.

Noah walks us to a restaurant on Main Street that I've somehow never seen before. I wasn't aware there was anything more than diner dining in the town of Heart Springs, but the restaurant he brings me to is all crisp linens and fine china and expensive wine. It's the kind of place I would visit at home, and it should be a good sign that Noah knew exactly where to bring me.

"Cheers." Noah holds up his wineglass. "To keeping our business and personal lives separate."

I raise one eyebrow but clink my glass against his. "Do you really think that's possible?" I ask after taking a sip of the smoothest wine I've had in a long time.

"Anything is possible if you want it badly enough."

That might have been my own personal motto before I woke up in Heart Springs, but this one similarity between us doesn't mean anything.

"So, Noah, what do you like to do when you aren't crushing the dreams of hardworking small business owners?"

"I feel like I could ask you the same, Ms. Andrews." He sips his wine, watching me over the rim of his glass.

I fidget with the napkin draped over my lap. "I enjoy working out." It's not the total truth since I haven't bothered to keep up with my regimen since being trapped here, but I figure it's something besides work that we might have in common.

"As do I." He passes me the breadbasket.

I take a piece, which is something I never would do back at home. But calories don't seem to matter here. All my clothes still fit despite the absence of my regular morning workout and the abundance of baked goods. "Do you like to travel?" I never have, personally, never wanting to be away from the office for more than a day or two, but it's a popular hobby and might be something Noah is into. Plus, maybe if he travels, he knows a way to get out of here that I haven't been able to figure out yet.

"I find I don't like to be away from my office for more than a day or two at a time."

Well then. I dip a piece of bread in olive oil and shove it in my mouth. Damn that's good.

Noah folds his arms and leans on the table. There wasn't a lot of space separating us to begin with and now we're close enough that I can see the flecks of crystal in the center of his dark blue irises. "You have to admit, Ms. Andrews, we have more in common than you might want to think."

"My name is Cam."

"Cam."

"Tell me what you want, Cam." His lip curls up in a smirk.

The undeniably sexual words and his voice and that smile should send a wave of heat through me. Emphasis on the *should*.

"I want to save Emma's bakery." I lean back in my seat and drink half of my glass of wine in one gulp.

Noah chuckles. "I'm looking forward to the challenge."

"You still think you're going to win?"

"I know I'm going to win. I always get what I want, Cam. And right now, I want only two things."

"What's that?"

"That bakery. And you." He refills both our wineglasses and raises his for another toast.

His confidence is something I normally would find attractive, and I try to give myself over to it. Across the table is a gorgeous man, an intelligent and driven man who wants to fall in love with me. I need to snap the fuck out of it and play the game so I can go home.

I raise my own glass. "To getting what we want."

LUCKILY, MY NEIGHBOR'S PORCH IS EMPTY WHEN NOAH walks me to my front door at the end of our date. This is the point when I would normally invite him in for a glass of wine and a fuck fest, but I need this relationship to be about more than just sex. I tell myself that feeling's not relief coursing through me. Because if I let myself really think about it, I'm not all that sure I actually *want* to have sex with Noah. Which is fine. It's only the first date. Surely the spark will grow.

I spin around in front of the door, making it clear that no man, no matter how hot and confident and on paper perfect, is going to be entering tonight. "I had a nice time tonight. Thank you for dinner." Platitudes that I mean, but platitudes nonetheless.

Noah gives me a wolfish smile and leans down, pressing a quick kiss to my cheek. He smells like fancy cologne, and the scent sticks in my throat. "When can I see you again?"

It's barely a question, but I know how I have to answer. "When do you want to see me again?"

"Is tomorrow too soon?"

I chuckle, impressed with his brazenness despite myself. "Maybe. How about this weekend?"

"Saturday night it is." He squeezes my hand and heads down my front path, walking backward as if he can't tear his eyes away from me. "Good night, Cam."

"Good night."

I open my front door, slipping in quickly before I'm tempted to let my eyes drift next door.

16

Soooooo, how was your date?" Emma squeals basically the second I enter the bakery doors the following morning.

"You do remember the man who took me on said date is trying to destroy your entire livelihood, right?" I hang my coat—the weather has turned full fall and the mornings are chilly—on the rack near the back door and slip an apron over my head.

Our routine is well oiled at this point and, as I take my place at Emma's side, we move with practiced motions around the kitchen, prepping the day's muffins and breakfast pastries.

Emma nudges me with her hip, her hands covered in flour. "If Noah turns out to be your true love, I promise I won't hold the destruction of my life's dreams against him. Besides, if he is your true love, maybe you can convince him to drop the whole thing."

I grimace. "I wouldn't count on that, Em."

"The true-love part or the him-dropping-it part?"

"Either."

Emma's head tilts to the side as she cracks a pile of eggs into a mixing bowl with one hand. "Did you write him off already?"

I sigh, taking the bowl and moving it into place on the stand mixer, turning the machine to low. "No, I haven't written him off."

"But?"

"But I don't know if he's the one." I'm fairly certain he's not the one, which is not really a thing I believe in anyway, but that's a conversation I don't think I want to have with Emma, who clearly not only believes in the one, but has found hers, even if neither of them will admit it.

"Well, are you going to go out with him again?"

"Yeah." I wait for a spark of excitement at the thought of a second date with a hot, successful man, but it doesn't come.

"So he's already doing better than your first two blind dates. Usually it doesn't take this long for Mimi to make a successful match. You must be a special case." The teasing lilt in her voice takes away the sting of her words.

"Haha." I take a tray of muffins from the cooling rack and head toward the front of the bakery. I have zero desire to continue talking about Noah and even less desire to be forced to examine my own feelings about the date.

I'm transferring the muffins to the display case when the door to the bakery opens. "We're not actually open just yet," I say without looking up from my tray.

"I'm not here for a muffin, though I wouldn't say no if you wanted to slip me one on my way out." Ben greets me with a sheepish smile, his hands shoved in the front pockets of his jeans.

"Hi." My chest flutters, and there's that spark that I was looking for earlier.

Fuck.

"Hi."

For a second, we just look at each other, until I finally clear my throat and pull my eyes from his. "What can I do for you?"

He takes a few tentative steps closer to the counter. "Mimi sent me to see how your date with Noah went." He can't hide the grimace, though his face looks like he's trying to, scrunching up like he smelled something rank.

Ah Mimi. So transparent.

"That was nice of her."

Ben's smile is genuine, unlike my sentiment.

There's another few seconds of silence.

"Do you actually want to know how my date with Noah went?"

"Do you want to tell me?"

"I don't know what I want anymore, Ben."

"Other than to go home?"

For the first time, the thought of returning to my old life isn't as appealing as it once was. But I know I can't stay in Heart Springs forever. This isn't real life, and at some point, something has to give.

"I do still want to get home. And I did make a second date with Noah." I soften my voice, as if that might stop him from hearing me.

"Good. That's good." His tone is flat and unreadable.

I shake out a bag and slip a muffin inside. "Thanks for checking in on me."

Ben reaches for the bag and our hands brush. There's another fucking spark, right where it shouldn't be. "Just trying to be a good friend." His eyes linger and neither of us moves to release the bag held trapped between our hands. He flashes me another small smile before finally breaking contact, heading out, the door thudding shut behind him.

"Oh, honey."

I spin around at the sound of Emma's sympathetic voice. I hadn't realized she'd come out to the front of the store, didn't know she was listening. Grabbing the empty tray, I push back into the kitchen, ignoring whatever she's implying.

"Anything you want to talk about?" she asks, following me to the back.

"Nope." I busy myself arranging a new tray of baked goods.

"Okay." She returns to the prep station, measuring a scoop of flour and dumping it into a mixing bowl, but I can hear everything unsaid in her one-word response.

And I should maybe talk to her about it. She might be the only one I actually could talk to about it. But talking about it would make it real, and if I continue to ignore whatever the hell is happening with my neighbor-slash-keeper, then I can keep pretending that it's all in my head.

I can convince myself to fall in love with Noah. I can dedicate my life to being the best baker's assistant to ever grace the kitchens of Heart Springs. I can get myself home and get Ben home. Once I do that, it'll be easy to put distance between us and I won't have to deal with phantom feelings for Dr. Ben Loving ever again.

MY SECOND DATE WITH NOAH GOES MUCH LIKE THE first. As does the third, and the fourth. And while pretending the two of us have fallen into madly blissful love would be a huge and total lie, I can at least admit he's growing on me. At least on the "pleasure" side of things.

When it comes to our business, I can't help but hate the man. Not because of anything he's done—beyond the obvious—but because I can't seem to find a way to beat him. And nothing is more infuriating than losing. I refuse to lose.

And yet, it's been three weeks since Emma first received that threatening letter and I'm no closer to finding her a solution.

While I'm not willing to admit total defeat just yet, the legal front is not looking promising in our quest to save the bakery. Which means it might be time to take things in a different direction. "What if we planned a big fundraiser?" I finally throw the suggestion out a week after it first popped into my head.

Emma frowns, kneading the bread dough in front of her a little kneadier. "I don't want to take people's money, Cam. I don't want to be some charity case."

Having expected this exact response, I have my rebuttal ready. "It's not charity, Em. The people of Heart Springs love you and they love this bakery. They don't want to see some corporate monstrosity move in to this space. Where is everyone going to get their muffins and birthday cakes and holiday cookies? Trust me, the people have very selfish reasons for wanting to save the bakery, it hardly has anything to do with you personally." Lie, but I do know how upset everyone would be were they to lose Emma's baked goods from their daily lives.

"I don't know. That seems like a lot of work, and it probably wouldn't even raise enough money anyway."

It's not a flat-out no, so I keep pushing. "You won't have to do any of the work, I will handle everything."

She raises one eyebrow and the disbelieving look she gives me is only mildly insulting. "You are going to plan a huge fundraiser all by yourself? This coming from the woman who has barely managed a few hours of community service?"

"Wow, Emma, don't hold back, I'm only offering to save your life's work here." I pull myself up to my full height. "I'll have you know I planned the firm's annual holiday gala for the past five years and have helped raise millions of dollars for charity." Anything for a tax write-off, am I right?

Emma's eyes widen. "Millions of dollars?"

"Yup." I rush to temper her beliefs. "We can't really expect that from this one, obviously. Our firm's clients are some of the wealthiest people in Manhattan. No one in Heart Springs can come close to their giving power."

Her newly found optimism is crushed. "Then what's the point?"

"We don't need millions of dollars. I'm confident we can earn enough for a down payment on the building, at the very least."

She eyes me skeptically. "And you'll do all the work? And keep up with your bakery shifts?"

My smile falters. "I was hoping that I could use some of my bakery hours to work on the fundraiser."

She opens her mouth, but I don't let her get a word in.

"But if that's what it takes to get you to agree, then sure, I'll plan the fundraiser in my off hours."

Good lord, what am I getting myself into?

It will be worth it, though, when we sign the contracts and shove our victory right in Noah's face.

"All right. If you think it can work, then I'm in."

I clap my hands together, sending a pouf of flour up in the air.

We both dissolve into a pile of laughter and something warm bursts in my chest. For a second, I think I might be having a heart attack or something, unsure what this foreign experience could be.

But then I realize it's just happiness. The realization sends another burst through my chest, and when Emma grabs me in a hug, jumping around in a happy and hopeful circle, I join in without a second's hesitation.

17

It doesn't take long for the happiness bubble to totally burst. In fact, it only takes as long as it does for me to compile a to-do list for the Save the Bakery fundraiser (snappier name to come). Because the list is long, and without Grandmother's black AmEx at hand, I don't know how I'm actually going to pull this off.

But Emma has looked so much happier in the few days since agreeing to give the fundraiser a shot that I force myself to keep going.

And I force myself to take a painful and probably ill-advised walk next door. Either I've been avoiding Ben or he's been avoiding me, but I haven't seen him since he came into the bakery.

Unfortunately, that hasn't kept him out of my head. I was sort of hoping for that whole out of sight, out of mind deal, but so far, the opposite has proven true. Now that I let myself somewhat sort of acknowledge a tinge of sparkly feelings, I can't seem to erase him from my brain.

So I continually remind myself that even if these feelings

were real (which they're not), it wouldn't matter because Ben is not one of my suitors and therefore, according to Mimi's decree, I can't end up with him. And even if I could end up with him (which I definitely can't), who's to say he would reciprocate said feelings. And even if he did reciprocate said feelings (which I know he doesn't), it wouldn't put me any closer to finding my way home. Mimi doesn't stand firm on much, but her rules are definitely at the top of the list.

So yeah. Deciding to go to Ben for help with the fundraiser is likely a colossally terrible idea, but after sitting with my to-do list for a few days and making zero progress beyond the first item (make to-do list), I know I'm going to need some real assistance. And who better to help than the man who mere days after arriving here planned an entirely successful event? Really, the fact that I'm also low-key dying for another spark-laden brush of skin contact has little to do with my decision.

I remind myself of this as I knock on Ben's door early on my morning off, ready with a notebook, two cups of coffee, and a tense smile.

"Cam, hey." Ben's eyes widen with surprise when he opens the door and finds me on the other side. "What's up?"

"I need you," I blurt out in a really embarrassing and not at all smooth way.

His eyes widen farther and it could just be the light, but they also maybe darken a little bit, and it's a sign of attraction when pupils widen? Right?

"I mean, I need your help." I hold up my notebook as if it were a vital piece of evidence. "I'm organizing a fundraiser to try to help Emma buy the bakery and I told her I would handle everything and also still manage all my regular shifts and I've planned events before but like with an unlimited budget and I obviously don't have that here and so I really need some help."

Ben leans against the doorjamb, a wide smile tugging on his lips. "Wait, did you just say you need my help?"

"Yes." I refuse to beg. And I refuse to let him get under my skin.

"Could you say that part again? About how you need my help and I'm the only person in town smart enough and clever enough and handsome enough to help you pull it off?"

"Don't really remember that last part, but yes, that's the gist of it. I need your help."

He pushes open the door and gestures for me to follow him inside. Taking the cup of coffee I offer as bribery, he leads me to a wood dining table. The style is similar to the farmhouse one in my own cottage, but this wood is about ten times more gorgeous.

Also, I can't recall ever thinking of a piece of wood as gorgeous before. At least not the kind that comes from a tree.

I run a finger along the knots before I realize I've been staring at this table for way longer than a normal person would. And Ben's been staring at me for the same awkward length of time.

"Did you make this?" I force myself to stop fondling his table and flip open my notebook.

He clears his throat. "Yup."

"It's beautiful."

"Thanks." He turns his gaze to his coffee cup, which

must hold some fascinating information buried in its depths from the way he's staring. "So. What do you have planned so far?"

I turn a couple of pages in the notebook until I land on my epic-poem-length to-do list. "Well, not much yet in terms of concrete plans, but I have some thoughts."

"Thoughts are good."

I blink at him, pointedly.

He smiles.

"Anyway. Since I know the town is so fond of all its festivals, I was thinking of like a Thanksgiving potluck kind of thing. Like everyone in town brings a dish, we all talk about shit we're thankful for and whatever. Something like that."

Ben nudges his coffee cup to the side, reaching for the list. He looks it over for a second. "Not a bad idea. How do you plan to make money from it?"

"Well, we could sell baked goods, of course. And I was thinking of asking everyone in town for donations so we could have some sort of silent auction."

His forehead creases. "Do you think that would get you enough money to save the bakery?"

I sigh and fall back in my extremely comfortable chair. "No. That's part of the problem. One, this is a lot more work than I expected. And two, even with everything I've thought of so far, I still don't think it will be enough."

"We could always put you back in the dunk tank."

"Ha-ha." I tap my pen on the table. "I'm serious about this, Ben. I need to help Emma. I don't want to let her down."

"And you don't want Noah to win."

"And I don't want Noah to win."

"I imagine this situation might cause some problems in your relationship."

"Are he and I in a relationship?" How many dates does a relationship make? It's been a long time since I've considered that question.

Ben clears his throat again. "I think that's probably a question for Noah."

"Right." I tug the notebook back to my side of the table. "So anyway. Will you help me?"

He leans back in his chair, cradling his coffee mug against his chest. "Of course. I am here to help you succeed in your tasks, after all."

I pretend like the reminder doesn't sting. "Great. Any bright ideas on how to make about ten times as much money as my current projection?"

His brow furrows. "That might be a little trickier. But let me think on it. I'm sure if the two of us spend some time together, we can come up with something."

"You're a genius." I bolt upright, the force of my brilliant idea almost knocking me out of my chair.

"I am?"

Clapping my hands together with excitement, I flip to a clean page and start writing furiously.

"Care to fill me in?"

When I continue to ignore Ben's pleas for information, he comes around to my side of the table, leaning over my chair so he can attempt to read my scribbles.

And I'm so focused on my project that it takes me a full minute before I realize the warmth of him is completely surrounding me. My pen clatters to the floor and I sit back, the sudden movement bringing me even closer into Ben's sphere.

He doesn't move. So I don't either.

My heart is pounding like it wants to knock itself right out of my chest.

Ben reaches out for the notebook, tilting it up so he can see my practically illegible handwriting better.

He still doesn't move.

His scent is fucking everywhere. And how come whatever woodsy natural smell he has is so much more appealing than Noah's undoubtedly expensive cologne?

"Wait a minute. Does that say what I think it says?" Ben's indignant tone yanks me out of my smell-induced reverie.

"Do you think it says Date Auction? If so, then yes, yes it does."

Ben drops his arm and backs away from me as if I smell like I bathed in Noah's cologne. "Sweetheart. Be serious. You do not actually mean to auction off people?"

I roll my eyes. "I'm not auctioning off people. I'm auctioning off *dates* with people. Think about it. Ethan would probably bid enough on a date with Emma to cover the whole down payment."

Ben pinches the bridge of his nose, falling into the seat next to me. "This is the worst idea I've ever heard."

"You'll probably bring in a good chunk of change yourself." Not from me, obviously, but surely someone in Heart Springs will be interested in a date with Ben.

"You are even more delusional than I thought, sweetheart. There is nothing you could do or say to get me to participate in this farce."

I stick out my lower lip. "Ben, come on. Don't you want to help Emma? Haven't you been on me the whole time we've known each other, trying to get me to consider other people and be a productive member of society and shit like that? Don't you want me to find my life's passion so we can get out of here and go home?"

"Yes, but not at the cost of my dignity."

"It's not my fault you're scared to think outside the box, sweetheart." I nudge him with my elbow. The pointy part. "Admit it, this has the potential to bring in some major cash flow. Cash flow that Emma desperately needs, I might add."

"Are you going to auction yourself off?"

"God no." I laugh, loudly.

Ben cuts me down with a single look. "If you want me to go ahead with this—and by that I mean not only participate but also help you plan it—then you, Campbell Andrews, are getting auctioned."

I glare at him for a solid minute, but he doesn't back down, and fuck if I don't kind of admire that. "Fine. I'll do it. In fact, why don't we take things one step further?"

Ben raises his eyebrows as if to say, *Bring it on.*

"I bet I'll bring in more money than you do."

A smirk curls up the ends of his stupid pretty mouth. "You think you—ruiner of weddings, destroyer of dates, grandmaster of the dunk tank—can bring in more money than me?"

"Yup." I pop the *p*, pushing my chair back and collecting my belongings, ready to make my dramatic exit.

Ben stands too, following me over to the door, which he opens for me like he can't help but be chivalrous. "You're on, sweetheart. Think about how the people of Heart Springs feel about me, the boy next door who spends his time healing sick children, versus you, who gave an eight-year-old nightmares."

I skip down his front steps, chuckling. "Oh Ben, you're forgetting one major piece of the puzzle here, my friend."

"What's that?"

I turn, halfway down the walkway, and find him perched against the doorjamb, a sexy smirk on his face and a blasted smolder in his eyes—and all of that could fetch a high price at the auction. I lose my confidence for a half a second, but then I remember exactly who I am. "I'm hotter than you."

I put a little extra sway in my step as I swing through his front gate. And because I couldn't possibly be so uncool as to turn around at this point, I continue marching straight ahead, as if I never meant to go home in the first place.

Oh well, I never say no to one of Emma's lattes and something tells me she might need a little convincing before she agrees to my oh so brilliant plan. To the bakery, it is.

18

To my absolute surprise and shock, Emma not only agrees to the Date Auction but seems to be fully in favor of the idea. She must really be desperate to save the bakery because she doesn't even put up a fight when I tell her a date with her is most definitely on the docket. Her excitement reinforces what I already knew was going to be a brilliant plan and I face down my to-do list with the kind of fervor I used to save for my biggest clients.

So plans for the Save the Bakery Date Auction barrel on, full steam ahead. With Ben at my side, everything becomes about ten times easier. Suddenly everyone is willing to donate their time, money, prizes, and themselves. Seriously, the man has been here just as long as I have—how has he managed to ingratiate himself to everyone in town so quickly? If he weren't on my team, I would hate him. But I obviously don't hate him because who could possibly hate Ben? He's charming and witty and intelligent and patient and a million other qualities I shouldn't even notice, let alone admire.

And something happens in those moments when we're working together. Something I don't want to examine too closely, but something that might resemble us opening up to each other. I've already shared more with Ben than I have with anyone else, but as we're recruiting daters and designing tablescapes, it becomes about the little things. Like how Ben had dreams of playing baseball before he broke his elbow in high school. Or how I envied my peers who took creative writing classes, something I always wanted to explore, but that Grandmother claimed was frivolous. We start to truly get to know each other in a way I haven't experienced with anyone else before, and it's nice. More than nice.

Being so busy with the fundraiser means I don't have a lot of spare time left over for dates with Noah, but after a week without seeing him, I finally give in and agree to meet him for dinner. I insist on meeting him at the restaurant since I'm already in town working on fundraiser stuff, not because I don't want Ben to see him coming to pick me up.

Noah leans in and presses a kiss to my cheek as I rush into the lobby, breathless from sprinting across the town square. "You made it."

I shrug out of my coat, draping it over my arm and doing my best not to tilt my cheek away from his kiss. "Sorry, got held up with some fundraiser stuff."

Noah's brow wrinkles. "It might be best if we don't talk about that tonight. Keeping the business and personal separate and all that."

"Sure." I follow the hostess to our table, barely noting Noah's hand resting on the small of my back.

We sit and peruse our menus. Order some wine and an appetizer. Make pleasant small talk about the weather. And then we stare. Not at each other, because that would be weird. But at the floor, and the ceiling tiles, and at my own reflection in the spoon.

Noah clears his throat. "So how are you feeling about everything?"

I take a small sip of wine to hide my grimace. "I'm afraid you might need to be a tad more specific. How am I feeling about what, exactly?"

He shrugs and waves his hands around aimlessly. "You know. Everything."

"What would you like to hear about first? My job at the bakery you're trying to shut down? Or the fundraiser aimed at stopping you? Those are the two main things happening in my life right now, Noah." I don't mean the words to sound completely bitchy. I can't help it if that's my natural tone.

He has the decency to look a little bit shamed. Not enough, but a little bit. "I know." He sighs. "I'm sorry for the bad timing and all of this bakery stuff. I guess what I'm really trying to ask is how you're feeling about us?"

I purse my lips together to keep from blurting out the real answer. I barely even thought about Noah in the week we didn't see each other because his absence has no effect on me. Which is probably not a good sign.

But I can't say that. One, because he actually looks sort of hopeful. And two, because this is my last chance. If I write Noah off . . . well I don't actually know what happens if I write Noah off because I'm too afraid to ask, but I know it isn't good.

I adjust my napkin in my lap so I have something to do

with my hands. "I don't really know how I feel about us, Noah. Maybe we just need to see how things turn out with the bakery before we can really give this a chance."

He spins his glass of wine around on the table before taking a long sip. "Maybe you're right."

"I usually am." I flash a playful wink so he knows I'm only sort of serious.

The server drops off our appetizer and takes the rest of our order. I dig into the pile of calamari, thankful to have something else to focus my attention on.

"Why don't you tell me a bit about what a typical day in your life looks like? Your life before you moved to Heart Springs, I mean."

I pop a bite in my mouth to delay having to answer the very simple question. My life outside of Heart Springs looked like one thing: work. It's a sentiment I know Noah will understand, and yet I'm hesitant to reduce my life to something so devoid of any feelings or emotions. Or people other than my colleagues, a group that includes most of my family, though I think of them more as co-workers.

"To be totally honest with you, my whole life has always revolved around my job. I work for my family's law firm and it's expected that we all work to make partner, which I did. I basically devoted my entire existence to the firm. I don't have much to talk about outside of my job."

"Do you miss them?"

"Who?"

Noah raises his eyebrows. "Your family."

My cheeks flush a little because, outside of the context of work, I've barely thought about my family. "Um . . . yes?"

Noah reaches out across the table and takes my hand in

his. "You know I understand being devoted to your job. I think we both know I share the sentiment."

"But?" My hand feels clammy in his and I want to pull away, but he seems to be having some kind of moment here.

"But family is important too. As are friends. As is having some kind of life outside of work."

I slip my hand from his, not caring if it's rude or not, reminding myself that Noah doesn't know the whole story about how I landed here and why. "Living here in Heart Springs is doing a good job of teaching me that."

Noah sits back in his chair. "I suppose."

For some reason his response pisses me off. "You know, I didn't ask for any of this. I didn't ask to go on a date with you. I didn't ask to be forced into a relationship."

He holds up his hands in surrender. "Whoa. Cam. I'm not even sure what you're talking about. Who's forcing you to be in a relationship? I'm just trying to get to know you better because Ben said he thought we would be a good match."

The words hit me right in the gut, a reminder who set me up with this man, and why.

A wave of total and complete hopelessness washes over me as I stare at Noah's gorgeous face and his perfect suit and his expensive watch.

Because I don't think I can ever fall in love with Noah. And if I can't fall in love with him—a man so perfectly suited for me, I might as well have picked him out of a catalog—I don't think I'll ever be able to fall in love with anyone.

That thought wouldn't have bothered me before I arrived here. Who needs love when you have money and success?

But now, in this moment, the realization makes me sad.

"I think I need to go," I say quietly, pushing back my chair. "I'm not feeling well."

Noah stands. "Let me walk you home."

I shake my head, already moving toward the exit. "No, stay and enjoy your dinner. I'll be fine."

I powerwalk through the main square and up the walkway leading to my cottage. As if the slight increase in speed will allow me to ignore the elephant on the porch next door. My hand reaches out to grip the doorknob, but I can't make myself turn it.

Instead, I turn to Ben, sitting in his gorgeous handmade chair, looking at me like he knows everything that just happened. And maybe somehow he does.

He pats the empty chair next to him in invitation and I take it, recognizing it as the chair from his workshop. Sinking into the wood that feels like it's been perfectly molded to my body, I don't bother trying to suppress my emotions any longer.

"We're well and truly fucked, Ben."

He hands me a full glass of wine. "It can't be that bad, sweetheart."

"I think I'm going to be stuck here forever." I take a long sip and lean back in my chair. "Which means, by default, you are also going to be stuck here forever."

"I'm sure nothing like that has ever happened here before."

"I have been known to break records."

We sit in silence for a minute, but it's a comfortable one; despite the turmoil in my brain, it's a peaceful one. I want to tell Ben everything. How much I don't like Noah. How much I think I might like *him*. How he is the man I look forward to talking to and laughing with and how just the sight of him sitting on his porch makes my stomach flutter. I want to tell him that I'll probably suck at this whole relationship and falling-in-love bit, but that if he could be patient with me, maybe this could actually be something. The thoughts roll through my mind and dance on the back of my tongue, but I can't seem to give them voice. We've spent so much time together recently working on the fundraiser that he has to feel it too. Even if we can't say it.

"I think you should give Noah another chance," Ben finally says, his eyes locked on a spot far in the distance.

One time I was so busy yelling at an intern over the phone that I tripped while walking on my treadmill and fell flat on my chest. It took two minutes to fully regain my breath and it felt like hours.

This is so much worse than that.

I study his profile since he is very purposefully not meeting my gaze. His advice and the way he seems to not even want to look at me suggest that whatever spark I might have been feeling between us is in fact one-sided. And holy fuck, does that hurt. I mean, of course it does. No one has ever rejected me before. Probably because I've never allowed myself to have actual feelings before.

So thanks, Ben, for reminding me why I keep the walls up.

I don't say anything because there's nothing to say.

Ben finally looks my way. "I met someone, Cam."

For a second, the words don't compute. I want to respond that of course he met someone, we've met a whole host of someones since waking up here in Heart Springs.

But then he keeps talking. "Mimi set us up. She thinks we're perfect for each other."

Why couldn't Mimi have thought he'd be perfect for me?

Maybe because I'm a selfish bitch who doesn't deserve him.

I force myself to say something, if only to keep any remaining minuscule shreds of dignity intact. "That's great. I'm really happy for you."

He offers me a small smile. "Thanks."

"Too bad it wasn't you tasked with falling in love or we'd already be on our way home." I down the rest of my wine and push out of my chair. "I guess I'll see you tomorrow?"

His smile turns pained. "Tomorrow."

"Think your new girlfriend will be okay with you getting auctioned off?"

"Hopefully she'll be the highest bidder." There's not a lot of conviction in his voice.

"She's going to have to have deep pockets if you think you're going to bring in more money than me."

"Here's hoping."

I hesitate at the bottom of the steps, not willing to drag myself away just yet. "I really appreciate all you've done for me, Ben. It probably sounds strange and maybe a little bit pathetic, but I think you might be the best friend I've ever had."

A wave of something like anguish washes over his face. "Cam . . ."

I force out a stilted laugh. "Okay, that actually was even more pathetic than I intended. Anyway, thank you for the wine." I turn and race down the walkway, for a second considering hopping right over the fence so I can get to my front door as soon as possible. But I know I'm not smooth enough to pull that off and the only thing that could make tonight worse would be falling flat on my face.

"Cam!" Ben's voice halts me in my steps, right as I reach his gate. He trails halfway down the path. "I don't have to go on a date. I could tell Mimi I'm not interested, if I had a good reason. Is there a good reason I should tell Mimi I'm not interested, or not available?"

I open my mouth to give him a hundred reasons why he should forget that other girl and choose me, but I close it just as quickly. I'm not good for Ben. I'm not good for anyone, really, but especially someone like him. I'm sure this girl Mimi has picked out for him likes kids and animals and is probably a kindergarten teacher or a librarian or a fellow doctor. Someone who knows how to help people. Someone who knows how to put others in front of her own selfish needs. Someone who is the complete opposite of me.

"Go on your date, Ben. I'm sure it will be great. I can't wait to hear all about it." I don't wait for a response, pushing through my own gate, barely making it through my front door before the tears start flowing.

Huh. Wasn't sure my tear ducts still worked. But if the rest of the night is any indication, they're going to make up for lost time.

There are no indications I spent the night huddled under the covers hysterically sobbing when I wake up the next morning. My skin is as clear and blemish free as every morning in Heart Springs. There aren't even any dark circles under my eyes like I normally have at home. It's like the whole thing never happened. Apparently all the bruises are internal, located right in my chest.

Maybe my outer self is on to something. Maybe I need to pretend like the whole thing never happened. Because really, what has changed between last night and this morning? I still need to save the bakery. I still need to somehow fall in love.

I still want nothing more than to get the hell out of here.

And I know the exact way to make that happen.

I swing by the bakery early, before even Emma has stepped on the premises. I make a latte and grab a muffin left over from the day before.

I find Noah right where I expected to: sitting at his desk, leafing through a stack of papers because even high-powered lawyers don't seem to rely on the internet here.

Forcing a timid smile across my lips, I hand him the latte and muffin. "I'm really sorry about last night. I shouldn't have run out on you like that."

He eyes me warily before accepting my offerings. "If you weren't feeling well, you weren't feeling well." He takes a small sip of the coffee. "Are you feeling better today?"

There are layers to his question, and I parse them out before answering so I can give him an honest response. "I had some things I needed to figure out, but I think my head is clearer now."

His smile is warm and crinkles the edges of his eyes. "Glad to hear it. I want this to work, Cam."

"Me too." I nod resolutely, as if that can make the sentiment be true.

But I know I can make it true. I wanted to be a lawyer, so I became a lawyer. I wanted to make partner, so I made partner.

If I want to fall in love with Noah Crenshaw, then I will fall in love with Noah Crenshaw.

"Do you want to try for dinner again tonight? Maybe something a little more low-key?" I offer, hoping if I fake the excitement for long enough, it will become real.

"Sure. Your place or mine?" He leans back in his chair, his hands laced across his stomach.

"Yours." The last thing I need is Noah coming to my place.

He studies me like he can see right through me, and I really hope this whole everyone-in-Heart-Springs-knows-everything doesn't mean they have some sort of emotional x-ray vision capabilities. "Why don't you come over at seven?"

"Sounds great!" With a smile and a wave that I hope look natural, I head out of the office and back to the bakery.

Emma greets me with her normal warm smile when I push through the door. "Good morning!"

"Morning." I do my best to keep the enthusiasm in my voice, but judging by the slight pull down of her lips, I don't do a good job.

"Everything okay?"

For a second, I think about confiding in her. Emma has proven to be nothing but a basically perfect friend, always with a warm smile and a warm hug and a warm cookie. But my walls are thick and high, long-standing and not so easy to knock down. If I let Emma in, I run the risk of her hurting me. Ben came close enough to breaking through my barriers and look how that turned out.

So instead of telling her the truth, I force another smile. "Everything is great! I went over to see Noah this morning, and he's going to make me dinner tonight."

He didn't actually say he's going to make dinner but I'm going to be at his house at dinnertime so I figure some kind of meal can be assumed.

Emma's eyes tighten. "Oh. Great." She turns away from me, heading back to the kitchen.

I follow her. I still can't claim to be great at opening up to people, but if anyone deserves insight into my feelings in this situation, it's Emma.

"I promise that I won't let whatever happens between me and Noah affect the fight for the bakery, Emma." I grab the bowl from the top shelf that she'd been standing on tippy toes trying to reach, and hand it to her before tying an apron around my waist. "You know I'm going to find a way to save the bakery, but I also feel like I owe it to myself to be open to falling in love." I come this close to spilling the whole thing to Emma, to telling her about my life back in New York and what I have to do in order to get home, but I manage to keep myself in check. "I never meant for my move to Heart Springs to be permanent, you know."

"Would staying be such a terrible thing?" She turns those big brown eyes on me and the genuine question softens them.

I hesitate before I answer, because I don't know how to answer. When I first arrived in Heart Springs, I could think of nothing I wanted more than to get the hell out. But despite my resistance, I've made a little life for myself here. I have a job I enjoy, even if it isn't necessarily one I ever envisioned for myself. I have friends in Ben and Emma, and maybe even Mimi, even if I do continue to hold part of myself back from them. And I have this thing with Noah. A man that is, on paper, perfect for me.

But this isn't my real life. Maybe there are things I'll want to do differently when I return home. Maybe there will be parts of Heart Springs that stay with me even when I make it back to New York.

And I do want to return to New York, to home. I think.

"I'll miss you if and when I leave, but I promise I won't go before making sure you and the bakery will be okay." I turn away from Emma's pleading look, grabbing ingredients from the fridge and setting up to mix fresh muffin batter. "And if I have anything to say about it, I'm also going to do my best to make sure you and a certain someone go on a date before I go." I will rig the date auction so that Ethan wins Emma's date if I have to.

"I don't know how many times I need to tell you that's a lost cause." She shoos me away from the muffin bowl, handing me a tray of cooling croissants to take out to the front. "Now get back to work." Her command lacks bite and is paired with a smile, and I know I will never have another boss quite like Emma again.

I DRESS CASUALLY FOR DINNER AT NOAH'S, IN JEANS and a soft sweater that when I tug it just right, slips off my shoulder. One thing is for certain: Noah is just my type, physically speaking, and maybe if we can find some chemistry, it will help open the floodgates to love.

Good god, I cannot believe the phrase *floodgates of love* just flitted through my mind completely unbidden. I need to get the hell out of here ASAP.

I close the front door, keeping my eyes firmly planted on the walk in front of me, avoiding any chance of a run-in with Ben.

But because my luck sucks, I hear the click of his gate as I'm latching mine.

I turn toward him before I can stop myself, and my breath catches in my chest.

Gone are the soft T-shirts and plaid flannels he typically wears. Tonight Ben is dressed in a dark green button down shirt, the sleeves rolled up to frame his forearms. His jeans have been exchanged for a pair of well-fitting gray slacks that are doing things to the shape of his thighs that are truly just unfair.

I force myself to stop ogling him, directing my eyes to his face. They land there just in time to see his own deep brown eyes lingering on the exposed hint of my collarbone.

"Hi," I manage to choke out, which seems to bring him back to the present.

His eyes fly to mine. "Hi."

"Hot date?" I joke before I realize that's probably exactly where he's fucking going.

"I suppose. You too?"

"I suppose."

We stand for a minute, just looking into each other's eyes, saying nothing and good lord, who knew one could experience so many emotions over the course of a single minute.

"I should go," I finally say, gesturing helplessly to the sidewalk in front of me.

"Yeah, me too." Ben turns and starts to head in the exact direction I need to go to get to Noah's house.

I fall in step next to him and ask the question I'm not sure I want the answer to. "First date with your new friend?"

Ben nods. His arms swing by his side, and I might be imagining it, but it feels like he leans in just a hair so that our hands brush.

A shiver races up my spine, and I put space between us.

Ben shoves his hands in his pockets.

"I'm sure the two of you will have a lovely date. Unless she turns out to be a total disaster like me." I'm not usually one for self-deprecating comments—I know who I am and what I've got—but something about Ben going on this date is seriously messing with my head.

"You're not a total disaster, Cam."

"Just sort of a disaster?" I joke with a mirthless laugh.

He pointedly ignores me. "It's just a first date. I'm not even sure why she's interested in me."

"She's interested in you because you're a good person, Ben. And you'll make a great date. And an even better partner."

"You don't have to lie to build up my confidence, sweetheart."

I stop in my tracks, reaching for his arm and pulling him to a stop next to me. "Why on earth would you think any of that is a lie?"

He looks at where his arm is still in my grip. I hadn't even realized I kept hold of him, as if trying to keep him anchored to me. His eyes lock on mine. "I guess it's hard for me to believe you would think those nice things about me."

I move a half step closer to him, letting the woodsy scent of him fill my nose. "I think you're maybe the best man I've ever met, Ben."

He sucks in a breath, and his eyes darken.

It's the closest either of us has ever come to acknowledging there might be something living in this blank space between us.

He told me to give Noah a chance.

I told him there was no reason for him to not accept his date.

And yet.

His lungs expand—my gaze is caught on his throat, the peek of bare skin where his shirt is unbuttoned, and I watch his breath stutter.

He takes a step back, shaking his head. "I should go. I don't want to be late."

Now I'm the one having trouble breathing. "Sure. Me too."

I gesture for him to go on ahead without me, knowing I can't possibly stomach walking by his side for another second.

Message from one Dr. Ben Loving clearly received.

He hesitates for a half second, his mouth opening and closing like he might have something to say, but he quickly spins on his heel and hurries down the path, leaving me behind without a second glance.

I dig my nails into the skin of my palms, using the bite of pain to center me, bring me back to the task at hand.

Noah Crenshaw. Falling in love. Getting the hell out of here.

20

Totally warm and delicious smells greet me the moment Noah opens his door. His house looks much like mine in layout but has been decorated in a more traditionally masculine fashion. His sofa is leather, his TV takes up the entire wall, and instead of a dated yet color-coordinated kitchen, his is all sleek marble and stainless steel.

And he appears to actually use said kitchen, which is something none of my past boyfriends have ever been able to say they do. To be fair, it's also something I have never been able to say.

"Wine?" he asks the second I've kicked off my shoes and made it through the front door.

"God yes." I follow him into the kitchen and accept the glass of red he offers.

"Tough day?" He flashes me a smirky smile and turns his attention back to the stove, which currently holds multiple steaming pots.

Since the only tough part about it was dealing with the

man I can't seem to make myself stop thinking about, I lie. "Oh you know, the usual. The bakery has been so busy lately, Emma and I are being run ragged." I slide onto a barstool at his kitchen island, sipping my wine and trying to look coy instead of depressed. Not an easy task.

Noah tosses me a knowing glance over his shoulder as he stirs something in the largest of the pots. "Glad to hear business is going well, should make it easy for her to invest in a new location."

I glare at his back. "Not going to happen, bud. And I thought we weren't going to talk business?"

He shrugs. "You brought it up."

I fold my arms and lean on the counter. "Can I ask you a serious question?"

"Of course."

"Does it ever bother you? Doing what you do?" Doing what *we* do, is what I really mean to ask. I need to hear his answer, to see if it's the same as mine once would have been.

He taps a wooden spoon on the edge of a pan and turns to face me. "Honestly? Not really. My clients hire me to do a job, and I do it. My loyalty is to the people who pay me. I can't think too much about what's best for anyone other than my clients."

I nod, not put off by his callousness because they're words I've thought to myself hundreds, if not thousands, of times. Why should I feel bad when I'm merely doing as my clients request? "Do you ever think about going into any other line of work?"

He arches a single eyebrow. "Do you?"

"I didn't. Not before I came to Heart Springs."

"Thinking about opening your own bakery one day?" he teases.

I laugh and am somewhat surprised to find that it's genuine. "Not hardly."

But it would be a lie to pretend that being here, watching Emma's struggle, hasn't made me second-guess some things about what I've chosen to do with my life. Emma has put her whole heart and soul into her bakery; there was no one there to give her a boost or a financial bailout when she needed one. She's spent her time and energy creating something where so much of my own time and energy has been spent tearing people down.

Noah leans over to refill my glass. "The way I think of it, it's not my job to make life better for everyone I encounter. That would be impossible. What I *can* do is make life better for my clients. And that's good enough for me."

It's a sound philosophy. Except when your clients are terrible people. As I suspect some of his are. As I know some of mine have been.

I swirl my wineglass and take another swig. "Well, that's enough of that line of questioning. Tell me something interesting about yourself, Noah."

"I once ate three whole pizzas all by myself."

My nose wrinkles. "Wow, you really know how to impress the ladies."

He shrugs, presenting me with a plate of bruschetta, tiny toasted bread rounds topped with bright red tomatoes and golden drizzles of olive oil.

I take a bite and flavors explode over my tongue. "Wow, you really know how to impress the ladies."

He laughs and his smile brings one of my own to my

face. And for the first time, I start to think this might not all turn out so bad.

OVER THE NEXT COUPLE OF WEEKS, LIFE IS SO BUSY, IT passes in a blur. But it's the good kind of busy, the kind where I fall into bed each night tired but happy. Maybe even a little bit proud. The bakery continues to take up most of my days, my usual duties split with time working on the fundraiser, which is just days away. All the plans are falling into place and when I show Emma the list of RSVPs, a hint of hope is restored to her eyes.

That alone is worth the long hours.

Noah and I don't spend every evening together—we're both too busy for that much contact—but we see each other often enough. We don't talk about business or lawyerly philosophies, our conversations instead revolve around getting to know the finer details about each other. And he's not a bad guy, Noah Crenshaw, business practices aside. He cooks and he reads and he makes interesting conversation. Sometimes he makes me laugh. Sometimes I truly enjoy being in his company.

The only thing missing is the spark. That undefinable, little something extra that makes you want to spend every second with a person. That sexual attraction that makes you want to throw a person against a door and kiss them senseless.

I keep telling myself the spark can grow. So can the attraction. It's not like I'm not attracted to him—the man is gorgeous. I just don't fall asleep each night envisioning our first real kiss. And I don't know that he does either, because he hasn't even tried to kiss me yet. A fact that I'm so okay with, it should probably be alarming.

All the fizzy, happy sparks seem to have abandoned me as of late. Every time I see Ben, the only man who's made me feel sparky since I arrived here, my stomach jolts, like I'm right on the edge of tossing my cookies. Luckily, I don't actually toss my cookies (at least I haven't yet), but it still doesn't change the fact that the sight of one of my only friends has turned into something so uncomfortable, I avoid him at all costs. And he seems to be avoiding me too.

At least, he is until the night before the Save the Bakery fundraiser. I trudge up to my front gate, feet aching, mind whirling, but heart happy. Everything is set up and ready to go. The only thing to do tomorrow is prep our daters to get auctioned off and hopefully make a lot of money.

I'm so surprised to see Ben sitting out on his porch when I get home, I stand and stare at him for at least a minute, like if I look long enough, I'll discover he's really an apparition and he'll disappear.

He watches me watch him, cocking an eyebrow and finally offering me a glass of wine. "I just opened a bottle of red."

I shift over to his gate, my steps slow as I make my way up his front walk. Partly because I'm sore and partly because I want to delay this conversation for as long as possible. "Thanks." I take the proffered glass and sink into my favorite chair with a contented sigh. "I missed this chair."

A bemused smile pulls at his lips. "It's been here the whole time."

I turn my head in his direction. "I wasn't aware I was welcome."

"You've always been welcome here, sweetheart." It could be me reading into it, but there doesn't seem to be the usual trace of sarcasm laced through his endearment.

"It is your task to keep tabs on me, after all." My words lack bite because I don't mean them to be cutting, but that doesn't stop Ben from flinching.

"I suppose it is." He takes a long sip from his own glass of wine. "Everything ready for tomorrow?"

I nod, turning my head to face forward so I can rest it on the perfectly sculpted back of the chair. "Barring any game-day emergencies, I think we're in really good shape. Knock on wood." I rap my knuckles gently on the arm of the chair.

"I never took you for the superstitious type."

"I'm not really, at least I don't think so. Force of habit, I guess." One I don't even know how I picked up because certainly no one in my family believes in shit like luck. We believe in hard work and solid plans and generational wealth. "I think the real question is, are *you* ready for tomorrow?"

"I was born ready, sweetheart." The teasing lilt of his voice doesn't hide the hint of nerves.

"Is the new girlfriend prepared to break out the big bucks? She's going to have to if she wants to match Noah's bid for me." I haven't actually talked to Noah about the date auction or bidding on me since that would violate our no-business-talk policy, but I would assume he plans to purchase my time.

"You think Noah is going to put up the big bucks when the whole goal of the fundraiser is to defeat his client? Don't you think that's a conflict of interest?"

Well, shit. I hadn't really thought of it that way. Not that I can let Ben know that. But Noah agreed to be my date to the whole shindig; surely he knows bidding on me comes with the territory.

"I'm not worried," I say, though I clearly am now worried. "How are things going with your new gal pal?" It's a testament to how much I don't want to talk about Noah that I change the subject to Ben's new girlfriend. It's a testament to how much time I've spent in Heart Springs that I use the phrase "gal pal."

"Lindsay."

"How are things going with Lindsay?" I hate to be that girl, but her name tastes sour in my mouth. Though I'm sure she's a lovely person.

"They're going well."

"That doesn't sound very enthusiastic." I sneak another peek at him. He's buried his gaze in his wine and refuses to meet my eyes.

"Sometimes it takes time to feel comfortable with a new partner."

"She must like you, otherwise she would've given you the boot by now. Think about how quickly I got rid of my first two dates." The realization turns my stomach. There must be something there between them.

"I suppose." He finally deigns to glance my way. Something uncertain is buried deep in the dark pools of his eyes.

I reach over, chancing a quick pat on his forearm before I think about all the reasons I should really keep my hands to myself. We're both wearing sweaters, and yet the brush of my hand against the soft fabric is enough to send a zing through me. Though maybe it's just the wine. "You know you can talk to me, Ben. Things have been weird between us, and I get it, but I'm still your friend, right? We're still friends."

He covers my hand with his and if my hand on his sweater created a zing, his hand on my hand sets off a lightning storm in my veins. "Of course we're still friends, sweetheart. You know we're in this together, for better or worse."

I shift my hand the slightest bit, allowing our fingers to interlock. "All I want is for you to get what you want, for you to be happy."

His fingers tighten around mine. "I want that for you too. Do you think Noah can make you happy?"

I open my mouth to tell him yes, whether I believe that fully or not. But the half-truth refuses to come out. "I hope so."

"What are you going to do when you get home?" he asks me softly.

I wait for him to move to untangle our fingers, but he doesn't, so I don't either. Instead, I enjoy the warm comfort of my hand in his. "I don't know really. I can't imagine anyone in my family is going to be too pleased with me."

His brow furrows. "They're going to be mad at you for something that's out of your control?"

"They're going to be mad at me for missing out on a huge deal and disappearing without a word." The truth is a biting one, one that makes my heart constrict.

"You don't deserve that, Cam." My name so rarely drops from his lips, it does something to me to hear it.

"Don't I, though? We both know I'm not a good person,

Ben. I wouldn't be here otherwise, and you wouldn't be stuck here with me."

He shifts in his chair, angling his body toward me. "Your priorities maybe weren't the best. But you still have plenty of time to be the person you want to be. The person I know you can be. Look at what you've done here, what you're doing for Emma. You've worked so hard, put in so many extra hours, all for the benefit of someone else. I'm so proud of you."

Wetness pools in my eyes, and we're sitting too close together for there to be any chance he might not notice.

"I'm sorry." He reaches out a hand, wiping the trail of tears with his thumb. "I didn't mean to make you cry."

"I don't think anyone has ever said that to me before." I whisper the admission.

His grip on my hand tightens, along with the lines around his eyes. "Your family sucks."

A tearful laugh escapes my choked lungs. "That I have heard once or twice."

His thumb rubs a soothing pattern over my knuckles. "You are doing great things, Cam. And you are capable of doing even greater things."

I use my free hand to swipe under my eyes. "Thank you, Ben. You're a pretty amazing guy. I hope Lindsay knows how lucky she is."

Saying her name breaks us from some kind of spell. We gently unlock our hands and scoot back in our chairs—and the small distance feels like an uncrossable chasm. We sit in silence for a few more minutes before I swig the last of my wine and rise. My body aches the moment it's separated from Ben's chair, the moment it's separated from

Ben. I would give up my morning espresso for the comfort of my hand back in the warmth of his.

"Good night, Ben. I'll see you at the fundraiser tomorrow?"

He nods. "I wouldn't miss it."

I offer him a slight wave before I head from his front porch over to mine. His eyes stay on me until I shut the door behind me, the weight of the evening pressing my back into the closed door.

21

So there's a chance that had I not screwed things up so royally at my first go round as a wedding planner, I might have actually done well in that career path.

At the very least, I'm kicking ass at this whole fundraising business.

I do a final walk-through, my eyes scrupulously examining every detail before dashing back to my cottage to change for the evening. Luckily, I don't have to worry about hair and makeup as the moment I stepped out of the shower after my bakery shift, I was ready to go, my normal makeup made more dramatic by dark liner, thick lashes, and a bright red lip.

Throwing open my closet, I realize in the moment I should have thought to plan out my outfit, but it turns out I didn't need to worry. The perfect little black dress is hanging right in the center of the closet, a pair of strappy heels resting on the carpet below. Diamond drop earrings and a dainty necklace sit atop the dresser just waiting for me. Dare I say, I may have gotten used to this on-demand stylist deal.

I change quickly, wanting to be back at the event site before any of the guests arrive. That doesn't stop me from lingering on the front porch for longer than it should take to close and lock my door. But there's no hint of Ben.

I stride down Main Street, smiling as the large clear tent set up in the middle of the green comes into view. The evening air holds a chill, but the tent is perfectly warm. The ceiling of the tent has been strung with tiny lights, and the combination of the lights and the clear view of the night sky above is absolutely magical.

The tables are set with simple china and lush floral centerpieces, the dance floor is gleaming, and the band is tuning up, everyone having donated their time and services to make sure the bakery survives.

"Everything looks absolutely amazing, Cam. I can't believe this." Emma's eyes are wide as she takes in the room.

"It turned out okay, yeah?"

She loops her arm through mine. "This is better than okay. It's incredible. How can I ever thank you for everything you've done for me and the bakery?"

"I'm happy to do it." I pull back a little, under the guise of checking out her dress, but mostly so we don't have to continue down the emotional route of this conversation. I don't know if this mascara is waterproof or not. "You look absolutely breathtaking, by the way."

She does a little shimmy, the swingy skirt of her bright red dress dancing around her legs. The crimson pops against her brown skin and the neckline is daringly low for Heart Springs. Ethan doesn't stand a chance tonight. "Thank you. You look gorgeous as usual."

"Thank you." I let her pull me into a hug because it's

just too hard to resist Emma's hugs. "I hope it's enough to save the bakery."

"It will be. I can feel it."

A server from the catering team approaches us, her steps timid. Which is a little dramatic as I've *barely* raised my voice at the staff. "The first guests are arriving. Did you want someone from our team to check them in?"

I shake my head and take the clipboard she hands me. "I'll do it. I want to have face time with everyone. You should come with me, Em. Remind the people why we're here."

She slides her arm through mine again, and we make our way to the entrance where a small crowd has already gathered.

Emma and I greet the guests and let them know their table numbers. Emma shines, her bright smile never dropping as she makes conversation with every person who enters the tent.

What's more surprising is that I do too. Pretty much everyone I greet has something nice to say about the event, and how happy they are to be there. Many of them offer me smiles and ask how I'm doing. No one threatens to push me into a giant vat of water, so things are much improved since our last community event.

It's almost time to get started, but some key players are still missing. Namely Ben and Noah. My stomach turns a little at the thought of Noah not showing up. I suppose he would be well within his rights, given the purpose of the event, but he told me he would be here, and who else is going to bid on me if he doesn't show?

Right before I can spiral into full-on panic mode, a pair of strong arms encircles me from behind.

"Sorry I'm late."

I pivot, the motion mostly not on purpose dislodging Noah's arms from my waist. "No problem, I'm just happy you're here." I make a show of checking his name off the list and searching for his table number, even though we're obviously seated together. He looks good, of course, the cut of his suit tailored and sharp, the blue of his tie an exact match to his eyes.

As I turn to lead him to his seat, my eyes catch on a couple entering the tent. My brain absolutely freezes, my feet along with it.

Ben's steps stutter as his eyes lock on mine, but luckily for his date, he doesn't lose his full range of motion.

I think Noah is trying to get my attention, but I can't be sure because I'm only capable of focusing on one thing right here in this present moment. And it isn't him.

It's *him*.

Ben wears a dark gray suit, clean and classic and simple in a beautiful way. He's paired it with a navy blue shirt, open at the neck without a tie. His thick hair, so often unruly, has been tamed in a way that makes me want to run my fingers through it and muss it up again.

It isn't until he clears his throat and gestures to the woman standing next to him that I regain any sort of motor function. I almost lose it all again when my eyes drift to the woman, Lindsay obviously. She's gorgeous, of course. Wearing a soft pink dress with a sweetheart neckline, her dark brown curls sweeping over her pale shoulders. She offers me a blinding smile and I wonder if she's as perfect as she looks, if she and Ben are as well suited in reality as they look together in this moment.

"You must be Lindsay." I direct my words to her, not

sure I have the ability to look Ben in the eye and make sounds come out of my mouth. I check off their names on my list and gesture toward Noah, waiting patiently by my side, though he is watching me with a questioning glint in his eyes. "Ben and I need to go get ready for the auction, but maybe the two of you could find your seats. We're all at the same table."

Noah's jaw tightens ever so slightly, but he flashes Lindsay a wide grin and offers her his arm. "You two have fun up there."

Without a second glance, our dates head toward the front of the room, chatting amiably along the way.

I finally allow myself to meet Ben's eyes. "Hi."

"Hi." He rocks forward on his toes a bit before shoving his hands in his pockets and leaning back.

"For a second I thought you might not be coming."

"And miss the opportunity to show you up out there? Not a chance."

A grin tugs on my lips and his face splits in an answering smile.

"You look beautiful, sweetheart." His voice is so low, I have to lean in to hear him. God, he smells good.

"You clean up pretty okay yourself."

The sound of a throat clearing pulls me from my Ben-induced haze once again. Emma's eyes flit between the two of us, something knowing and worried lurking in the depths of them. "It's time to start the auction."

I pull back from Ben, straightening my dress, though not a stitch is out of place. "Great! Let's go!" My voice is overly cheerful, but they both blessedly ignore it and follow me toward the stage.

Our group of auctionees is waiting off to the side, and

after a quick run-through, I accept the mic from the emcee and climb up on the stage.

"Hello everyone," I begin, giving the crowd a couple of seconds to finish their conversations. "Thank you so much for coming out tonight to our Save the Bakery fundraiser." I hold for applause and am granted a rousing chorus of cheers. "I know it means so much to Emma to see you all here supporting her tonight. Now, I promise we have a fun night of dinner and dancing ahead of us, but before we can cut loose, it's time to raise some money!" This round of cheers is louder than the first and I make a mental note to tip the bartenders extra as they clearly have done their jobs well. "And what better way to kick off this auction than with the woman of the hour herself: please give it up for Emma!"

This time the yells and hollers are so loud, I have to force myself not to cover my ears.

Emma climbs to the stage with a look on her face that can only be described as pure and unadulterated terror. She steps toward me and turns to face the audience, her hands clasped in front of her.

"Smile," I whisper fiercely in her ear.

She obliges, but it's definitely not the winning grin she usually sports.

"All right, everyone. Let's start this off with a bang. Who's willing to give a hundred dollars for a date with this gorgeous woman? If you ask nicely, she'll probably bring some baked goods!"

Several hands shoot into the air, and we're off. It doesn't take long for Emma's numbers to climb. I'm so busy keeping track of the bids that I don't notice the disappointed look in her eyes until we're down to our final two bidders, two men I don't recognize, neither of whom are Ethan.

I reach for her hand, squeezing gently as I announce, "Going once, going twice—" I spot Ethan standing in the back of the room, his hands shoved in his pockets, his face pinched. I flash back to our conversation about his lack of funding and how it made him feel like he doesn't deserve Emma. And I make a decision. "What's that I see in the back of the room? Another hand? You'd like to bid a thousand dollars, tall guy with the brown hair?"

Emma's eyes widen and she moves to grab the mic, but I'm too quick for her.

"Sold to that guy in the back!"

Ethan looks confused for a minute, but he finally catches on and a grin spreads across his face. He politely pushes his way through the crowd, offering Emma his hand and helping her off the stage. She throws me a confused but gleeful look over her shoulder and I flash her a thumbs-up in return. Yeah, I'll have to throw in the cash myself, but what difference does it make when the money isn't real? The happiness on Emma's face *is* real, and that's worth every penny.

The rest of the dates aren't quite as exciting, but we continue to make a ton of money and maybe even a love connection or two.

Finally, we're down to our last two biddees—me and Ben. I'm about to call Ben up to the stage when Emma takes the mic from my hand and nudges me off to the side. "I'll take it from here," she whispers to me with a wink.

I don't like the look of that wink.

"Before we get to our final two daters of the evening, I

wanted to take a minute to tell all of you how thankful I am for all of your love and support." Emma's barely begun her impromptu speech and tears are already gathering in her eyes. "The last several weeks have been tough, but the care you all have shown me, throughout that time, but especially tonight, has truly made me feel like there's nothing I can't do."

Aw fuck. Now tears are also gathering in my eyes.

Emma turns toward me and I know instinctively there's no hope for my mascara. "And Cam. To say that none of this would have been possible without you is the understatement of the century. When I needed help, you were there for me, without question. You've put aside your own personal business"—her eyes flit in the direction of Noah, but don't linger there—"to make sure my business has a chance to be saved. I can never thank you enough for the sacrifices you have made for me." She tucks the microphone under her arm and leads the crowd in a round of applause.

And something weird happens in my stomach as I watch this room of people, most of whom have hated me at some point in time, cheer for me like I'm a homegrown hero.

"I hope you're proud of yourself, sweetheart," Ben says, his lips an inch from brushing the shell of my ear. He said something similar to me once before, but without the ring of sincerity.

I let myself take in the room at large, and for one single moment, let myself feel proud. Because I did this. Not for me, or to suck up to my grandmother, or to piss off the rest of my family. I did this for Emma. For someone who truly deserves it.

If this is what it feels like to do good, I may have been going about some things all wrong.

But before I have the chance to introspect too far, Emma is calling Ben up to the stage. His hand squeezes mine as he makes his way past me and up the stairs, and there's that fucking shiver again.

My eyes dart to our table, the one I have yet to sit at. Noah and Lindsay are chatting, but once Ben takes the stage, she has eyes only for him. She does a little fake stretch, like she's going to need to be in top condition to win this auction. Ben sees her and a smile tugs on his lips.

My empty stomach roils at the sight, and I probably should have eaten something before this moment, but it's too late now. I tried to cloak this whole thing in competition vibes, like watching Ben rake in the money was going to somehow be fun and silly.

Now I realize what I'm watching is Lindsay staking her claim.

Which is fine, I tell myself. Ben is a good person and maybe my first real friend ever and I want him to be happy because I'm not a total and complete asshole. At least, not anymore. And as much as I want to get out of Heart Springs, as much as we both want to go home, it doesn't mean he doesn't want a chance to find his person. He deserves that chance.

And yet.

When Emma opens the bids and Lindsay raises her hand, some force greater than my well-honed logic completely takes over my brain.

"A thousand dollars!" I shout from the side of the stage.

The silence lasts only a second, but fuck, is it deafening.

Emma recovers first. "A thousand dollars! Do I hear eleven hundred?"

"Eleven hundred!" Lindsay echoes. Of course she does and she should and I should shut the fuck up right now and let her win.

"Twelve hundred!" I call before Emma can even ask for it.

She shoots me a look, but Emma's not dumb and higher bids means more money for the bakery, so she keeps going.

Every person in the room is staring at me.

Well, every person but one.

Ben hasn't looked at me once since the auction for his date started.

Were my attention where it's supposed to be, I would also notice that Noah is avoiding looking at me, his gaze buried in a glass of whiskey.

Finally the tension becomes too much for me. "Five thousand dollars!"

The room inhales a collective gasp.

Lindsay looks properly defeated, which should not make me as happy as it does.

"Sold!" Emma cries with a triumphant bang of our ceremonial gavel. "And on that note, our dating auction has come to an end!" She passes the microphone back to the emcee before anyone can protest.

"Thank you, Heart Springs, for those amazing bids!" The emcee's soothing tone booms through the tent. "Let's get all of our auctionees and our winners out on the floor for a celebratory dance."

Shit.

I'm frozen here at the side of the stage, my eyes locked

on Ben's. He hasn't moved from his position on the stage itself. His expression is unreadable, but there's no mistaking the heat in his gaze.

What the fuck did I just do.

I can't even make myself look at Lindsay, let alone chance a glance at Noah. He must be furious, and rightfully so.

"Come on, sweetheart, let's give the people what they want." Ben's voice rumbles low in my ear and burrows down under my skin. His hand finds a place on my lower back, and he guides me to the dance floor.

More than one curious pair of eyes finds their way to us, but most people are more interested in their own partners and the attention slowly shifts away.

Ben places a hand on my waist, linking his other hand with mine. For a minute, all we do is sway to the soft swells of the music surrounding us.

Then I allow myself to look at him.

The music and the people and the bright lights and the sheer mortification fade away and I tuck myself closer into Ben's embrace.

"Why did you do that?" His words are barely a whisper. I have to move in closer to hear them. He adjusts his hold on me, keeping me there, our bodies pressed together in a way that kicks my heartbeat into overdrive.

I don't answer right away because I don't have an answer. "I'm sorry," I finally say. "I shouldn't have. I should have let Lindsay win. God knows she deserves you more than I do."

He shakes his head, dislodging one of his brown curls from his carefully coiffed locks. "Don't do that. Tell me why."

I tentatively reach for the stray curl, tucking it back into place. "You know why."

"Let's pretend I don't." He takes our joined hands and presses them to his chest. His heart is pounding just as fiercely as mine.

"Does it matter why, Ben? If we want to get out of here, if we want to make it back home, we have to follow Mimi's stupid rules." I watch his eyes, looking for some hint of hope.

He lowers his head, the two of us no longer dancing so much as we are hugging with a little swagger. "Maybe I'm sick of following the rules, sweetheart."

My breath catches and my eyes flutter closed as I press my cheek to his. His warmth is everywhere, but it isn't just the heat of him, it's the comfort and the safety and the utter peace I find wrapped up in Ben's arms.

Peace that is shortly destroyed by the emcee once again taking to the mic. "Now how about everyone dances with the person they came with!"

Everyone on the dance floor looks confused, none of the couples separating at the emcee's command.

Ben and I are the only two forced to separate by this declaration and my cheeks heat at the realization that everyone else either came single and bid or bid on the person they came with.

A strong pair of arms tugs me away from Ben, who doesn't fully look like he's willing to let me go until Lindsay steps into his line of sight.

I reluctantly step into Noah's arms, keeping significantly more distance between the two of us than between me and Ben. I wait for him to say something, to put me out of my misery, but he really has learned how to best torture me given the short amount of time we've spent together.

"I don't know what came over me, Noah." I can't seem to make myself apologize because I'm not actually sorry.

Noah puts even more space between us, forcing me to look him in the eye. "This was never actually going to work, was it?"

I shrug, turning away from his piercing gaze as if that will hide the tears beginning to pool in my eyes. "I really did try. I wanted this to work."

"But it was never going to."

"It was never going to," I say softly. I halt our motion, needing to put an end to the farce. "I really am sorry, Noah."

He shrugs, and I try not to be offended by how easily he takes it. "It is what it is." He adjusts the cuffs of his suit jacket and strides out of the tent without a backward glance.

I do my best to avoid looking at Ben and Lindsay, but they're right there in front of me. Ben catches my eye over her shoulder, and I layer a million questions in that look. *What are we doing here* and *Am I the only one feeling this way* and *Want to get the hell out of here please*?

His eyes are unreadable.

I wait for him to come to me, to gently set Lindsay to the side and take his rightful place in my arms, but the two of them continue to sway while I stand in the middle of the dance floor alone, looking like the complete moron I must be.

I catch his eye and mouth the words *Can we talk?*

He looks pained, mouths *I'm sorry.*

Wow. I turn on my heel and make for the exit, keeping my head down so I don't have to make eye contact with anyone along the way. Technically this is my fundraiser and I should not be abandoning Emma, but I can't stay here for another minute. Not when I've realized what's been right in front of me this whole time. Not two minutes ago, we were wrapped up in each other's arms, our heartbeats synced, and now he's sorry?

Maybe this is what the whole purpose of Heart Springs really is, to show me what it feels like to be treated as disposable, like I have treated so many others. Well, joke's on Heart Springs because I've been disposable my whole life.

I don't run, and I keep a smile plastered on my face until I'm free and clear from the town square. As far as anyone else is concerned, I could be dashing to the store to pick up more ice.

But the only thing I need right now is to get away.

Thoughts swirl around in my brain like some kind of tornado, and parsing them out, making sense of them while my chest feels like it's been caved in with a hammer, doesn't seem likely.

I reach my front door just in time. As soon as it's safely closed behind me, I dissolve into the kind of tears I don't remember crying as an adult. The kind of hopeless sobs that come easily when you're a teenager and you've just caught your boyfriend making out with your best friend, the ones you typically don't have much occasion for as a grown-up.

At least I haven't had much occasion for these kinds of tears as a grown-up because that would mean I would have to be emotionally invested in something other than my career.

And this right here is as good a reason as any to keep my emotions walled off because look what happens when I start to feel things.

My chest is still heaving, I'm still struggling to catch my breath when there's a knock on the door. I should have suspected Emma would come look after me, but I'm not about to let her risk her big night for my dumb feelings.

I open the front door, ready to tell her to get back to her party, that I can lay all my problems on her tomorrow.

But Emma doesn't stand on my front stoop.

"I'm so sorry, sweetheart." Ben steps through the front door, takes my face in his hands, and kisses me.

22

I melt into the kiss, fall into it, sink into it, only for it to end a second later.

Ben keeps his hands on my cheeks, wiping away the remains of my tears with his thumbs. "I didn't mean for you to leave. I just needed a second to tell Linsday it isn't going to work out between us."

My hands find the lapels of his coat, hanging on like he's a life jacket and I've just been thrown overboard. "Just to clarify, the *us* it isn't going to work out between would be you and Lindsay, right?"

A small smile tugs on his lips. "Yes, sweetheart."

I tilt my head up, searching for another kiss. He doesn't make me beg for it, his lips brushing against mine with the softest of flutters. And it's perfect and zingy and I want more. I rise up on my toes, circling my arms around his neck as I deepen the kiss. His arms cinch around my waist, pulling us so close together, his heartbeat thrums through my chest.

We kiss for what feels like hours before we part, chests heaving, needing to catch our breath.

Ben presses his forehead to mine. "Maybe we should slow down for a minute."

I groan, sliding my hands down to his chest. It's firm underneath my palms, and I want to feel it without the layers of fabric separating us. "Or, alternative plan, we should keep going at this rate and see where the night takes us."

He leans down, planting a gentle kiss on the curve of my neck that makes me shiver. "Trust me, that is most definitely what I want to do."

"So then what's the problem?"

He puts a small sliver of space between us, but it's too much space. "I feel like we're in uncharted territory here. We don't really know what's going to happen tomorrow. What might happen if we were to . . . you know."

"Consummate the relationship?"

His eyes flutter closed for a second, like I just whispered a litany of dirty words in his ear instead of describing sex in the most absolutely bland way possible. "God, Cam, I don't know what the answer is here. All we've been trying to do since we got here is get back home."

"And now I've gone and broken all the rules." I infuse my tone with a teasing lilt, trying desperately to lighten the mood, though his words leave a shadow of doubt hovering over me. "Maybe you're right. It's probably a good idea to take things slowly, see how some stuff plays out."

His thumb returns to my cheek, tracing the line of my jaw. "Sometimes you are very wise, Ms. Andrews."

I scoff. "Excuse me? Sometimes? How about all the time, thank you very much." I gesture to the couch. "Now, how about we sit down and pretend to watch a movie and make out a little more?"

He chuckles, leaning down to kiss me on the cheek. "Sounds perfect. Let me just run next door to change first."

I turn my head, capturing his lips with mine. "Don't take too long."

Five minutes later we're curled up on the sofa, which I swear has widened to somehow magically fit us both comfortably. We can't be in too much trouble with the Heart Springs gods if the furniture is morphing to accommodate us.

I flip on the TV to its one channel, ready to burrow down and not watch whatever sappy movie is playing today, but Ben seems to have other ideas.

"I don't know what's going to happen tomorrow, or the next day, or in the long term, sweetheart, but if tonight is all we get, then I want you to know that it's been you for me from the beginning." He smooths back a lock of my hair, tucking it behind my ear in a move no one has ever really tried in real life before.

"That is so not true, and we both know it." I slip my hand under his navy blue hoodie. "You couldn't stand me when we first met."

He shrugs with a grin. "You were a pain in the butt, but somehow I knew you were destined to be my pain in the butt."

I roll my eyes and wrap the string of his sweatshirt around my finger. "I don't think you would be saying that if we never got stuck here. If our only interaction was our one terrible date."

"Believe it or not, I've had worse."

"Of course I believe it. Dating is awful."

He adjusts his position, turning on his side so we're

facing each other on the sofa. "So maybe it's a good thing we ended up here. If not, I might never have seen you again."

The thought of that makes me unbearably sad. "I never thought I would be grateful for Heart Springs."

"Me either."

"What do you think Mimi is going to do?" I tug a little on the string of his hoodie, needing another reaffirming press of Ben's lips to mine. "Is she going to kill us for breaking the rules? Is she going to sentence us both to a lifetime of Heart Springs purgatory?"

"Probably." He kisses me again, deeper this time. "But it'll be worth it."

We quit talking then, and I force myself not to worry about what might come tomorrow. The absolute worst that could happen is that I never find my way back home, and really, at this point, the thought doesn't sound so terrible. I've got a job I like, a friend or two, and a man whose lips are currently finding their way down my neck, causing a trail of goose bumps to explode in their wake.

I bring Ben's lips back to mine, threading my fingers through his soft hair and tugging just gently enough to make him grunt. His tongue teases the seam of my lips and I open for him.

It's the kind of kiss you feel absolutely everywhere. Heat pools in my belly and I press myself closer into his embrace, needing more contact and more kisses and more Ben. He rolls me flat on my back, his weight sinking down on me like the most perfect blanket. I groan, rolling my hips, searching for more of him. He slides his thigh in between my legs, giving me the smallest measure of relief.

"I want you so badly, sweetheart." He mutters the words into my skin, his mouth trailing down my neck, nipping at my collarbone. His position shifts and the hard length of him nudges my hip. "I've wanted you for so long."

"I want you too, Ben." I shamelessly press my aching core to the firm muscle of his thigh. "I need you."

Our lips come together again, both of us searching for more, for relief.

I break the kiss, letting my hands trail down his chest until my fingers are dancing along the waistband of his gray sweatpants. "I know we just said literally five minutes ago that we should take this slow, but you also said you don't know what happens tomorrow, so if we only have tonight then maybe . . ." I'm not going to beg, but I have no problem putting my powers of persuasion to good use if it means getting what I want, and what I want right now is Ben.

A war wages inside the deep brown of his eyes.

He's on the verge of capitulating, I can see it. Normally this would be the point where I would push just a little bit further, to make sure things go exactly in my direction.

But something stops me. I don't want Ben to have to give in. I don't want him to do this if he's not truly ready.

So I kiss him softly instead. "Let's wait until we both feel comfortable."

He nods, relief washing over him. "Yes, I think that's a good plan."

I drop my hand an inch lower. "Maybe for tonight, we could do this instead?" My fingers dance to find what I'm looking for. "It's not actually going all the way."

"Not going all the way *is* taking it slowly, if you think

about it." His eyes flutter closed and his hand reaches for mine, guiding me to stroke him with more pressure. He groans, his forehead falling to mine. "Can I touch you, sweetheart?"

"Fuck yes you can."

He laughs as his lips find mine again. This kiss is deep and dirty, and I whimper with aching for him.

"Where did you learn to kiss like that, Dr. Loving?" I ask when we finally come up for air.

His mouth moves down the column of my neck. "The only person I want to be thinking about right now, Cam, is you."

A few minutes later, I can't even remember my own name. Ben tugs the fabric of my shirt aside, his lips tracing the faintest path over the curve of my breasts before his tongue swirls over the peaked bud of my nipple. The contact makes me gasp and I don't ever want him to stop, yet I need that mouth in other places.

Ben's fingers dance down the expanse of my stomach, dipping into my waistband. "Is this okay?"

"Fuck, Ben, everything is okay. Please touch me."

A sheepish smile tugs on his lips as his fingers drift lower.

I grasp both the pants and my underwear and shove them down to my knees. I haven't been this horny for someone in a long time, and I need some pressure, some relief before I go absolutely mad.

Ben drags a single finger over me, his sheepish smile turning to something that looks a little like awe. "You're so wet, sweetheart."

I take his hand in mine, trying to direct him where I

need him most. "I want you, Ben. Have I not made that clear up to this point?"

His finger circles my clit as he watches me, finding the perfect spot, the one that makes my breath freeze in my lungs. "It's nice to hear you say it."

"I want you, Ben. Please touch me, give me more." My voice is breathless and borderline pornlike, but I don't care. He pulls his touch from me, and I glare at him. "That is the opposite of more."

He chuckles, his hands dragging down my legs to where my pants still rest at my knees. He removes them completely, tossing them to the side and pushing my legs open. "Patience is a virtue."

"We both know I'm not exactly vir—" The word gets caught in my throat when his tongue slips through my folds, tracing me, opening me. My back bows off the couch, pressing me closer to his mouth.

He groans and the vibration of it sends a bolt of heat through me. My hips buck, but he doesn't stop his total assault of my senses. He licks and teases until my vision is hazy. My fingers lock in his hair, holding him to me, not that he shows any intention of breaking away. He slides first one finger, then another into me and I cry out at the fullness. Then his lips focus in on my clit, sucking until I see stars and I completely shatter beneath him, calling his name over and over as the orgasm rockets through me.

His licks turn gentle and almost soothing as I come down from the highest of highs. He kisses a trail up over my stomach. When he's within reach, I take his face in my hands, kissing him deep enough to taste myself lingering on his tongue.

"Holy shit," I say, putting enough space between us so I can look him in the eye. "I might actually need to know who taught you that so I can send them a thank-you present."

He laughs, kissing me again, lighter this time. He holds his weight off of me, but I tug him down, reveling in the feel of being pressed beneath him. He's still hard, and I rock against the length of him, far fewer layers separating us now.

"Can I touch you?" It's a question I don't know that I've explicitly asked before. Anytime I've been in this position in the past, it was clear to both parties exactly what was going to be happening. But with Ben, I don't want to push things. I know there is more at stake here than a one-night hookup, and I can think of nothing worse than him waking up tomorrow and regretting what happened here on this couch.

He hesitates for only a second before he nods. "Please, sweetheart. Have your way with me."

"I hope you know what you're getting yourself into." I flash him a wicked smile, rotating us so he's lying flat on his back. Normally I rush through this part of the equation, but with Ben, I want to take my time. I want to find the spots that make him shiver, find the best way to bring him pleasure. I want to make him feel as good as he made me feel.

Which might be the most selfless thing I've ever thought.

Also, it will be fun to torture him.

I tug on his sweatshirt, yanking the whole thing over his head. I take my time, taking him in. The lean muscles of his stomach are defined, his chest covered with a smattering of dark hair. My fingers trace over the lines of his pecs, down to his abs, hovering over the vee pointing me south.

I pay attention to the rise and fall of his chest, to the goose bumps that pop up after I stroke a particularly sensitive part of him. "You're kind of beautiful, did you know that?" I pull my eyes from his bare skin and meet his gaze.

The look he's giving me stops my heart in my chest, just for a second. Huh. I didn't know hearts could literally skip a beat, but the heat in Ben's gaze is enough to do it.

He reaches up, twining a lock of my hair around his finger. "You're the most gorgeous woman I've ever seen, Cam."

The words do something to me. Not because I haven't heard them before, but because I know Ben doesn't just mean what he can see on the outside. And that somehow means more than any compliment I've ever received before.

"I was already planning on going down on you, you don't have to flatter me." I don't really want to brush off his words, but instinct overrides my better judgment.

Ben rolls his eyes, tightening his grip on my hair and bringing me down for a kiss.

I don't tease him as much as he teased me, moving my lips steadily down the plane of his chest and over his stomach, tugging on the waistband of his pants, freeing him.

It was hinted at from behind the fabric, but when Ben's cock springs free, my suspicions are confirmed. It's perfect, and I want to take him inside of me like now.

But I exert some self-control, lowering myself instead, swiping my tongue around the head and relishing the low, guttural moan Ben releases. I spend some time exploring him before taking him fully in my mouth. Wrapping my hand around the base of his cock, I squeeze gently as my lips work over him.

"Jesus, sweetheart, that feels so fucking good." It's the first time I've ever heard him cuss and I love that I drove him to it.

It doesn't take long before Ben's hips are bucking, thrusting him deeper into my mouth, his groans echoing around the room and spurring me on.

"I'm going to come, Cam," he gasps a minute later, giving me space to pull away.

But I don't, wanting to experience the full breadth of his pleasure. He explodes a second later, and I slacken my grip, placing soft kisses on every part of him I can reach while he regains his breath.

He wraps his hands around my arms, tugging me up and into his embrace, burying his face in my hair. "That was beyond words."

I nuzzle into him, throwing my leg over his and snuggling as deep into his arms as I can manage. "For me too."

For a few minutes, there's nothing but peaceful silence between us. I've never been a cuddler, but lying here in Ben's embrace is nothing short of pure bliss.

Until a pesky thought burrows into my brain. "Ben? Are we going to wake up tomorrow back home in our own beds?" I don't know why the thought sends a burst of fear through me, but suddenly I can think of nothing worse than waking up tomorrow in my own apartment, Heart Springs lost to us forever.

"I don't think so."

I pull away the slightest bit so I can look him in the eye. "You don't think so? So there's a chance?"

A slight frown tugs on his lips. "I mean, I guess there's a

chance, but I wouldn't count on it. Technically you haven't experienced true love yet." A hint of something darts through his brown eyes, and I must be hallucinating because it looks a little like doubt.

That doubt must be because *he* doesn't feel it yet. Maybe he won't feel it ever. It would make sense, Ben is a wholly good person who spends his time helping others. Lust is one thing, but how could he ever fall in love with someone like me?

In fact, maybe now that he's gotten his rocks off, he'll disappear from my life completely. And then where will I be? Stuck here in Heart Springs with no boyfriend, no best friend, and no orgasms.

I pull away more.

It's not like I'm in love with him either. If I fell in love with every man I'd awarded a blow job, well I probably wouldn't have ended up here. Or maybe I would have. Maybe I was meant to find Ben all along.

It's a sobering thought, given the turmoil in his eyes, like he's worried about having to let me down easy.

I practically leap from the sofa, finding my underwear and pants and sliding them back on.

Ben sits up, dragging his own pants up over his thighs, though he doesn't bother to search for his shirt. "Talk to me, sweetheart."

"What is there to say?" I perch on the edge of the armchair across from the sofa, wrapping my arms around myself to further ward off any trace of feelings. "You can't fall in love with me, I've known that from the beginning. So it shouldn't really matter that you don't want to."

"Hey." He pushes off from the couch and crosses to the chair, kneeling in front of me. "Why would you think that?"

"We both know I'm not the right person for you. Mimi sure as hell knows it, or she would have paired us up from the beginning. And you know it too." I ignore the pleading look in his eyes, but I don't pull away when he takes my hand in his.

"No one is perfect, Cam. Not even Mimi. This time she got it wrong. You and me, I think it was always meant to turn out this way." He sounds so sure, so confident, that it takes me a minute to fully process his words.

"Wait. What are you saying, Ben?"

"I don't want to say it, at least not until we know more about what's going to happen." His grip tightens on my fingers. "But it's there, Cam. I wouldn't be putting our return home at risk if I wasn't completely sure. God, I feel like I've been holding back from you for so long, trying to let you fall for someone you were supposed to be with."

It's a foreign feeling, this open and honest communication. One I don't know that I've ever experienced with anyone in my life, ever.

It makes me want to be open and honest as well, but Ben is right. We don't know what's going to happen tomorrow, how this magical little hell hole might react to us going completely off script.

"I've been fighting it too." I place a hand on his cheek, my thumb stroking along the strong edge of his jaw. "I wouldn't have thrown away my best chance of getting out of here if I wasn't sure too."

Ben rises up on his knees, bringing us level and pressing his lips to mine. The kiss deepens, but he pulls away after a second. "I would very much love for this to continue, but I think it might be best if I head back to my place."

I pout, though I know he's right. His kisses reach deep down inside me, stoking flames in both my heart and my pants. If we were to even cross the threshold into my bedroom, I don't think either of us would be able to resist the natural next step. "What if I wake up in the morning and I'm not here? What if we both wake up at home and have no memory of ever being here?" Somehow, I don't think it's physically possible for me to forget Ben, he's so deeply ingrained on my soul, but nothing about Heart Springs makes sense.

He stands, leaning down to drop a kiss on my forehead. "I'll find you. Wherever we end up, I promise, I will find you. You, Campbell Andrews, are unforgettable."

I stand, tucking myself into his arms because I'm not quite ready to let him go yet. "That was the sappiest thing anyone has ever said to me."

The rumble of his laugh vibrates against my cheek. "Something tells me that's not an especially high bar."

"I don't deal well with sap."

"Well, you're going to have to get used to it."

"You lured me in with all your sarcasm and banter. I feel like I've been deceived!" I tug myself out of his embrace, missing the warmth of him instantly.

He leans down and kisses me. "I promise to still be plenty sarcastic, sweetheart."

This time I pull away from the kiss. "I'll see you tomorrow?"

He nods, sure enough for the both of us. "Tomorrow."

23

I keep my eyes screwed closed for several minutes when I wake up the morning after the fundraiser. The morning after I kissed Ben. The morning after Ben showed me exactly what that smart mouth of his can get up to.

I finally open just one eye, just a sliver. Just enough to check for sunshine and lace and a mountain of throw pillows piled in the corner of the room, where I ceremoniously toss them every night, where I leave them every morning, yet somehow by the time I'm ready to go to sleep, they've made their way back to the bed.

My vision catches on the sunshine first. It's bright, beckoning through the sheer white curtains. The light somehow seems more blinding this morning, and I wonder if I've just fallen into some kind of love bubble where the flowers smell sweeter and the sun burns brighter.

A wave of relief washes over me when I open both eyes, take in all the details, and realize I'm still in my bedroom in Heart Springs. Still warm and cozy yet cool enough to sleep under the butter yellow covers. Still hair and makeup ready despite sleeping like the dead the night before.

I don't stop to think about why I'm happy to still be here, despite the previous night with Ben all but fulfilling my final task.

The only noticeable change is in my wardrobe. When I throw open the doors of the closet, I'm faced once again with a brand new set of clothes. Everything hanging in the closet is in shades of red and green, a couple of gold sweaters and spangly silver dresses tucked in among the holiday spread.

I dart into the living room, which has been transformed overnight. A huge Christmas tree, reaching the ceiling, stands in one corner, already decorated with blinking white lights and a flurry of ornaments. Presents I definitely didn't buy or wrap stand ready under the tree and the whole house smells like cinnamon and pine.

It sort of reminds me of Ben's scent.

Just the thought of him brings a smile to my face.

And apparently just the thought of him brings the real him to my door.

I answer the knock, taking in a sleep-rumpled Ben with a grin. His eyes look tired but bright, and he offers me a mug of coffee in case I didn't already think he was the greatest person in the world.

"You're still here." He says it with a relief that lets me know his confidence the night before wasn't totally legit.

"We're still here." I take the coffee and gesture for him to come in.

But he shakes his head, softening the rejection with a sweet and all too closed-mouth peck. "You need to get to work."

I raise my eyebrows. "Everything okay?"

"Now that we've gone rogue, I think it's essential that

we focus on making sure your other tasks are thoroughly and unarguably completed."

I stick out my lower lip. "But work is boring and kissing you is way more fun."

He laughs and leans in to kiss the pout off my face. "I'm glad you think so. But work is not boring. Don't you want to check in with Emma anyway? See how the rest of the fundraiser went?"

I nod, begrudgingly. "Yes. I suppose." I actually do want to—need to—talk to Emma so I can apologize for running out on the event and leaving her to fend for herself.

Plus, I need to see how she's feeling about her upcoming date with Ethan.

I finish the final swig of my coffee, handing Ben my empty mug. "All right then. Be off with you so I can strip off these PJs and get dressed."

His pupils widen, my words having their desired effect.

I pop a button on my pajama top, just to see if I can get him to break, but he shakes his head and focuses his eyes on mine.

"We should go see Mimi at the café later today."

That's enough to halt my fingers. "You were expecting to end up back home this morning, weren't you?"

He shrugs, but his eyes can't hide the truth. "I don't really know what to expect anymore, Cam, but whatever ends up happening, we'll deal with it."

"Is this where you tell me we can face anything as long as we face it together?"

"You really are an asshole sometimes, aren't you?"

I grin, leaning in to leave him with a lingering kiss. "The sooner you accept that, the easier your life will be."

"Have a good day at work, dear."

"Have a good day playing doctor since no one in this town ever seems to get sick or hurt."

He rolls his eyes, bounding down my front walk with a spring in his step.

I take a minute to enjoy the view of him walking away before ducking back inside and getting dressed for the day. Skinny jeans and a red sweater and knee-high brown boots. Nothing I ever would have picked out for myself before, but when I check my reflection in the full-length mirror on the back of my bedroom door, I have to admit, it doesn't look too bad.

I double back for a real coat once I step outside and realize that along with the wardrobe update and décor explosion, the weather has changed once again, a chill in the air and heavy clouds in the sky, the kind that look like they might open up and dump a snowstorm on you at any moment.

Pushing into the front door of the bakery, I slip out of my coat and hang it on the rack that yesterday stood empty, but today is dotted with scarves and jackets.

The bakery is crowded, a line extending almost out the door, so I jump behind the counter and start pouring coffees. "Sorry I'm late," I call to Emma over my shoulder as I grind espresso beans and tap them into their little pod, which I now know is called a portafilter, ready to slot into the machine.

"We will be discussing the reason for your tardiness in great detail." She offers a harried smile and a bag of muffins to the customer at the counter. "As soon as we get through this line!"

I hand one of our regulars his pumpkin spice latte. "Here you go, Fred!"

"Thanks so much, Cam! Great event last night!" Fred takes his first sip and sighs with pleasure. "Perfectly made, as always!"

I wave to him as he exits the store and turn to help the next customer.

It takes longer than usual for the bakery to calm down, people continuing to come through the door long past the typical end-of-the-morning rush. The delay could be chalked up to the fact that everyone wants to talk about the fundraiser, nothing but effusive praise directed at both me and Emma, but mostly me, if I'm being honest.

Finally, around midafternoon, the door closes behind our last customer and Emma flips around the "Open" sign, even though it's a half an hour before we usually close for the day.

We collapse at one of the tables, neither of us bothering to wipe the sticky trail of crumbs the last person sitting here left behind.

I hoist myself up again a second later, needing a second boost of caffeine more than I need a break for my feet. "I can't believe I've been standing next to you all day and I still don't know how the fundraiser turned out. Please tell me you can forgive me for bailing on you early."

Emma stays put at the table near the door, but even from across the room, I can see the sadness in her eyes. "I hate to say this, Cam, and I really hope you don't blame yourself, but unfortunately . . ."

My stomach drops, and despite her preface, I don't know if I'll be able to forgive myself if the fundraiser was a failure. I never should have left, but typical selfish Cam had only one person on her mind—me.

"Unfortunately, you're going to have to keep working at

the bakery for the foreseeable future because we made more than enough money to buy the shop!" She jumps out of her chair, joining me behind the counter.

I don't even resist when she grabs my hands, jumping up and down with excitement. The motion forces me to jump up and down too, or maybe it's just the sheer joy of the moment seeping through and working its way into my formerly cold and dead heart.

"Emma! I'm so fucking excited for you, I can't even stand it!" I throw my arms around her, squeezing tightly.

"I'm so excited for me too!" She spins us around in a circle, breaking my hold on her when the espresso machine beeps for attention. "A bakery and a date with Ethan, all in one night." She pours each of us a shot of espresso, though I've never seen her drink anything less sweet than a flavored latte piled high with whipped cream and a chocolate drizzle on top. I must be rubbing off on her, and that thought makes me a little bit proud. "I never could have done this without you, Cam. Seriously, with all the work you put into the fundraiser, all the money we made, you've completely changed my life."

I clink my tiny espresso cup against hers, and we both swallow the rich, bitter brew. I hide my teary eyes behind the mug. Between Emma and Ben, I'm hearing things about myself that I still don't know if I can fully accept.

A tap on the front door draws my attention away from my thoughts. A grin splits my face when I see Ben waiting for me in front of the bakery.

Emma nudges me. "Don't think you've escaped this conversation; you will be telling me what happened with

Dr. Loving. I want all the details." She winks at me, the move more adorable and endearing than salacious.

"I'll tell you everything tomorrow, promise." Though it strikes me that I maybe shouldn't make that kind of promise anymore, one that I don't know that I will be able to fulfill.

Emma wraps me in another hug before I can turn to leave. "Thank you again, Cam. For everything. Bringing you into the bakery was the best decision I ever made!"

I don't want to remind her that it wasn't her decision at all—I was forced on her by Mimi just like I've been forced on everyone else—but she doesn't really know that. Instead, I return her hug, letting her gratitude warm my core.

Which is useful, because it's fucking freezing outside. The moment I step through the front door of the bakery, I have to tuck my hands inside my coat pockets and burrow down into my collar. I guess the scarf and mittens hanging on my coatrack at home this morning weren't just there for ambiance.

Luckily, Ben seems to be my own personal furnace. He tugs me into his embrace, placing a soft kiss on my cheek before tucking me into his side for the short walk to Mimi's.

"So . . . don't keep me in suspense, how did everything work out for Emma last night?"

Another wide grin splits my face—I can't seem to stop them today; they just keep on coming. "Amazing! She made enough money to buy the shop! She's going to be able to keep the bakery open. And we were packed today. It feels like everyone in town came in at some point."

"That's amazing, sweetheart. I'm so happy for both of you."

"Thanks." I don't voice the worrisome postscript in the back of my mind—that I'm actually a little bit sad I won't get to see the true fruits of our labor. At some point I'm going to go back to New York and I won't get to work with Emma any longer.

But at least I can leave knowing I helped her secure her dream. And a date with her man, which we didn't even get to talk about today. I'm going to miss catching up with her and seeing all of her happiness come to fruition.

"Hey." Ben nudges my ribs with his elbow. "We're going to get some answers, okay? Not knowing is the hardest part."

I hope he's right about that, because right now it feels like leaving might be the hardest part. Then again, there's no guarantee that we will be leaving. I might have totally destroyed that possibility by hooking up with Ben last night. Though I don't think either of us would consider what happened to be merely a hookup. And if I've irreparably screwed up my chances at accomplishing my tasks, what does that mean for Ben?

The bell over the café door tinkles as Ben pushes it open, holding it for me before shutting out the cold behind us. As usual, the homey space is bare of people. Mimi waits for us at our regular table, two mugs already sitting and waiting for me and Ben. I can practically hear the ominous tones underscoring our entrance.

We slide into our seats like kids waiting for a punishment from the principal. Which is ridiculous, really. We haven't done anything wrong.

I wrap my hands around my mug and take a careful sip. The brew inside is pepperminty and chocolatey and I really wish I didn't find it so damn delicious.

Ben sits stiffly next to me, his hands shoved in the pockets of his jacket, his face tight with some unreadable emotion. "Look, Mimi—"

Mimi stops him with a pointed glare. "Well. You two have managed to get yourselves into quite the little pickle."

I peek to my left, but Ben's eyes are now firmly locked somewhere in the distance over Mimi's shoulder. So I guess it's up to me to present our defense. "Believe it or not, Meem, I didn't exactly set out to break all the rules here."

One of her eyebrows arches like a Disney villain's. "Why do I find that hard to believe?"

I refuse to let her fluster me. I have stared in the face of way more foreboding characters than Mimi, and most of the time, I've come out on top. Except when facing off with my grandmother, of course. Who, now that I think about it, does bear a slight resemblance to Mimi herself.

But none of that matters. I pull back my shoulders. "Look, Mimi, if we approach this whole situation logically, you'll see that really, I've done exactly what was asked of me. I found a job I'm passionate about—look what we accomplished with the fundraiser last night!" I inject cheer into my voice, but Mimi's face doesn't give me even an inch. "Everyone has been super nice to me lately, and they don't even seem to be pretending!"

Mimi offers me a mere grunt of assent, but doesn't bother to expand beyond that.

"And . . ." I look to my left again. This time Ben meets my eyes and the softness in his gaze bolsters me. He pulls a hand from his pocket, taking mine in his and squeezing gently. "And you told me to fall in love, Mimi. And I did."

I sort of hate that the first time I'm saying the words out

loud, it's not just to Ben. But on the other hand, it makes it easier having a buffer here. In case he's wised up since last night and changed his mind about me.

Mimi sits back in her chair, her eyes flitting back and forth between the two of us. "You're in this then. Both of you? For real?"

I hold my breath, waiting to hear Ben's answer.

His grip on my hand tightens and for a second, fear sinks my stomach. But then he lifts our joined hands, kissing mine before looking right at Mimi and saying, "I couldn't be more in this, Mimi." Ben hesitates for a minute before speaking again. "I've waited a long time to find someone who felt like a match for me. I've watched so many of my friends and colleagues find their partners, and for years I thought I was doomed to never find one of my own. But I knew from the moment I first saw Cam that she was different. Even if she was a complete jerk that night." He shoots me a grin. "Getting stuck here together seemed like it might be the worst thing to ever happen to me, but it didn't take long for me to realize that Cam is the one I've been waiting for, that being here was really just bringing us together. She's my best friend."

I know the man himself told me to be prepared for more sap, but good god, could he at least break me in gently? Is there anything worse than tearing up in front of Mimi as he makes a declaration of love so grand even Hallmark would call it cheesy?

Mimi's eyes soften as she listens to Ben's speech. She leans forward, resting her arms on the table between us. Then her entire face changes, going from soft to smug.

And a realization dawns on me. "This was your plan the whole time, wasn't it?"

Mimi shrugs, tossing her gray curls over her shoulder. "I admit nothing."

"You are the one who brought us here." I point a finger at her. "You assigned me men you knew I wouldn't fall for and told Ben his only task was to help me."

A smile pulls on Ben's lips. "Ensuring Cam and I would spend plenty of time together."

I cross my arms over my chest, not nearly as amused as he is. "This was your plan from the beginning. Fess up, Meem."

She sighs, smiling. "All right, fine. I knew when I saw the two of you at that café that there was something between you. You were both just too stubborn to see it. So, I decided to give you the push you needed to bring you together." She gestures to the table, where our joined hands rest. "Don't pretend to be mad when it clearly worked."

She has a point there, but I'm not ready to hand it to her yet. "Why didn't you just tell us that from the beginning? Save us the trouble?"

Mimi snorts. "Like that would have worked. When in your life have you not done things your own way, Campbell?" She turns her all-too-observant eyes on Ben. "And you. You say you've been looking for love, but being in love requires vulnerability. It requires opening up to people and letting them see who you really are."

It took a long time for Ben to open up to me. I mostly thought that was because it took me forever to ask him questions about himself, but maybe that wasn't the only reason.

"It's been hard to let people in," Ben admits. "Sometimes my job requires me to compartmentalize. Maybe I was doing it so much, I forgot to turn that part of my brain off."

"Why do you think it was different with me?"

His eyes meet mine, and his whole heart is reflected in his gaze. "Everything is different with you, Cam."

"Just as I expected, you two were made for each other."

Okay, fine. Another point for Mimi.

"So what happens now?" Ben asks, his grip on my hand tightening.

Mimi hesitates before answering. "When the tasks have been completed, then you'll both go home."

Ben and I exchange a look. "So I haven't completed the tasks yet?"

"Not yet."

"And what happens when we get home?" Just asking the question makes my stomach spin, but if Ben and I aren't going to come out on the other side of this together, I think I need to know now.

Mimi's face softens, but her eyes betray nothing. "You'll just have to wait and see."

Ben releases my hand and sits back in his seat. "How long are we going to be stuck here, Mimi?"

"That depends on you."

"Depends on me, you mean." My hand feels empty without Ben's in it. Here we are, just getting started together, and I already feel like I'm failing him.

"Yes," Mimi confirms.

"I realize that the way I've gone about things might be a little unorthodox, but you know what?" I scoot my chair closer to Ben's. "I don't do this whole love business, okay? I go on occasional dates. I hook up when the mood strikes. But I don't open myself up to people. I don't let anyone in. And Ben did that for me. He cracked me open like a freaking walnut in a Christmas nutcracker, which is maybe not the best metaphor but whatever, you get the point. And now you're telling me we can't go home until I what, build my own fucking bakery? Spend my whole life doing community service? Why should he be stuck here because of me? This is bullshit." I finish my tirade like I'm finishing closing arguments, waiting for some kind of similarly rousing response.

Instead, Ben is full on fucking beaming and Mimi looks proud, despite my harsh words aimed directly at her.

"That was beautiful, Cam." She pushes back her chair, coming around to our side of the table and hugging us both, the motion squishing our faces together. "I'm so happy for you guys, really, and I promise all hope is not lost. You can still find your way home."

I gently tug out of her embrace so I can, you know, breathe again. "Thanks, Meem. We appreciate your support."

"Yeah, we appreciate you," Ben says, standing and taking my hand back in his, yanking me out of my seat. He pulls me along, the two of us practically running down the street toward our houses.

"Dude, where's the fire?" I can barely get the words out.

Ben throws open his door, shutting it behind us just as quickly. "No fire, I just really needed to do this."

And with that, my back hits the door as his lips crash down on mine.

24

Days pass, and there's no other word to describe them aside from blissful. The snow eventually falls, blanketing Heart Springs in fluffy whiteness, the kind of snow that sticks but doesn't slush, the kind that's perfect for snowball fights and building snowmen but doesn't get all gray and dirty.

Lights are strung up throughout the town, a ginormous tree erected in the town square, right next to the equally large menorah that gets lit in a nightly ceremony for the eight days of Hanukah. Each morning Emma slides holiday-themed treats onto the trays in the display case and by the time we're ready to close up shop each day, all of them have sold.

A couple of days after Ben and I met with Mimi, Emma asks me to accompany her on an errand after closing. I agree, of course, because there's not much I wouldn't do for her.

She locks the front door of the bakery and turns to link her arm with mine. "So we only have a few-minute walk, but I need to know everything about you and Ben. What happened and how's it all going?" We've been so busy lately, we've barely had time to breathe, let alone gossip.

I swear, all anyone has to do lately is say the name Ben and I'm grinning like an idiot, and today is no exception. "I don't really know how it all happened, other than the two of us became friends and then it became clear that it was really something more."

Emma sighs wistfully. "Ugh, just the way your voice changes when you speak about him is so freaking romantic."

I nudge her with my elbow. "Well, pretty soon, that's going to be you. Isn't your date with Ethan this weekend?"

She grins and nods. "It is. I'm so excited, but also like super nervous. I never thought he would ask me out, but it's finally happening."

I don't kill her buzz by reminding her he didn't actually ask her out; I basically forced him into making the date. "It's going to be fine. The two of you are perfect for each other." I don't really know enough about Ethan to be making such a claim, but Emma is amazing, and the little time I did spend with Ethan made me believe he'll be just as amazing as she is.

"Have you and Ben . . . you know, taken things to the next level yet?" She waggles her eyebrows up and down, and I can't help but laugh.

"No, we have not taken things to the next level yet." Not that I haven't wanted to. Not that he hasn't wanted to, either. We've spent every evening together since our chat with Mimi, but we've been holding back before going all the way.

I think a large part of our hesitation stems from the unknown. What happens if we sleep together and wake up the next morning back in the real world? What happens if we don't? If we do find our way back home, how do we know we'll remember our time here in Heart Springs? What if opening myself up to love, opening myself up to Ben, somehow also leads to the greatest heartbreak I can imagine—losing him.

So yeah. For now, there will be no sexy times happening. Luckily, we have fingers and hands and mouths, and exploring the ways we can make each other come without going all the way has been a challenge we're more than happy to face head on. I realize the whole thing is an extremely heteronormative way of looking at sex, in line with a lot of the other outdated rules about dating present in Heart Springs, but it's allowed us to have the time to explore each other in a way I've never done with any other partner.

Just thinking about it sends a little shiver down my spine.

And then I see where Emma is taking us, and that shiver goes from hot and horny to cold and dready.

I pull Emma to a stop outside of Noah's office, willing to stand in the freezing snow rather than make our way to the warmth inside. "Really, Em?"

"I'm sorry, I'm sorry." She bites her lip with worry. "I wanted to tell you, but I figured if I did, you wouldn't come with me."

"You figured right." I try to dislodge my arm from her grip, but with a surprising amount of strength, she keeps me locked in place.

"Please, Cam. I have to go in there and sign paperwork

and didn't you tell me not to sign anything without having a lawyer read it first?"

"I didn't know I would be the lawyer in question. And I didn't know all the paperwork signing would happen at my ex's office," I grumble, though I push through the door of the office, succumbing more for the promised warmth than anything else.

Noah greets both of us with a pleasant but fake smile, leading us into a conference room much cozier than any I've been in before, with cushy chairs, a large oak table, and windows overlooking actual nature and not the concrete jungle of Manhattan.

He slides a stack of papers across the table. "I'll give you some time to look through everything. Let me know when you're ready to discuss."

As soon as he leaves the room, I glare at Emma. "You're lucky I love you."

She gives me a stiff grin in return. "You're the best, Cam."

Luckily, the paperwork Noah handed me is pretty straightforward, documenting the sale of the bakery to Emma for an agreed upon price. I haven't looked at a lot of real estate contracts lately, but I remember enough from law school to make my way through. By the time we leave Noah's office a couple of hours later, everything is signed and Emma has the metaphorical keys in her hands.

We've barely stepped outside when we're stopped by Noah's receptionist.

"Wait!" she calls, grabbing her coat and shoving her arms into her sleeves.

I assume we must have forgotten to initial something and turn back with a sigh.

But the receptionist, Celeste, I think her name is, doesn't beckon us back into the office. "You're Campbell, right?" she asks, though she obviously knows exactly who I am.

"That's me." I tighten my scarf around my neck. There's something about the cold here that's just colder than it is in New York.

"I have a favor to ask."

I raise my eyebrows, but don't say anything, gesturing for her to continue.

"It's not so much for me, but for a friend of mine. Anna. She's been working at the local toy store for years and she wants to take over the business since the owner has passed. He basically promised her he would leave her the shop, but now his long-lost nephew is coming back to town and claiming he has more of a right to it than she does." Celeste pushes out the words in a rush, as if she doesn't believe I'll stand there and listen.

"I'm not sure what you'd like me to do."

Celeste gestures to Emma, who's standing next to me and flashing me weird looks. "We all saw what you did for Emma. I don't think anyone in this town has ever bested Noah before, and you managed to bring him down in just a few weeks."

"I didn't exactly bring him down." Though I obviously knew from the beginning there was no way I was going to let him take the bakery from Emma. "And really, Celeste, that was a one-time thing. I don't think we can expect everyone in town to shell out for fundraiser after fundraiser."

Celeste shakes her head. "Anna doesn't need money. She has money, she just needs someone who can represent her, be her advocate."

"I don't know." I feel myself starting to waver because I can't lie—helping Emma felt good. More than good. It unlocked something inside of me that has been buried for a long time.

Celeste must feel me wavering too because she clasps her hands together and flashes me a huge smile. "Please, Cam, just talk to her. Any advice you could give her would be much appreciated."

"I don't have time to full on take her case," I warn. "I work at the bakery full-time and then I . . ."

Celeste's smile turns borderline salacious. "And then you have to get home to Ben. I know."

"Great, well, love that everyone in town is talking about my personal life, but—"

"We're all just so happy to see both of you happy!" Celeste insists.

I roll my eyes, though I know the sentiment is genuine. "Fine. I will go talk to her. One time."

"Amazing! Thank you!" Celeste looks for a minute like she might throw her arms around me, but then thinks better of it, offering us a two-handed wave before bouncing back into Noah's office.

Emma and I turn to walk back toward the bakery, and I can practically feel her vibrating with excitement.

"Oh my god, just say what you need to say, Em."

"This is perfect!" she squeals.

"The entire town is now going to be coming to me for free legal advice and that screams perfect to you?" The minute people find out you're a lawyer, they all want free legal advice.

"Who says it has to be free? Celeste said that Anna has

money, she just needs your representation. Therefore, she has the ability to pay for said representation."

"Representing clients is a full-time job, Emma. More than full-time, if we're being real. And, as you might recall, I already have a full-time job."

Not to mention, Mimi might blow an actual gasket if I break another rule. She straight up told me I'm not allowed to practice law anymore, lest I be settling for a career I'm not "passionate" about.

"I've been thinking about bringing on some extra help anyways, now that the building is mine, and with how busy we've been. Maybe this would be a good time for you to become just a part-time employee."

We stop outside the bakery in question, the soft glow of the lights warming the pastel interior, the smell of fresh-baked goods seeping out through the front door and tickling my nose. Maybe working in the bakery isn't my greatest life's passion, but I've felt content here, and at home. There's a certain sense of accomplishment that comes with a long day of hard, physical work that I never used to feel after eighty hours of sitting in front of my computer at the law firm.

"I'll talk to Anna, but don't you dare go cutting my hours and giving them to some pimply-faced teenager just yet." I bend down to give Emma a hug, all on my own, without her urging at all. "You heading back inside?"

She nods. "Yup. I've got some prep to do for tomorrow."

"Want help?"

She shakes her head, her eyes tracing over the soft purple letters on the door, *Emma's Eats and Treats*. It all really belongs to her now, and I wouldn't be surprised if there's no actual prep needing to be done. I think Emma really just wants a minute to stand inside her bakery and relish the fact that it's hers.

Some kind of warm goo flows through my body as I realize that none of this would have happened without my help. Emma put in the time to build her successful business, and I helped her take true ownership. For a minute, I let myself revel in the pride.

"Get on in there, then," I say when the time for pride has passed. "I'll see you tomorrow."

Emma just nods and unlocks the door, stepping into her domain like it's the very first time.

25

I leave Emma at the bakery, tuck my hands into my coat pockets, and take my time walking back home. There's a strange feeling in my chest, one I'm not entirely familiar with. It expands, warmth flooding through my frozen veins, as I smile and wave to everyone I pass. As they smile and wave to me.

For the first time, maybe ever, everything in my life seems to be going right.

It should bring on nothing but elation, but instead, it stokes a little niggling fear in the back of my brain. Because if everything is going so right, there's only one possible way for things to go from here: down.

And with so much left unknown, I don't even know what down looks like.

It's an unsettling feeling, and the more I wallow in it, the more my brain runs away with itself. Sure, it's easy to think about never going home, or going home and not remembering Ben. But what about all the ways things could go wrong with Ben, here and now?

What if he doesn't actually love me? What if all of this has just been a ploy to get me to fall for him? I know Ben has no chance of getting out of Heart Springs without me fulfilling my tasks. Maybe he saw how hopeless things were with me and Noah and decided to swoop in and solve that problem for himself.

My stomach turns at the thought of Ben somehow duping me. I want to believe such a thing isn't even possible.

And yet, when I see him waiting for me on his front porch despite the frigid temperature outside, I can't help the doubt tornado that rips through first my head and then my chest.

I accept the glass of wine he hands me, but rather than sinking into my favorite porch chair, I push open the front door and escape into the warmth of his home.

"Everything all right?"

I collapse onto his sofa, tucking my feet underneath me. "I don't know."

He sits down next to me, extending his arm around my shoulders and pulling me into his embrace. "Talk to me, sweetheart."

"What if we just don't go home?" I blurt the question without fully thinking it through. I'm grateful for my instincts though, because how Ben answers might give me the insight that I need.

Ben sighs, his fingers tracing soothing circles over my shoulder. "I've been thinking about that too."

"You have?"

He nods, setting down his own wineglass on the coffee table. "Ever since we had our talk with Mimi. I don't know what else there is for us to do, Cam. From my perspective, you've more than fulfilled all three of your tasks."

"And yet, we're still here."

"We're still here."

I swirl the dark-colored liquid in my glass. "And how do you feel about that?" It's obvious fishing, but I don't much care.

He takes in a long breath, taking my wineglass from me and setting it next to his. He shifts so he's fully facing me, taking my hands in his. "I think I would be okay with it."

I release a breath I didn't realize I was holding.

He continues on, probably interpreting my confusion for anger. "Hear me out. I know how important it is for you to go home, and I want that for you, I really do."

"But?" My voice is little more than a whisper.

"But I think a part of me would rather stay here with you than risk going home and never being with you again."

Before, Ben had managed to put a whole lot of cracks in the hard shell around my heart. But with those words, he takes a sledgehammer to the remaining glass, destroying the barrier and leaving me open and raw. It should feel vulnerable, and scary as fuck, to be so exposed, but with my heart safely in Ben's hands, I know there's no chance of it being damaged.

"I love you."

It's the first time either of us has ever said it, plain and straightforward and cutting right to the heart of it.

His chocolate eyes lighten, and he takes my face in his hands. "I love you too, sweetheart."

His lips brush over mine in the softest, sweetest kiss, and I lean into it. Lean into him.

He tucks a strand of hair behind my ears. "It feels good to finally say that out loud."

"It does." I shift on the sofa, turning so my legs drape

over his lap. "I do still want to find a way for us to get home, Ben. But if it doesn't happen, if we are stuck here forever, then I know I can be totally happy being stuck here with you."

"Are you sure? What about your job, your family?"

"I guess let's worry about that later. I know for sure I've fulfilled the love task. We can look at my other two tasks and see if there's something we're missing." I smooth away the wrinkles on his forehead with my finger. "What about your job and your family?"

He frowns. "I would miss them, of course; I can't lie about that." Ben shakes his head. "But that's a problem for tomorrow." He shifts my weight in his lap so I'm straddling him, one of my thighs tucked on either side of his.

We both wear jeans and thick sweaters and yet the heat of him burns through my clothes, warming me to my core.

"Tonight there's only one thing that matters."

I rope my arms around his neck. "And what's that?"

"You love me."

"I do."

"And I love you." Ben dots a kiss on my right cheek, then my left, then my forehead, then the tip of my nose. "I've never said those words to anyone else."

"Me neither." I twine my fingers through his hair. "And I truly mean it, Ben. I've never felt this way about anyone before." I know then that any doubts I had about Ben's feelings for me are unfounded. He's never given me any reason to not trust him, and even though it's scary and foreign, I do trust him. With my whole, formerly ice-cold heart.

His forehead falls to mine. "I want to make love to you tonight, Cam."

Said by any other man in any other circumstance, I would have groaned at the cheesiness of the sentiment. But here, with him, I want nothing more than to lose ourselves in each other.

He presses a lingering kiss to the side of my throat. "I want to feel what it's like to be buried inside you." His lips trail up to my jaw, tracing over the smooth skin with little nips of his teeth. "I want to make you scream out my name."

"Jesus, Ben. Where have you been keeping all this dirty talk?"

He grins against my neck, his tongue tracing maddening circles on the sensitive skin there. "I've got to keep you on your toes, sweetheart."

"Mission accomplished."

He brushes another lingering kiss across my lips. "So, what do you say?"

"What do you mean, what do I say? Yes, let's fuck, let's make love, let's do whatever will get you out of those clothes and naked in bed the quickest."

He chuckles, pushing up from the couch, my legs wrapped around his waist, his hands supporting my butt. "Oh sweetheart, there's going to be nothing quick about tonight." He carries me into his bedroom. It's not the first time I've been in here, but already tonight feels different. Heavier, and more important somehow. I see the room in a new light. How the soft flannel sheets are a lot like Ben himself, comforting and warm. When I'm tucked underneath his covers, I feel safe and protected.

Ben sets me on my feet at the edge of the bed, and I rise up on my toes so I can kiss him properly. I try to get to the good stuff, teasing the seam of his lips with the tip of my tongue, but he grins against my mouth and shakes his head. Rather than opening to me like he normally would, he lets his lips move gently against mine, delivering kisses that are as soft as those flannel sheets I want to be in between right now.

My instincts tell me to fight him, to shove my hand down his pants and stroke him in the way I know gets him hard and ready. But for once, I tell myself to not be the contrarian. Ben and I will only ever have one first time together, and I want to enjoy it, let myself really feel and experience it.

Ugh, the whole thing is so sweet and tender, it almost makes me sick.

But then Ben's kisses drift down to my neck and I forget about everything but the sensation of him. His fingers tug on the neckline of my sweater and his mouth drifts over my exposed shoulder. I wasn't aware shoulders were erogenous zones, but I'm quickly disabused of that notion.

My fingers rake through his hair and my eyes flutter closed. I lean into him, breathing in his woodsy scent, relishing the scrape of his stubble over my smooth skin. His mouth makes its way back over the trail of my neck, landing on mine once again. This time it's his tongue teasing the seam of my lips, and I open for him, falling into him as we explore each other.

This isn't our first kiss, not by a long shot, but it feels like I'm learning a whole new Ben tonight.

He cups my cheeks in his hands, his mouth breathing new life into me. "You're so beautiful, I can hardly stand it, sweetheart."

I can't seem to make my brain formulate difficult things like words, so I say nothing, showing him my feelings instead. He reaches for the hem of my sweater, and I don't hesitate before yanking it over my head. When we separate out of the sheer necessity of needing to take each other's clothes off, I find myself caught in his gaze. His eyes are so dark, they almost look black and they trail over my chest, wrapped in a lacy black bra because the only thing I find in my drawers these days are matching sets of pretty lingerie.

I reach around my back to unhook it, letting the straps slide off my shoulders. His eyes burn as they trace over me and my nipples harden under the intensity of his gaze.

But I need more than his eyes on me. I take his hand in mine, bringing it to my breast. He knows my body well enough by now to know just how to stroke the sensitive skin around my nipple, teasing me with his fluttering touches before he cups my breast in his hand and brings his mouth to my skin. His tongue swirls around the peaked bud and my knees weaken. Luckily, he's there, a firm hand on my lower back keeping me upright as his teeth graze over me, making me shiver.

My fingers latch on to the waistband of his jeans, needing an anchor while also needing more of him, needing all of him. I fumble with the button and he doesn't pause his ministrations to help me, leaving me to attempt to get him undressed all while his mouth works its distracting magic.

I finally free him from the denim and my hand cups the hard length of him through the fabric of his boxer briefs. He grunts and the vibration of it on my nipple nearly sends me over the edge. I manage to shed my own jeans before pushing him away just enough to climb onto the bed. He perches over me, both of us down to our underwear but it's too much left between us.

Instead of removing that final barrier, he lowers his head and kisses me again. This time there's nothing soft or sweet about it. Our tongues tangle, our teeth nip at each other. I tug him down so the weight of him presses me to the bed. My hips thrust, searching for relief, searching for him, and I find him, rubbing against his hardness until we're both panting.

I reach in between our bodies to shimmy out of my underwear and, mercifully, Ben frees himself of his boxers.

"You sure you're ready?" I wrap my hand around him, stroking slowly until his eyes flutter with arousal.

"I've never been more sure of anything in my life, sweetheart. Are you sure?" His hands gently press my thighs open and I sigh with pleasure when his fingers dance over me, finding that perfect spot and stroking me until I can barely see straight.

"I'm really fucking sure, Ben. I need you inside me," I pant, desperate for him and for relief that can only come from him pressing into me.

His weight disappears for a half a second, but when he returns, he's got a condom in his hand. He makes quick work of opening the package and rolling it on.

He takes his cock in his hand, hovering at my entrance, teasing me, driving me absolutely mad. "I love you, Cam."

His declaration is more than enough to make me forgive him for making me wait. I reach up to cup his cheek in my hand. "I love you, Ben."

He pushes inside me in one slow thrust, both of us releasing matching moans when he's fully seated. I bring his mouth to mine and let the thrusts of our tongues mimic the thrust of his hips. It's slow and delicious and I never want this feeling to end.

"Jesus, Cam, how do you feel so perfectly made for me?" he mutters into my neck.

"I was perfectly made for you. Just like you were perfectly made for me."

He pulls away just enough to be able to look in my eyes. "That was some sappy shit right there, sweetheart."

"Don't get used to it." I wrap my legs around his waist, pulling him deeper into me.

"Can you come like this?" he asks as his hips move faster, mine rolling up to meet his every thrust.

"I don't know," I pant. I can feel the orgasm building deep in my belly, but penetration alone isn't usually enough to get me off.

Before I can say anything else, Ben flips us so he's flat on his back and I'm on top. His hand slips between us and he strokes my clit with his thumb. His other hand reaches for my nipple, pinching and plucking just on the borderline of being too much. My head falls back as the combination of sensations overwhelms me. My hips rock over him and he hits me right where I need him.

"Fuck, Ben, I'm going to come." I can barely get the words out, but I want him to know, want him to feel just exactly what he's doing to me.

"God, Cam, yes, let me feel you come on my cock."

It's his words that send me over the edge. I tighten around him as the orgasm moves through me, a slow burn of an explosion unlike anything I've felt before. My movement slows and stutters, but Ben grabs my hips, thrusting deep inside me until his own orgasm overtakes him a minute later.

He rocks his hips while we both ride out the aftershocks. Then he sits up, wrapping his arms around my back and burying his face in my neck. "How was that even better than I ever imagined it could be?"

I laugh, stroking his slightly sweaty hair back from his face. "It was for me too."

We kiss for a few more minutes, Ben's hands smoothing soothing circles over the bare skin of my back. Finally, he lifts me from his lap, disappearing into the bathroom for a minute to dispose of the condom before coming back to bed.

"Will you stay here tonight?" He pulls me into his embrace.

I haven't slept over at his place before, and he's never slept at mine—we both knew what would happen if we spent the night together when we weren't fully comfortable with taking our relationship to the next level. But nothing sounds better than waking up tomorrow morning in Ben's arms.

I nuzzle deeper into his chest. "I would love to."

Despite the truth in my words, there's also a little fear hidden deep inside. What if trading those three little words with Ben, or taking things all the way, really was the missing link? What if I wake up tomorrow not in Ben's bed but back in my apartment? What if when that eventually happens, Ben is nowhere to be found?

There are no guarantees here, and I want to refuse to let my doubts dampen what we just experienced. But I can't seem to stop my mind from racing after Ben dozes off the minute he closes his eyes. All this time, I thought I was brought to Heart Springs to learn some kind of lesson. Like how not to be a totally horrible asshole of a person who goes around destroying people's businesses. Like how to actually care about someone other than myself for a half a second.

But what if I got it all wrong? What if I didn't come here for a lesson, but a punishment? I can think of no greater punishment than losing Ben now that I've finally learned to love him. It would be a fitting way to pay me back for all of the terrible things I've said and done to people over the years. Classmates and colleagues. Interns and associates. So many people have been victims of my casual carelessness.

I need to reach out to a lot of people and apologize, honestly.

But will any of that really be worth it if Ben isn't by my side?

Ben stirs, turning over on his side and forcing me to turn with him. He tucks himself behind me, making me his little spoon. "Everything is going to be fine, Cam," he mutters, his breath tickling my neck.

"How can you know that for sure, though?"

"I don't know for sure, I just have to believe it." He kisses the slope of my shoulder. "It would be a cruel world to bring you into my life only to take you right back out."

"Hate to break it to you, sweetheart, but the world is just that cruel sometimes." I'm that cruel sometimes—or I was anyway—I think but don't say.

He adjusts the covers, tucking me back into their warmth. "It's okay if you don't believe it right now. I'll believe it enough for the both of us."

"Ugh, you've really got to stop with the sap. I just threw up in my mouth."

He chuckles, but it's laced with sleep. "Charming."

"You know it." I wiggle a little. "Also, I'm never going to be able to fall asleep like this. There is such a thing as too much cuddling."

He doesn't offer more than a muffled grumble.

But a few minutes later, still wrapped firmly in his arms, I fall asleep.

26

There's a minute when I wake up the following morning that I think I must have found my way back to New York. There's no sunshine beaming through the curtains and I'm definitely not in my Heart Springs bedroom. It isn't until Ben tugs on me, pulling me tighter against him, that I remember where I am and what happened the night before.

A shiver of heat runs through me as the memories flood my mind. The warmth spreads through my veins as the sexy times fade to the background, replaced by the sweet memories, the declarations Ben and I both made to each other.

I love him, and he loves me.

We cemented that love for each other last night, and yet, I'm still here in Heart Springs.

Somehow, I haven't managed to fulfill my tasks yet.

I scoot out of Ben's bed, needing the bathroom and a minute alone to think. If the bakery isn't truly my passion, then what else am I supposed to do? I ran through my other job options, and it's not like I can go back and try being a bookseller or wedding planner again. As far as I know, my options were limited, and the bakery has definitely been the best of them.

So it must be the third task, find myself a useful and productive and valued member of the community. I've volunteered at events and saved the local bakery. People say hi to me when they see me on the street. I ask genuine questions and converse freely with our customers at the bakery, and yet it still doesn't seem to be enough.

"Story of my life," I mutter under my breath.

No matter how far I reach, how much I change myself to try to fit in the mold others have deemed the only acceptable version of me, I can't seem to get it right. I never found acceptance from my family, despite the thousands of hours and millions of dollars I brought to the law firm. Why would I expect acceptance from total strangers?

There's a gentle knock on the door. "You okay in there?"

I open it sheepishly. "Sorry, didn't mean to wake you up."

Ben leans on the doorjamb. He's put on a pair of flannel pajama pants, but he hasn't bothered with a shirt. His hair is sleep-rumpled and sticking up in several messy directions. "Don't apologize. I just wanted to make sure you weren't freaking out."

I narrow my eyes because how dare he know my tics so well. "I'm not freaking out about us if that makes you feel any better."

"Marginally." He reaches for my hand, and I let him pull me closer. "What's going on in that beautiful and sometimes self-destructive brain of yours?"

"It is too early for a call out like that. I haven't even had coffee yet."

He tilts his head toward the kitchen. "We can fix that."

A few minutes later, we sit across from each other at the dining table, steaming mugs cupped in both of our hands.

Ben waits for me to speak, which is annoying and also does exactly what he wants it to.

"I sort of expected to wake up back in the real world this morning." I take a sip of coffee, but it's still too hot to drink and so I'm forced to keep talking. "And that was scary in a lot of ways, because I can't imagine not having you in my life anymore when this is all done. But now that I know for sure that it's not the love thing keeping me here, I can't help but feel like a total failure." My voice drops on that final word, the worst word, one that's haunted me my entire life. I've been working since I was a kid to avoid failure, and yet here I am.

Ben reaches across the table for my hand, his thumb delivering soothing strokes over the skin of my palm. "You're not a failure, sweetheart. We're going to figure this out. And over the next few days as we get a handle on things, whenever you feel down, I want you to think about how far you've come since you've been here."

"I'm still the same terrible person I was before. Only now I know I'm terrible and I mostly don't want to be terrible, I just don't know how to stop."

"You're not a terrible person, Cam." He doesn't elaborate, but he sounds so certain, and Ben is nothing if not trustworthy and reliable. "So what's your plan for today?" He steers the conversation away from my existential crisis like it's all been resolved.

Which it definitely hasn't, but I don't know what more I can do to fix it today. I pull my hand from his grip, wrapping it around my mug again and sitting back in my chair.

"I'm going to the bakery this morning and then meeting with Anna in the afternoon."

Ben raises his eyebrows just the slightest bit. "Are you going to work with her on her case?"

I shrug, though even the thought of it stirs a little something exciting in my brain. "I don't know. I need to see what kind of paper trail she might have showing her claim to the store. But I probably won't do more than this one meeting. The bakery is a full-time job, and I don't want to commit to something if I can't follow through."

Ben nods, but doesn't say anything further. We finish our coffees to the tune of amiable meaningless chatter and teasing, after which I kiss him and head back to my own house so I can dress for the day.

The bakery is busy once again, and before I even have time to stop and catch my breath, Emma is flipping the sign to "closed" and pointing me in the direction of the toy store.

I push through the front door, waiting for the tinkle of a bell to accompany the movement as it does in every other shop in Heart Springs. Instead, I'm greeted by a loud train whistle, which scares the shit out of me.

The woman at the counter laughs at my jump scare, but it's not unkind. "Wait until you leave, that one's even better."

I try not to grimace, but I'm probably not very successful. "You must be Anna."

"And you're Cam. I was at the fundraiser for the bakery; you truly did such a magnificent job. Emma is so lucky to have you."

I'm not one to usually shy away from praise, but I brush off her words. "It was nothing. Emma deserves it." I make my way slowly over to the counter, taking in the space. It's hard to move through the store, as the shelves are practically overflowing with toys. Baskets stuffed full of even more goodies line the aisles. It's cluttered but cozy, and I can see how every kid in town must love coming here.

Anna watches me take it all in, a small smile on her face. "I know it's a lot in here."

"It is, but it's cute. And obviously, it's working out for you. Or it's working out for the store, rather."

Anna's small smile shrinks further. "I've been working here since I was in high school. I love this place, and the thought of a stranger coming in and selling it for parts makes my stomach turn."

My eyebrows raise. "Is that the nephew's plan?"

Anna rolls her eyes. "He hasn't said that explicitly, but he doesn't live in town and there's no way he's going to relocate to Heart Springs to work in the store. He wouldn't know the first thing about it."

"People can learn to run a business, you know. And who knows, maybe this nephew is looking for a change in his life and does want to move here." Despite trying for so long to get out of this place, I certainly am no longer a stranger to its appeals.

"If we can prove that that's the case, I'll happily leave him to take over ownership of the store. But I want to make sure if I'm walking away, I'm leaving her in good hands."

"Fair enough." My eyes flit around the room, looking for some kind of office. "Is there somewhere we can go to chat in more detail? I don't know that I can be of much assistance, but I'll take a look through whatever paperwork and evidence you've gathered."

Anna leads me to a closet-sized office in the back of the store. There's barely room for both of us and her tiny desk, but she hands over everything she has. And luckily, she actually has things to hand over. Letters and documented conversations with the former owner of the store, who passed away a few months ago.

"So do you think you can help me?" Anna asks after two hours of shuffling through papers, a tinge of hope in her voice.

I don't want to let her down, and she does have a good case. It's going to be tricky because the nephew is family, but his uncle made his intentions pretty clear. Of course, he could have helped everyone out by leaving a will, but the time for that has passed.

"You have a good case, Anna. Have you reached out to Noah Crenshaw at all? He's actually the town lawyer and he could devote way more time and resources to your case than I could."

Her nose wrinkles. "I did reach out to him, but he told me my case wasn't financially worth the time it would take."

I flash her a sympathetic smile. I've delivered the same response many times myself. I open my mouth to reply but Anna cuts me off.

"I can pay you for your time, obviously. I have plenty of money, that isn't the issue here. I just need someone to fight for me, to help me get what I was promised. I care about this store, and I care about this town. Please, Cam. I need your help."

Well, fuck.

I pinch the bridge of my nose, hoping I don't regret this. "All right, Anna. I'll help you. But I need you to keep in mind that I still have to keep up my hours at the bakery, and I can't promise you a win here." I pretty much never lose when it comes to getting the best deal for my clients, but this isn't technically my job anymore.

Anna jumps out of her seat, an impressive feat in the tight space. She circles around the desk and throws her arms around my neck. "Oh my gosh, Cam. Thank you so much. You have no idea how much this means to me."

I awkwardly pat her on the back. "I know what it feels like to be invested in a business and I'll do what I can to help you save yours."

She leads me back through the store, where she hugs me again. I promise to keep her updated.

I push open the front door of the toy shop and almost have a heart attack as the sound of a thousand quacking ducks explodes around me. I shoot Anna a dirty look over my shoulder, but she just smiles and waves, and how does she listen to that all day long?

The people in this town really are something else.

TIME PASSES LIKE SOME KIND OF A HAZY DREAM. IN THE mornings, I work my bakery shifts, though Emma lets me go earlier and earlier each day. She hires two part-time employees who come in to pick up the slack. At first, I hate that these newbies are taking my place, but the more I get to know them, the more I like them. And their presence leaves me with more time to work on Anna's case, which invigorates and stimulates my brain in a way nothing else in Heart Springs has.

I spend my afternoons organizing our case, and I'm confident we're going to come out of this victorious. We're only a few days away from presenting all of our evidence to the nephew's team and if they're smart, they'll take a look at everything we have and turn tail and run.

The weather outside stays crisp and snowy, and though it's clearly the holiday season, I still have no idea when Christmas will actually be upon us. Instead, we seem to be trapped in a perpetual snow globe, and Ben and I take full advantage. We spend our time together ice skating, and having snowball fights, and strolling through the winter marketplace that occupies the town square each weekend.

When I let myself sit and really think about it, I realize how content I am here in Heart Springs.

Waking up next to Ben each morning is blissful in itself, then I get to fill my days with people whose company I truly enjoy, doing work I feel truly proud of. I come home each night to a man who loves me and knows exactly how to satisfy me.

I start to forget why I would ever want to leave this place.

I wake up the morning of our big meeting to Ben dotting soft kisses along my shoulder. His hardness is nestled against the curve of my ass, and I instinctively push back against him.

"I have to get up and get ready for my meeting," I mutter as I turn my head to meet his kiss.

"I know. I figured you might need a little stress reliever before then." He grins against my lips as his hands drift down to work their magic. He pushes into me from behind, his fingers working over my clit until I'm gripping the pillow and calling out his name. He finishes a second later, the two of us so in sync these days, our orgasms are almost always simultaneous.

"You really are the best alarm clock I've ever had." I kiss him before throwing off the sheets and hopping out of bed.

I open the closet, knowing the ideal outfit is going to be there waiting for me. And it is. A sharp gray pantsuit, perfectly tailored and matched with a killer pair of red heels. The only thing different from my standard wardrobe back home is the polka-dotted blouse that ties in a floppy bow at the collar. I wish I could say I hate it, but it actually adds the perfect amount of flair. As I dress, I catch sight of Ben's reflection in the mirror. He's still in bed, the sheets draped over his waist, and he's watching me like he can't believe how lucky he is. Slipping into the suit feels a little like slipping into the old me, but I know the old me would never look at this life we've made in Heart Springs and feel grateful for it.

I slip in a pair of gold stud earrings and turn back toward the bed. I lean down and kiss him again, letting this one linger. "Wish me luck."

"You don't need luck, sweetheart. You've got this in the bag."

I throw him a wink over my shoulder as I head out. "I know."

He laughs and the sound follows me to the front door. Most days lately we sit and share a cup of coffee in front of the Christmas tree, enjoying the cozy morning together, but today I don't have time for that.

Instead, I push through the café, hoping Mimi is around to provide me with the necessary caffeine. She waits behind the counter, though, as usual, there're no other customers waiting for a drink.

Her eyebrows raise when she sees me. "Espresso shot?"

"Actually I'll take one of those peppermint mocha things." What can I say, I've developed an addiction to sweet coffee.

Her eyebrows rise even farther, but she turns to prepare my drink without further comment about my change in tastes. "You look nice."

"Thanks. Anna and I are meeting today with the nephew's legal team." I refuse to acknowledge the man has an actual name, only referring to him as *the nephew.*

"How's it going to go?"

"Well, we don't really know that until the meeting is over."

Mimi gives me a sharp look as she hands me my drink in its reusable cup. "How's it going to go?"

I grin. "I'm going to kick his ass."

"Good."

I spin around, heading to the front door. "I'll bring the cup back on my way home."

"Make sure you do," she says, though there's several layers of teasing in her voice. "Oh, and Campbell?"

I stop by the front door, turning to face her.

"I'm proud of you. For taking this on, and for helping Anna." She offers me a small smile and a wave, dismissing me like she didn't just completely rock my world.

Her words run through my mind over and over as I stroll toward the toy store. Really, for a meeting like this, we should be meeting somewhere neutral, but the only place I know of in town like that is the conference room at Noah's office and I'm not about to ask him for the space for obvious reasons.

Anna is anxious when I arrive at the toy store, but we run through everything one more time, and it seems to soothe her nerves.

And the meeting goes exactly as I predicted it would.

By the time we've finished presenting our evidence, the nephew's lawyers are shooting each other knowing looks. They tell us they need some time to discuss and consider their options, but it doesn't take more than an hour before they're calling and capitulating.

I'm ready for Anna's hug this time and accept it with no qualms. She has tears in her eyes, and I have to blink away my own because I do not get emotional over cases. Especially ones I've won.

I leave Anna with strict instructions to not say or do anything more until all the paperwork is signed. And I don't even jump when the squad of ducks hollers at me as I exit the toy store.

Ben is waiting on the front porch of his house with two glasses of champagne, and we toast my victory and kiss under the mistletoe he's hung over the front door.

It's a perfect day in what's become a very long string of perfect days.

And it blends into yet another perfect night.

BEN AND I STROLL THROUGH THE WINTER MARKET IN the town square a couple of days later. The ground is blanketed in snow, but none of it encroaches onto the paths snaking between the stalls, making it easy to stroll hand in hand from booth to booth. We sip on hot chocolate and say hi to everyone we encounter. It's another fairy-tale-esque winter day.

We're making our final loop around the town square when we pause to admire the giant tree that's the centerpiece of the town's holiday decorations. The tree towers above the buildings, blanketed in lights and swathed in ornaments that each bear some sort of tie to Heart Springs. There's a whisk and a mixing bowl for Emma's bakery, a stack of books for the bookstore. One of the favorite pastimes of the holiday season in Heart Springs is everyone finding the ornament that represents them.

I haven't been able to locate mine yet, but Ben assures me it's there somewhere. We found Ben's easily the first day the tree went up. It's a red heart shaped by the handprints of all his patients and the kids who benefitted from his carnival event. It's basically the cutest thing I've ever seen, and I hate it a little more each time we see it. Not because he doesn't deserve it or hasn't earned it, but because he's clearly so loved by everyone in this town, and despite the strides I have made, despite the acceptance I've felt recently, I still am not.

"Dr. Loving!" a voice calls across the square just as we're about to head home.

We both stop and turn, and my blood chills a little when I see the absolutely drop-dead gorgeous woman waving to Ben from the other side of the tree.

I would say I try not to let the jealousy overtake me, but that would be a lie.

The woman jogs over to us, a wide smile on her face like she doesn't know I'm silently planning her murder.

"Taylor, have you met my girlfriend Cam?" Ben asks the second she lands in front of us. Damn, this guy is smart.

She turns to me without dropping her smile, no hint of malice anywhere on her perfect face. "I haven't, but that's actually the reason why I stopped you. I wanted to talk to you, Cam."

"Oh?" I manage to keep the hostility from my voice, which Taylor is making easy with her warm smile and the way she doesn't even look at Ben after he introduces me.

"I heard what you did for Anna and for the bakery, and I was wondering if I would maybe be able to hire you to represent me?" The hope is clear in her bright blue eyes, and I hate to be the one to dash it.

"I'm sorry, Taylor, but I'm not actually a practicing attorney anymore. Those were sort of one-off occasions."

Taylor clasps her hands together, making her look like an actual Disney princess. "Oh please, Cam. I really need your help. My ex-boyfriend is claiming that he gave me the idea for the business I own and trying to get me to buy him out when the man never spent a single cent or lifted a single finger to help me start it."

"Have you talked to Noah Crenshaw?"

Her face hardens. "That's the jerk who's representing him."

I do my best to morph my face into a sympathetic smile. "I really wish I could help, Taylor." And I do. Her ex sounds like a total dick. "But I don't think I have the time to take on anything else right now."

Ben nudges me. "Your case with Anna is done, and Emma already hired the extra help for the bakery."

"I'm aware." I glare at him, wondering if he's being swayed by Taylor's pretty face.

"Give us a second." He shoots Taylor an apologetic look and pulls me off to the side. "What's with the excuses, sweetheart? You can try to hide it if you want, but I know how much you enjoyed working with Anna. Why not take on Taylor's case and help her stick it to the man?"

"Don't you think we've pushed our luck enough, Ben?" I whisper the words fiercely, making sure my voice is low enough so no one can overhear us. "Mimi made it very clear to me that lawyering is not a career option. I don't think I should be breaking any more rules."

His eyes soften and he reaches out to tug gently on a strand of my hair. "I think you should do what makes you happy, Cam. Fuck the rules."

I tap my foot impatiently as I mull it over, not sure which is swaying me more, Taylor or Ben using the word *fuck*. Looking back at Taylor, who's watching the two of us with a hopeful expression on her face, I sigh. "I guess there's no real harm in taking a look at what she's got."

Ben grins and before I can say another word, Taylor is back at my side, throwing her arms around me.

I'd like to say I've become accustomed to the hugs, but this one still catches me off guard. "No promises." I lace my words with serious warning.

She holds up her hands and begins walking away from us, like she wants to escape before I change my mind. "Understood. I'll come find you at the bakery on Monday and we can talk more!"

Taylor darts off into the crowd, though she leaves a trail of squealing in her wake that makes me think she did not take my warning all that seriously.

Ben's smile is triumphant and a little smug as we start our short walk home.

"You're the worst," I tell him as he pushes open the front door to my house.

"You know you love me."

"I hate it when you're right."

27

The day after I agree to take on Taylor's case, she comes into the bakery with a binder full of evidence. Surprising no one, it turns out her ex really is a dick. I want to punch him in the balls for his overall audacity, but I'll settle for making him cry in court.

Two days after that, Emma fires me.

Okay, it's not so much a firing, but a gentle push out the front door with my promises to devote my full attention to Taylor's case. Emma has always seen me clearer than I've seen myself, but even I can admit this go around that she's right.

It might not be the way things were "supposed" to turn out, but helping the women of Heart Springs get theirs has become something I'm legitimately passionate about, and something I don't want to turn away from.

The morning after I get fired, I still wake up and go to the bakery first thing. But I don't put on my apron and hop behind the counter. Instead, I grab a pastry and a coffee, give Emma a hug, and head back home, where I've spread out the contents of Taylor's binder across my kitchen table. It's not exactly the corner office of my old life, but for now, it will have to do. An hour later, when I get up to use the bathroom, I find a new doorway, leading to an office space. It's sparse, but comfortable, and once I move all the materials Taylor brought me, it's the perfect space.

I work throughout the entire day, making notes and reading until my eyes sting and compiling a list of questions I have for Taylor. I don't stop until Ben physically removes the pen from my hand, guides me out of my chair, and takes me next door to his place for dinner.

He pours us each a glass of red wine and dishes up plates of spaghetti. Both are delicious, and I sigh with pleasure when the first bite of garlic bread hits my tongue.

Ben watches me with a bemused smile on his face. "Good day at the office?"

I roll my eyes, but there's no true annoyance in the motion. "I got a lot accomplished if that's what you're asking."

He swirls a bite of pasta on his fork. "I was mostly asking if you enjoyed yourself."

"I mean, it's hard to enjoy a day buried in paperwork." Even as I say it, I know it's a lie, because I did in fact enjoy my day. Yes, there were moments that were exhausting and some that were even frustrating, but at the end of it, I felt good. Content. Happy with the work I'd put in.

Ben, of course, can read me like a freaking book at this point. "Happiness looks good on you, sweetheart."

I decide not to argue with him for once. "Thanks, babe."

After dinner we move to the couch with our second glasses of wine. Ben turns on the TV, though we both know we won't be paying much attention to whatever movie we're stuck watching today.

I tuck myself into his side, nuzzling farther into his warmth when his fingers twine in my hair. The soothing motion of his hands in my hair almost puts me to sleep, but there's still wine to finish, so I force my eyes to stay open.

"Ben?" I mutter, my voice laden with sleep and wine and an overwhelming feeling of peace.

"Hmm?"

"Do you think that we might be wasting our time trying to find our way back home? Are we better off at this point just accepting that this is where we belong?"

His fingers stop, his hand dropping to my shoulder as I pull away just enough so I can look at him, read the response on his face. "Do you really want that, sweetheart? To be stuck here forever, never seeing your home or your family again?"

I shrug, hiding my discomfort with another sip of wine. "Does it make me a terrible person if I admit I don't really miss my family all that much?"

He sets his wineglass on the coffee table and shifts so he's facing me. "It doesn't make you a terrible person, Cam. I know life with them wasn't exactly easy for you. But they're still your family. Don't you think they miss you?"

"I don't actually know, which sort of makes me think they probably don't. What I do know is that if I were to go home, I would miss everyone here. Emma, of course, and Mimi." I take another long gulp. "And you."

Ben reaches for my hand, lacing our fingers together. "I fully stand by my theory that we will remember everything that happened here. But I understand how you would miss everyone else. And miss the town. I will too."

"And, I know you already know this, but just sit here quietly and let me have this moment of discovery, okay?"

He mimes zipping his lips and throwing away the key.

"I like what I'm doing here. With Emma, and Anna, and Taylor. I like using the skills I've been practicing my whole life for good instead of evil. I like that I'm making a difference in these women's lives." Fuck, it feels good to say that out loud.

Ben's smile is knowing but not smug. "You know you could do something similar when we get home."

I shake my head, finishing my wine and setting the glass down next to Ben's. "I don't see how. My whole life is working for my family. I don't see how I could possibly break away from that."

"You can do anything you set your mind to, sweetheart."

"Except get out of here, it seems."

Ben shrugs. "Maybe part of the problem is that you don't truly want to get out of here. Maybe it's easier to stay here than to change the things that were making you unhappy in your real life."

"Okay I'm going to need you to take it down like twelve notches."

He smiles my favorite smile, the one that's a little lopsided. "Too perceptive?"

"Always."

And he might be right, though I'll never voice those words out loud. Maybe it is easier for me to stay here where everything is easy than attempt to go home and deal with thirty-four years of family trauma. I shudder just thinking about a heart to heart with my grandmother that ends with her thinking I'm nothing but a disappointment. And an indescribable sadness presses down on my chest when I think about picking up the phone and calling my mom. I think she and I need to have a long conversation. I think I might have seriously misunderstood so many things about our relationship.

Ben scoots closer to me, taking my cheek in his hand, his fingers clutching the nape of my neck and bringing our lips together. "Whatever you decide, Cam, you know I'm right there with you."

"But you think we should still try to get back home." It's not a question, because I already know his answer.

"I think that as happy as we are here, you could be even happier if you find a way to have your family in your life, even if it's not the way you once would have thought. Think about the kind of life we could build together."

I listen to his advice—really I do—but when the thought of facing my family on the other side of this starts to fester in my brain, I climb into his lap instead. "I think that's enough talking for one evening."

"Well, you're not going to get any arguments from me there, sweetheart."

THE CALENDAR THAT ONLY SEEMS TO OPERATE ON Heart Springs time keeps on ticking until finally we arrive at Christmas Eve. It feels like we've been prepping for the holiday for months, something that would have driven me crazy in my real life. But here, I find myself relishing all the moments of winter wonderland cheer. I might even be sad when it's all over.

As soon as it gets dark outside on Christmas Eve, Ben and I bundle up and stroll hand in hand to the town square. Everyone is gathered around the tree, waiting for the lights to turn on. Carolers are singing, and really, the whole thing couldn't be more idyllic.

As beautiful as it is, I don't look too closely at the tree. I still haven't found my special ornament, and the whole thing feels like an all too familiar slight. But Ben walks us right up to the edge, getting us a front-row seat to the tree lighting. Even though the tree is lit every night, tonight's ceremonial lighting is the one the whole town has gathered for.

Emma and Ethan nudge in right next to us, their smiles bright and their arms linked.

I lean over to give Emma an unprompted hug, mostly because I miss the smell of baked goods and it seems to be permanently embedded in her skin. She grips me tightly in return. "I miss you too, Cam."

Pulling away with a grimace, I hold up my hands in retreat. "Whoa, whoa, whoa. Let's not get carried away. I mostly just miss your lattes, is all."

"Uh-huh." She loves me enough not to press the matter further.

I take a second to look at the people circled around the tree. I make eye contact with several, all of whom offer me smiles and waves, all of which I return. Even Kate the wedding planner doesn't seem totally unhappy to see me.

After a rousing rendition of "Jingle Bells," Mimi steps up to flip the oversized switch that powers the tree lights. They come to life in a burst of color and everyone gasps like we haven't all seen the same sight for weeks now.

But I guess it doesn't really matter how often you see it; it is a magical feeling when the lights first blink on, brightening not just the tree but the faces of the crowd around it.

"Hey, sweetheart." Ben nudges my elbow, drawing my

attention from the glittery star at the top of the tree. "Check out that new ornament."

My eyes immediately fly to where he's pointing and my breath catches in my chest. There is indeed a new ornament, now visible thanks to the lights shining upon it. It's one of those ones we used to make as kids out of popsicle sticks. The kind my grandmother refused to display on her professionally decorated tree. This one is in the shape of an angel, with yellow yarn on top of her head and a wide red smile on her face. But the most spectacular thing about this angel is her dress. It's made up of a collage of photographs—and though I've never once seen a camera in Heart Springs, I don't stop to question how they were acquired. Because each photo is tied to me, in some way. There's one of Emma and me in front of the bakery. One of Anna holding the key to the toy store. One of me sitting on the ledge over the dunk tank.

And my favorite, one of me and Ben during our dance at the fundraiser.

It would be impossible to try to stem the tears welling in my eyes, so I let them flow down my cheeks, not even worrying about mascara tracks because certainly such a thing doesn't exist here in this perfect little town.

"It's beautiful," I finally manage to choke out.

Ben hands me a tissue and wraps me in his arms. "Almost as beautiful as you."

By the time I free myself from his embrace, wiping hastily at my eyes, the crowd around us has dissipated.

"Ready to go home?" Ben asks.

I don't really want to leave just yet, content to stand here and stare at the beautiful tree and my perfect ornament for the rest of the night.

"I'll give you your present . . ." Ben knows just the thing to tempt me.

We don't rush, waving happy holidays at everyone we pass. When we get back to my place, Ben pours us each a glass of wine and we settle in front of the tree.

"You first," I say, handing him a flat rectangular package.

"My, my, my, how selfless of you." Ben shoots me a wink before ripping through the paper like the Tasmanian Devil.

I watch his face closely for his reaction, and my heart warms when I see the genuine smile tug on his lips. I struggled to find the perfect gift for him because what does one get for the man who truly has no needs and doesn't ever express his wants beyond wanting me to be happy? In general, I love that for me, but it did make the gift-buying process difficult.

But I came across the perfect thing one day at one of the little shops in town. It's a small canvas, painted with the town's main street. It captures not only the buildings and the people, but somehow also the warmth and the love that radiate from this special place.

"This is amazing, Cam. I love it." He leans in to kiss me, still holding the painting in his hands.

I give him ten more seconds of enjoying his present before I clap my hands together. "My turn."

Ben drags a large box out from under the tree and sits back with a proud smile.

I tear into the paper with even more fervor than Ben, ripping off the lid of the box underneath and digging through the tissue paper. My hand hits smooth leather and I pull out the gift with a bit of a pit in my stomach.

It's a bag. A beautiful bag, the leather a honey brown

and supple and smooth, the clasps gold and elegant. It's the perfect size to carry all my files for the legal work I've taken on.

And it looks just like the bag I used every day back at home.

"You don't like it?" Ben seems confused by my silence, probably because it's an uncommon occurrence.

"No, I love it, Ben. It's gorgeous. It's perfect." I run my fingers over the front of it, marveling at the similarities. "It's just, this bag is *just* like one I used to have back home. I used it every day. My grandmother got it for me when I graduated from law school."

"I'm sorry, sweetheart."

I carefully place the bag back in the box before I lean in to press a soft kiss to his lips. "Don't be sorry. Clearly you know exactly what I like."

"I didn't mean to get you something that would make you sad."

"You didn't, I promise."

And I'm not lying, because I'm not sad. I'm just confused. Seeing that ornament up on the tree all but cemented my decision to stay here in Heart Springs. That kind of love and acceptance is something I've never really felt before and I found it tonight, in the town square, surrounded by my friends. The kind of friends who are just as good as family.

But seeing the bag brings a wave of homesickness, something I haven't felt here in a really long time. Something I didn't think I was ever going to feel again once I decided to make Heart Springs my home.

And so I lose myself in Ben's kiss, rather than try to parse out my feelings further. He follows my lead, pulling me into his arms and opening to me. He rolls me to my back, holding his weight over me as his mouth trails down my neck. I wrap my arms around his waist and tug until he covers me fully, pressing me into the soft fabric of the rug in front of the tree.

He unbuttons my cardigan—who would've thought I'd ever wear a fucking cardigan—and slips it from my shoulders. I tug his sweater over his head, relishing in his groan as my fingers trace over the planes of his torso. His mouth moves from my neck to my collarbone and down to my chest. He lingers there, his eyes locked not on the red lace, but on the center of my chest, where my heart thrums an impossibly frantic beat.

He kisses the space between my breasts softly and reverently and it's too much. He's too much, and too good. I unhook my bra and toss it to the far corner of the room, and Ben's pupils widen in response, like he's never seen anything as miraculous as my tits, though he sees them literally every night.

Sensing my impatience, he makes quick work of trailing his mouth down my stomach, to the button of my jeans. He unsnaps it quickly, frees me from the denim just as fast, but once he's perched between my thighs, his pace slows. He kisses me through my lace panties and the brief contact makes me gasp. I try to move the fabric, but he captures both of my hands in one of his, keeping me from messing with his plan to torture me.

And torture me he does. He tongues me through the fabric, and the lace is just open enough for me to feel the slightest hint of pressure. It's exquisite and electrifying and simply not enough. He drives me to the brink, the fluttering of his tongue and the slickness of his mouth giving me everything except that one thing I need.

My thighs tighten around his head, and I choke on my plea. "Ben, please."

His hand releases mine, and his fingers tug the sopping lace to the side. When his tongue finally makes contact with my clit, the moan that escapes me is guttural and borderline mortifying, but I'm too far gone to care. I'm coming before he even slips his fingers inside me and the orgasm doesn't stop as he strokes into me.

I finally have to guide his mouth away from me when it all becomes too much, the sensitivity overtaking me. I practically rip the blasted panties from my body, and Ben, being the smart man that he is, frees himself of his jeans and boxer briefs.

He pushes into me with one sharp thrust that leaves us both breathless.

He moves maddeningly slowly inside me at first, rocking his hips so with each thrust his pelvic bone brushes against my still sensitive clit. I spur him on, grabbing his ass so he knows to go harder and faster. His mouth finds mine and we careen over the cliff together, every part of us mingling, tangling, so closely woven together I don't know that we can ever come apart.

It takes several minutes for our heartbeats to slow, our bodies to disengage, our kisses to soften.

I look at Ben, really look at him, and wonder how I could even for one second think there is anything missing in my life here. Because when I have him, I have everything.

He pulls out of me with a groan and hops up from the

rug, reaching a hand down to help pull me up. "Come on, we're too old to fall asleep on the floor."

I scoff, knowing he's absolutely right. "Speak for yourself."

We go through our nightly routine, showering and brushing teeth and climbing into bed. It's domestic but not boring, and I relish every minute of it. Ben drifts off to sleep basically the moment the covers are tucked around us, but for once, I don't immediately join him.

Ben stays sound asleep, despite my tossing and turning, until I finally can't lie there for another second. I carefully slide out of bed so as not to disturb him, closing the bedroom door behind me.

I curl up under a blanket on the couch, reaching for a book Ben has left on the coffee table. If one of his boring medical books can't put me to sleep, I don't know what can. I open the pages, picking a spot at random to begin.

Only to find stuck between the pages something that catches my breath in my chest. Two somethings, actually.

The first is the check from Two Hearts Café, the one Mimi left for us that first night. It should surprise me that he kept it, but maybe Ben really did know from the beginning that we were meant to end up here.

The second thing is an old photo, one that someone took the time to print out and not just leave stranded in the cloud. The paper is worn and creased, like it's been handled, carefully, but often over the years. I study the four people in the picture, my heart cracking open as I take in the details.

The man who has Ben's thick brown hair. The woman with his whiskey-brown eyes. The little girl with the wide grin and a skinned knee, looking up at her older brother like he hung the moon.

My eyes linger the longest on Ben. He must be about twelve years old in this picture, but I would know that smile anywhere. It's the same smile all four of the people in the photo share—open and warm and real.

This is the kind of family I've never allowed myself to want. Not because it's not appealing, but because I know it's out of reach.

But Ben has that family, the perfect one, the one where people fight, but make up. Where they tease, but also show love. Where they show up for one another, support one another, truly enjoy one another's company.

My finger traces over Ben's face, his cheeks still a little rounded with youth, smattered with a spray of freckles that have faded as he's gotten older.

Ben can't go the rest of his life without these people, without his family. He doesn't mention them often, and I assumed it was because they're not close, that he misses them as little as I miss my family. But I think I had that all wrong. Maybe he doesn't talk about them because it's too painful, because the missing them is too overwhelming.

And yet, he told me he's willing to stay here in Heart Springs. With me.

He would give up his family to be with me.

And I would let him. I would stay here, where everything is perfect and easy, if it means never having to face my grandmother. Never having to tell her I no longer want the legacy she's built for me, never having to face her disappointment.

If I never have to tell her I'm running away, just like Mom did, then maybe I won't have to face that disappointment. Never have to deal with the fact that maybe I am like my mom, and maybe that's not such a bad thing.

But I can't do that to Ben. He won't leave me, would never think of trying to find a way out of here that doesn't include me. He would put me first, above his own needs, always.

I stick the photo back between the pages and close the book, mind made up.

It's time to go home.

28

The next morning, I stride down Main Street with a purpose. It's technically Christmas Day, but I have a feeling the one person I really need will be right where she always is.

Mimi sits at our usual table at the café, one mug in her hands, another waiting for me in front of my chair.

"Do you really not have any other guests in town whose torture you oversee?" I slide into the seat across from her and immediately reach for my mug.

She chuckles. "You are more than enough for me, Cam."

"I take it you know why I'm here?"

"I think I can take a guess."

"Good, so then let's cut to the chase. I've done everything asked of me. I'm a part of this community, I found a career that helps people and that I'm truly passionate about. And I'm in love with Ben." I can't utter that last sentence without smiling, but I quickly wipe the smile from my face so Mimi knows I mean business. "I want to go home, Mimi."

"What changed your mind?"

"What do you mean?"

"If I'm not mistaken, you were seriously thinking about making a life for yourself here in Heart Springs. So what changed your mind?"

I don't even bother asking how she knows because of course she knows. For a minute I think about lying, or brushing her off, but instead I decide to try just being honest. "Ben needs to see his family. As happy as we are here, I know he'll never truly be happy without them in his life."

"So this is about Ben, then?" She watches me over the rim of her mug.

"Yes." I take a deep breath. "But I think it's also about me. I can't hide from my own family forever, even if it would be easier. I have some things I need to say to them. So will you please help me figure out what I'm doing wrong so we can go home?"

Mimi flashes me a knowing smile. "Do you remember the exact words I said to you on your first day here?"

I roll my eyes. "You said a lot of words, Meem, and to be totally honest, I probably wasn't listening to at least half of them."

"You heard these ones. When I told you your third task."

I can't roll my eyes again or they might get stuck, so instead I open them very wide to help convey my annoyance. "You mean how you told me I needed to find a partner and fall in love, and I've absolutely done that?"

"I didn't tell you you needed to find a partner and fall in love."

I chug the rest of my coffee so that my mouth stays busy for a minute and can't scream at her. Slamming my empty mug down on the table, I do my best to stay calm.

"If you didn't tell me I needed to fall in love, then what did you tell me?"

"I told you you needed to experience true love, Campbell."

"Oh my god, what is the difference, Meem? Fall in love, experience true love, those are literally the exact same thing."

She shrugs. "Are they?"

I shove my chair back. "Here I am trying to be nice and selfless, and you are giving me nothing. Thank you, as usual, for being zero help."

"Just think about it, Cam." She sips calmly from her mug. "And if I don't see you again, it's been a real pleasure getting to know you. Mostly." She winks at me.

I glare at her, stomping out of the café and heading right for the one place that will make me feel better.

The bakery is warm and welcoming and smells like heaven, and by some miracle of miracles, the front door is unlocked but no customers wait inside. Instead, Emma sits at a table, a croissant and a peppermint mocha waiting for me.

I slip into the seat across from her and start to get a really weird feeling in the pit of my stomach. "Did you talk to Mimi?"

Her lips purse, and I watch her lie to me. "No, not today."

Whatever. I'm not going to let it stop me from enjoying the deliciousness in front of me. I chomp into the croissant. "I need to move back to New York." I don't wait until I've fully chewed and swallowed, so the declaration comes out muffled.

Emma ignores my terrible manners. "You have the tools to go home whenever you want, Cam."

"Oh my god, you totally did talk to Mimi!"

"I might have," she admits with a sheepish grin.

"Rude." I take a sip of the warm chocolatey coffee to make myself feel better.

"Look, Cam, if you really want to leave Heart Springs and move back to the city, you can. No one is keeping you here but you."

I cross my arms on the table and let my head fall on top of them, wishing I could be fully honest with her. "If only it were that simple. Everyone knows that I really, truly love Ben, right? Like no one thinks I'm faking or anything?"

She pats my hair in the soothing way most mothers would. "I know you're not faking it. You love Ben, and he loves you."

"Then why isn't that enough?" I raise my head to level her with my pleading gaze.

"You are enough," she says, her eyes softening along with her voice. "Just remember that, okay? You are enough."

I nod, pushing back another chair from another table. "I'll let you enjoy your Christmas. See you tomorrow."

"See you soon."

The cold air bites at my cheeks as I make my way back down Main Street, toward home.

Well, that was a total bust.

At least I got two cups of coffee out of it.

"Cam! Merry Christmas!"

I turn toward the toy store and catch Anna waving at me from the doorway. "Merry Christmas to you too!"

"I still can't thank you enough!" she calls.

I wave off her thanks. "It was my pleasure!"

She waves again before ducking back into her store, which can only be open in case some parents majorly screwed up Christmas. Too bad for her that she has to work, but she didn't look upset at all. She seemed thrilled to be there actually, and it helps warm me up, to think I had some small part in that.

Ben is waiting for me on the porch when I return. The cold is still bitter, but I sink into my favorite chair anyway.

"Rough morning?"

I slipped out of bed before he woke up, wanting to have some good news for him, but I can't help but feel like this whole thing is a bust. I need to find a way to get Ben home, but I'm no closer than I was last night.

I let my head fall back against the perfect curve of the chair. "I was trying to figure out a way to get us out of here, but no luck, I'm afraid."

"What changed your mind about going home?"

"I found the picture of your family." I turn my head in his direction. "You don't talk about them much."

"You don't ask." There's no anger or sadness or frustration behind the sentiment, just the simple truth of it. He sighs. "And honestly, after hearing about your family, I didn't want to rub it in."

"That you have a perfect family?"

He shrugs and reaches for my hand. "No family is perfect."

"But you love them. You miss them."

He squeezes my hand. "I do."

"Then I'm going to find a way to get us home."

"Hmmm."

"What's that supposed to mean?"

"It means, I think the answer is right in front of you, sweetheart; you just have to be willing to see it."

"Did everybody take an extra dose of cryptic pills today?

Jesus." I lace our fingers together, so he knows I'm just being a cranky bitch and I still love him.

He stands and drops a kiss on the top of my head. "I'm going to do some work in the garage, but you know where to find me if you need me."

He heads inside, leaving me alone to fester in my own thoughts. I play back my conversation with Mimi, but nothing she said was remotely helpful.

Closing my eyes, I let the cold wash over me, hoping it will sharpen my brain function and bring me the clarity I need. Shockingly, it doesn't work.

I don't want to disturb Ben with my melancholy, so I head back over to my own house. I curl up in the armchair in front of the tree. My bag still sits prominently front and center, the perfect replica of the one my grandmother gave me when I graduated from law school. She never told me she was proud of me for finishing at the top of my class, but she did tell me she hoped I would prove to be worthy of the family name.

"Seems like even here in Heart Springs I'm not enough," I mutter.

The words echo in the empty room.

And I bolt upright in my seat.

"Holy shit."

Maybe the answer really was right in front of my face this whole time.

Mimi was right. She didn't tell me I needed to fall in love with someone else. She told me I needed to experience true love. She never mentioned the need for another person in this equation. Just love. True love. Not love for someone else. For myself.

The voices of my friends bounce around in my head.

Mimi saying I'm more than enough for her.

Anna telling me she can't thank me enough.

My dear, sweet Emma telling me I am enough.

And Ben. Ben, the man I fell in love with without even trying.

He has always believed in me, that I am enough.

It was never about him. It was about me.

I push out of my chair and head to the front door. My stomach feels a little woozy, and my lungs compress when the cold air hits them. But I need to get to him. I vault over the fence separating our yards and burst right through the front door without knocking.

I'm light-headed, black dots clouding my vision, but he's there, right there, to catch me before I collapse.

"I just needed to figure out how to love myself." I can barely manage to get the words out, my lungs so tight they're starting to burn.

Ben holds me close, his eyes clouding with tears. "I knew you would figure it out, sweetheart." He presses his forehead to mine. "I love you so much."

"I love you too, Ben. And I'll find you, I'll remember. I promise." I just manage to brush my lips over his, right before the blackness overtakes me.

29

There's a suspicious lack of sunshine when I open my eyes.

The room is dark, the sheets are crisp, and when I swing my legs over the side of the bed, there are no fuzzy slippers waiting for me.

My hand drifts up, searching for the long curly locks I've grown accustomed to. Instead I find the blunt edge of my sharp bob.

That's when the realization sinks in.

I'm home.

I grasp for the switch on my bedside lamp. Once the room is illuminated, the truth of it all smacks me in the face. I'm back in my own room, the walls a soft eggshell, the only hint of color in the space coming from the abstract art over my bed, a single crimson slash on a black canvas in a gold frame.

Gone are the cozy flannel pajamas, my body instead in a black silk nightgown trimmed with lace.

At least Ben will like my sleepwear, I think to myself.

Ben.

My Ben.

Thank god I didn't forget about Ben.

I check the other side of the bed, as if I could have somehow missed seeing him next to me.

I still remember him, but he isn't here.

Is he back in his own apartment? Does he still remember me?

If he does, is he grateful for this clean break? The fact that he won't have to let me down easy because I have no clue how to get in contact with him?

No. I'm not going to let myself think like that. What Ben and I had was real, and I will find him. Sure, Manhattan's population is huge, but the island is only thirteen miles long. If I have to knock on every door, I will.

A piercing ring erupts from the nightstand, and I practically jump out of my skin.

My cell phone sits on the white marble tabletop, blaring at me to pick it up. It's loud and obnoxious and jarring.

To think there was a moment in time when I missed having it in my hand.

I swipe to accept the call. "Hello?"

"Where are you?" It may have been months since I've heard her voice, but there's no mistaking my grandmother's tone.

"I just woke up."

"Just woke up? Jesus, Campbell, it's almost ten o'clock. We have the meeting with Coleman and Sons in half an hour. Get your ass here, now."

"Right, will do." I hop out of bed, my almost Pavlovian

response to her commands kicking in. "I'm so sorry I've been gone for so long, I'm sure you've been wondering where I was."

"I saw you yesterday. Right before you left the office."

"Yesterday?"

"Yes, you had a date with that doctor. How did it go? He'd make a perfectly respectable partner, he's handsome enough. You aren't getting any younger, Campbell, and I want to make sure the future of the firm is secured."

"Wait." It takes a minute for my brain to put the pieces together. "My date with Ben was last night? The meeting with Coleman and Sons is today?"

"Good god, Campbell, are you drunk? Do you seriously not know what day it is?"

"I have to go."

"Be here in fifteen minutes," she commands, her directive echoing in my ear as I close out of the call.

But I have no intention of making my way to the office.

I'm home. No real time seems to have passed. But I remember Ben. I remember Heart Springs. I remember everything.

I race to my closet, throwing open the door, and expecting the perfect outfit to be there waiting for me. But this is my regular old closet, so I have to rifle through the racks of suits to find normal clothes.

Ben doesn't care what I look like anyway, I tell myself as I grab the first pair of jeans I find. A quick look in the mirror reminds me I no longer wake up with my hair and makeup done, which really is a shame, but I don't care enough to spend time putting myself together. I need to see Ben, and if he made it back home, if this whole thing was real, if he woke up and remembered everything we went through together in Heart Springs, then there's only one place he'll be.

Stepping out of my building onto the busy streets of Manhattan should feel like a screech of a wake-up call. And it is, but after a few deep breaths of city air, I realize how good it feels to be home.

I raise my arm to hail a cab, but one look down the traffic-filled street lets me know it would take an hour to get the few blocks I need to travel. So, I put my arm down and start walking, ignoring the cabbie who'd been about to pull over for me as he yells "Bitch!" out the window.

I let the familiar sights and sounds of the city wash over me as I break into a light jog. No one makes eye contact with me, let alone smiles or returns my hellos. I don't let the rebuffs dampen my spirits; I know if I collapsed on the street right now, there would be a swarm of New Yorkers stopping to help me. Sometimes kind is more important than nice.

I slow my pace as I approach my stop, nerves suddenly swarming in my stomach. There's a good chance I'm going to walk through the door and not find what I'm looking for.

But I also know that, if the worst does occur, I would be okay. I have the tools now to break down my walls and let people in. I've proven I can make friends and help others. I can become who I want to be.

I hold my breath the tiniest bit when I push the door open. A bell tinkles, something I didn't even notice when I was here the night before.

I spot him immediately, sitting at the same table where we shared dinner, just a few hours ago. A few hours, and for us, many months ago.

He stands when he sees me, his warm smile spreading across his face. "Hi, sweetheart."

I fold myself into his arms, leaning into his warmth, letting my nose fill with his woodsy, comforting scent. "Well, hello again, Dr. Loving."

He separates us, leaving just enough space for him to cup my cheeks in his hands and bring our lips together. The kiss starts soft, and maybe a bit unsure, but once his mouth brushes mine, any doubts are cleared away.

He's here, my Ben, and this is most definitely real.

"So, I had the strangest dream," I say when we finally part.

He chuckles. "Must have been something in the water." He pulls out my chair for me before taking the seat across the table. "I'd love to hear all about it."

A server approaches our table, ready and impatient to take our orders.

"Is Mimi working this morning?" I exchange a look with Ben, and his smile turns encouraging. "She was our server the last time we were here, and I don't think we left a proper tip."

How much cash do I owe the woman who fully changed my life?

"Mimi?" The man's nose wrinkles. "There's no one working here named Mimi."

"Are you sure?" Ben asks. "We weren't here that long ago."

"Listen, I've been working here since I was fourteen, my aunt owns this place. There's no one here named Mimi, never has been. Now do you wanna order or not?"

"I'll have a coffee and a bacon, egg, and cheese." Ben hands the man his menu, his friendly smile never wavering.

"I'll also have a BEC, and I'll take a large honey lavender latte."

The man takes my menu, rolling his eyes and muttering under his breath about ridiculous coffee orders.

Ben and I both burst out laughing. I slip my hand into his, and he laces our fingers together. We drink our coffees and eat our breakfasts, sharing our favorite memories from our time together in Heart Springs.

When we finish our meal, the server brings us our check. I check the front and back, but there's no message from Mimi, no directive about loving ourselves or living life to the fullest. Maybe she's already turned her attentions to some other poor soul. I hope for their sake that they take her advice.

We link hands again as we stroll out of the café and down the street. I know I need to make my way over to the office, not to make the big meeting, not because my grandmother threatened me, but because she and I need to have a real talk. Some things are going to need to change in my life, and my job is the biggest among them.

Because I don't want to spend my life buried in paperwork, racking up more hours in the office than not. I want to enjoy the time I have, be able to go out for breakfast with my boyfriend, and not feel like I'm letting my whole family down if something job-related doesn't go exactly right.

I want to help people who really need it, not a bunch of corporations who take more than they could ever possibly give back.

It's not going to be an easy conversation to have with her, but Grandmother is going to have to understand.

Ben nudges me with his elbow as we stroll down a quiet walkway in Central Park. "What's going on in that beautiful brain of yours?"

"Just thinking about some career changes I'd like to make."

"Oh yeah?" He pulls me to a stop. "Is it too early for me to ask for a change?"

My heart thuds in my chest. Nothing he's said throughout the day today would lead me to believe he doesn't want our relationship to continue, but I can't help but jump to the worst-case scenario. "Go ahead."

He runs a hand through his hair. "I know in the real world we've only known each other for like a day, but I know how I feel about you, Cam, and I don't want to waste any time. What do you think about moving in with me?"

My eyes flutter closed for a second because I must have misheard him.

When he senses my hesitation, he starts talking again. "We don't have to, obviously, I know it's early, and if you still need time—"

I cut him off with a kiss. "I would love to live with you, Ben."

"Yeah?"

I nod. "Yeah."

"I love you, sweetheart."

"I love you too."

We resume our walk, our pace leisurely, our hands linked.

"I hope you know I'm not exactly an easy person to live with."

Ben barks out a laugh. "You don't have to tell me that. I

think at this point, Campbell Marie, I know you better than you know yourself."

And he loves me anyway. That part doesn't need repeating, because I know it, deep in my bones.

"I don't know, babe, I think right now, I know myself pretty damn well."

EPILOGUE

Eighteen months later

"Do we really need to walk all the way to Rockefeller Center again?"

"It's two blocks away, and you know it makes me happy."

"It's just a Christmas tree, sweetheart."

"First of all, how dare you. Second of all, you know you love it just as much as I do." I loop my arm through Ben's, tugging him in the direction he already knows we're going to end up going. Because if I don't see the tree at least once a day, the holiday spirit just seeps right out of me and we start catching glimpses of the old Cam.

Okay, not really, the old Cam is well and truly buried at this point, but you definitely don't want to mess with me before I've had my morning peppermint mocha.

"How are things going with the case?" Ben pulls his scarf up, burrowing down into the cashmere. My grandmother gifted him the scarf last Christmas and it became his instant favorite.

When we got back from Heart Springs and I told my grandmother I didn't want to work for her anymore, she took it a lot better than I thought she would. Or at least, she did after she had some time to calm down. While she will never fully understand why I wanted to give up my stake in a multi-million-dollar law firm, the one thing she understands better than most is the need to make something for myself.

Also, I find it way easier to get along with not just her but the rest of my family, when we're not all working together. Our relationships are still a work in progress, but at least we're working on them.

And speaking of working on them, after I had my come-to-Jesus moment with Grandmother, I made a phone call I never expected to make: to my mom. I opened the conversation by letting her know I was leaving the firm, and well, I guess you could say that opened the floodgates. I always blamed my mom for leaving, but there was much more to her relationship with Grandmother, things I never witnessed and never knew. Our relationship is far from perfectly settled, but I'm set on finding space for her in this new life I'm creating.

It didn't take long for me to decide to open my own law firm. We specialize in helping the little guy (metaphorically, the majority of our clients are women and nonbinary folks) take down the man (not metaphorical, pretty much all of our opponents are straight white dudes). We've only officially been in business for about a year, but already the job is making me happier than just about anything in my life.

At least happier than anything aside from the man walking next to me.

Ben is everything he was to me in Heart Springs, and more. Despite both of us working demanding, time-consuming jobs, we always make time for each other. Ben makes us dinner at least twice a week and I plan our date nights, sometimes at fancy restaurants, sometimes at smaller cafés. He's the first person I call when I have something to celebrate and I'm the one he turns to when the stress of his job starts to take a toll. We're both there to pull the other one back when the temptation to become completely absorbed in our jobs strikes. He knows me better than just about anyone, and he accepts me and loves me just the way I am. He did even when I couldn't accept and love myself.

But I don't have any issues with that anymore, the lessons I learned in Heart Springs still ingrained in me.

"Want a gingerbread latte before we get to the tree?"

"Do you even need to ask me that question?"

"I think there's a new bakery that just opened up on this corner. Let's check it out."

My heart squeezes just a tad. I got to keep Ben and all of our memories from Heart Springs, but I still miss the other friends I made there from time to time. The painting I bought Ben for Christmas somehow ended up back at his apartment, hung on the wall, and I often wonder how Emma and Ethan might be doing, what Mimi and the rest of the townspeople might be getting up to. Did life for them keep right on rolling along without us? Do they even remember us?

Ben jerks to a stop, halting me with him.

I was so lost in my thoughts of Emma, I didn't realize we were already in front of the new bakery. It's got a purple and white striped awning and adorable yellow café tables and chairs out front.

I walk up to the door and gasp when I see the name stenciled on the glass. Throwing open the door, I stride right up to the counter, searching for brown eyes and lustrous curls.

"Emma?"

The woman turns around and offers me her brightest Emma smile.

"Holy shit, it's really you. I can't believe you're here." I reach behind me, needing Ben's hand to keep me grounded.

Emma's brow wrinkles. "Have we met before?"

My heart sinks. Ben's fingers squeeze mine.

Of course. Something had to give. Having Emma here in the real world would make things just a little too perfect.

"Wait, aren't you that lawyer?" Emma's eyes study me, and her lips curl back into their usual smile. "I read an article about you; you opened that law firm to help small-business owners."

I smile right back. "That's me."

"What can I get you? It's on the house today. I have to say, I love what you're doing." She turns and starts prepping my order before I've even given it to her.

"Thank you. Believe it or not, I think I get more out of it than my clients do."

She spins back around and hands me a lavender to-go cup. "It's Campbell, right?"

I nod. "My friends call me Cam."

"Well, Cam, I hope you come in again soon. I'd love to chat with you more."

"I'd love that too."

I stare at her for an awkwardly long minute, until Ben tugs on my hand, pulling me from the shop.

"That really just happened, right? You saw her too?"

Ben releases my hand so he can tuck me into his side, his arm wrapping firmly around my waist. "I saw her too."

I tilt my head up expectantly, waiting for a kiss.

He drops one on my lips as we cross the street to see the huge Christmas tree, the centerpiece of the holidays in New York.

We may have left small-town living behind in Heart Springs, but even in New York, the holidays are full of magic.

And so are we.

ACKNOWLEDGMENTS

First and foremost, so many thanks to my incredible editor Kate Dresser. You were handed this book knowing absolutely nothing about it and you really helped make it shine. Thank you for bringing this one across the finish line with me!

My agent, Kimberly Whalen, continues to be a literal agenting rockstar. Kim, thank you so much for the continued support. You have shaped my career in ways I couldn't even fathom, and I couldn't do it without you!

Tarini Sipahimalani, assistant editor extraordinaire! Thank you for being so incredibly on top of your game and keeping me on track!

Kristen Bianco, Molly Pieper, Brennin Cummings, and the entire Putnam publicity and marketing teams, thank you for making sure people actually want to read my books! So much of your work goes unseen, but none of it is unappreciated.

Andrea Peabbles, Danielle Barthel, Quinn Cosio, thank you for catching all my typos. One day I will learn the difference between *further* and *farther.*

Sanny Chiu, your covers continue to blow me away. Thank you for putting so much love and care into the design of these books.

To everyone else at Putnam who made this book possible—Leah Marsh, Maija Baldauf, Emily Mileham, Shannon Plunkett, Lorie Pagnozzi, Christopher Labaza, Ivan Held, and so many others—thank you for your continued support.

Cinco Paul and Ken Daurio, chances are you'll never see this, but thank you for the gift of *Schmigadoon*.

Corey Planer, you continue to save my butt every time I get stuck. Thank you for loving this book as much as I do.

Courtney Kae, chatting with you is the highlight of my week, every week. Thank you for being the brightest light in Romancelandia.

Ashley Hooper, thank you for always remembering to check in on me. I appreciate it more than you know. Brianna Mowry, thank you for always showing up. To all my IRL friends, you're amazing and I love you.

I really want to list all my writer pals here because I truly could not do it without you, but I'm so afraid I'll forget someone and feel terrible, and also, the list would be long! So if you're a fellow writer, thank you for keeping me sane! Special shout-outs to Erin LaRosa, Elissa Sussman, Kate Spencer, Lacie Waldon, and Lauren Kung Jessen for keeping it real in the group chat, and MA Wardell for screaming with me about literally everything.

To the Bookstagrammers, BookTokers, and influencers, thank you for sharing your love of books. Every time I see a gorgeous picture of one of my books, it absolutely makes my day. Thank you for the time you invest in authors. To the librarians and booksellers, thank you for all you do. I wouldn't be here without you.

My family continues to be the most supportive. There are not enough thanks, but please know you have them.

Canon, thanks for continuing to be the coolest kid ever. I still have no plans to write a book you can read, but I hope I still make you proud.

Matt, there is no way I could be publishing my fifth book if I didn't have you by my side. You have never once doubted me or my dreams and your unwavering support makes this all possible. Thanks for being a real-life book boyfriend.

And to you, dear reader, thank you for picking up this book. I hope it brought you some joy.

DISCUSSION GUIDE

1. Cam Andrews hates love. Why do you think this is the case? What are your views on love and romance? Do you believe in true love?

2. When Cam wakes up in Heart Springs, she is distraught at the untimely displacement from her strict routine. How would you react if you found yourself in such a situation?

3. Cam wakes up in Heart Springs perfectly groomed, which lightly pokes fun at the ways in which romantic heroines are often portrayed in TV, movies, and books. In what ways do we expect our heroines to be "perfect" in the love stories we consume?

4. Cam's task to find true love is particularly daunting. In what ways is her instruction to find love emblematic of everyone's struggle in today's dating world?

5. Heart Springs is described as a perfectly kept town, filled with white picket fences and "intentionally charming" shops and cafés, or as Cam calls it, "pastel purgatory." Why do you think it feels grating to Cam? Would you like to live in Heart Springs?

6. Noah is one of Cam's suitors. Discuss what Cam learns from this relationship.

7. Cam and Ben end up nurturing a strong friendship together during their time in Heart Springs. To what extent do you believe this outcome was dependent on being in Heart Springs? Do you think they could have been friends in the "real world"?

8. *Change of Heart* features some of the most popular rom-com tropes: small town, fated mates, matchmaking. If you could choose one of these tropes to be your love story, which one would you choose? Discuss.

9. The title *Change of Heart* aptly speaks to Cam's journey. What other themes or images does the title recall?

ABOUT THE AUTHOR

Photograph of the author © Brianna Mowry

FALON BALLARD is the author of *Lease on Love, Just My Type, Right on Cue,* and *All I Want Is You,* and cohost of the podcast *Happy to Meet Cute.* When she's not writing a romance book, reading a romance book, or talking about romance books, you can probably find her at Disneyland.

Visit Falon Ballard Online

falonballard.com

FalonBallard

FalonBallard